Her eyes had a red sheen; like blood on bronze.
Elmien Grove

Love and lemons collide: a romantic story with a nifty mauve bag!
Ryhen E Knight

Jessica stood with the door handle in her hand and looked back at the door, seeing the mangled remains of the lock mechanism, shredded metal and splintered wood. How would she explain this to her mother?
H J Kruger

A story set in the last fortress of humanity in a harsh desert landscape, where a chance encounter with a future human being forces the age old question as to which is more palatable; a certain doom, or an uncertain future?
Caldon Mull

Four days from Jaht-Ni until he might die. Four days from Jaht-Ni until he knew for certain what his life was worth.
Natalie Rivener

Draca is a story about the dangers of obsession and the foolishness of egotism. It will tear you in many directions as Draca faces the reality of his curse.
Andrea Vermaak

The world is going to hell, and it's up to the Angels to mitigate the damage.
Richard T Wheeler

The Flight
of the
Phoenix

Elmien Grove ♦ Ryhen E Knight ♦ H J Kruger
Caldon Mull ♦ Natalie Rivener
Andrea Vermaak ♦ Richard T Wheeler

Edited by Natalie Rivener

SIYGRAH

First published in South Africa in 2015 by Siygrah Books
Pretoria

Ifrit also appears in *The Estuary Tales* by Caldon Mull and is available from
Smashwords

Cover illustration by Elsabé Viljoen

Cover design and layout by H J Kruger

ISBN: 978-0-620-65229-2

To Annette, Robyn and Tiaan for their unwavering faith

CONTENTS

Acknowledgments

Introduction   *Natalie Rivener*

Gargoyles   *Elmien Grove*   15

Albert has everything he ever wanted; a
good job, a nice car and a beautiful wife.
But lately when she looks at him, he gets
scared.
Her eyes are different.
Instead of the familiar rich brown he has
known all these years, they have acquired
the red sheen of blood on bronze.

And they are watching his every move.

The Dragon with the Girl Tattoo   *Ryhen E Knight*   43

Every boy has a dream of a girl and
sausages. Every girl has a tattoo and
smell of wet grass. And usually every boy
and every girl do not meet. Not in the real
world. Unless they stumble upon a
grumpy giant with an old Beetle backseat
strapped to his back.
And then it happens!

The Phoenix Syndrome   *H J Kruger*   71

After an unknown epidemic called PS
spread across the globe with strange and
dangerous side effects, the military
declares a national man hunt for all of the
'infected' individuals. A young girl
named Jessica has to flee persecution and
gets tangled in a liberation struggle for
those living with 'Phoenix Syndrome'.

Ifrit *Caldon Mull* 119

A story set in the last fortress of humanity
in a harsh desert landscape, where a chance
encounter with a future human being forces
the age old question as to which is more
palatable; a certain doom, or an uncertain
future?

Captive *Natalie Rivener* 153

When Fyhnn, an Yrthullian student of
magic, hears stories about the sometimes
dangerous Beyonders, he feels the
irresistible urge to go find out about them
firsthand.
He didn't bargain on being a sought-after
commodity, however, and now has to
fight for his life just for the slim hope of
seeing his homeland again.

Draca *Andrea Vermaak* 185

When Draca discovers that a golden cup
has been stolen from his cursed hoard, he
is torn between leaving his lair in search
of his cup, or living a doomed life trying
to protect the rest of his hoard.

Guardian Angel *Richard T Wheeler* 209

Angels are not welcome, but they've got
a grim duty to do before they crack and
punch their ticket home. Obsidian Edge
has been an Angel longer than anybody, a
freaking legend, but now the secret to his
resilience is about to be exposed.

ACKNOWLEDGMENTS

It takes a whole lot of hard work to put together an book. And an anthology is really a whole stack of books in one.

This publication would not have been possible without the generous contributions in time and creativity of the following people:

Beta readers:
Beatrix Naudé, Dina Steyn, Robyn Grimsley, Natalie Myburgh and Richard Wheeler

Language practitioners:
Dina Steyn, Robyn Grimsley, Natalie Myburgh, Ida Els and Andrea Vermaak

Artists and designers
Elsabé Barnard, Hernes Kruger and Ida van Os.

INTRODUCTION

You're really lucky, you know that? Finding an anthology like this is not an everyday occurrence.

In these pages are stories by seven gifted South African writers, each with their own style, each with undeniable talent.

You might wonder what a bunch of South African writers are doing writing fantasy, science fiction and horror. After all, that is hardly what you'd typically associate with Africa. But, the fact of the matter is, we love these genres and have spent countless hours of our lives reading books, watching shows and movies, and playing games set in fantasy, science fiction and horror worlds.

We love it just as much as you do…if not with a little more of a crazy glint in our eyes.

I hope you enjoy reading these stories as much as we enjoyed writing them.

If you'd like to see more work by the writers featured in this anthology, check out the author biographies and the subscription page in the back.

-Natalie Rivener

Gargoyles

♦ Elmien Grove ♦

"The planet has been through a lot worse than us. Been through earthquakes, volcanoes, plate tectonics, continental drift, solar flares, sun spots, magnetic storms, the magnetic reversal of the poles ... hundreds of thousands of years of bombardment by comets and asteroids and meteors, worldwide floods, tidal waves, worldwide fires, erosion, cosmic rays, recurring ice ages ... And we think some plastic bags and some aluminum cans are going to make a difference? The planet isn't going anywhere. WE are."

- George Carlin

23 September 2011

The first time it happened was in September.

There was an alien sound coming from downstairs. Sam could not remember ever hearing it before. Rising from a cloud of sleep, he lazily tried placing it.

Gurgling. But with tone. A monotone rhythmic gurgle, verging on a growl.

Poltergeist. Must be a poltergeist. This was the last sleepy thought he had before realising Gertrude was not next to him in bed.

The next thing he knew, he was hurtling down the stairs still half asleep, already saying the prayer of adrenaline: *Oh please God please God oh no please help me let it be okay make it okay God please...*

His prayer stopped short halfway down. On the kitchen floor, a creature was coiled backwards onto its head. It faintly resembled Gertrude but the angle of the body was not human. The face was twisted in a bizarre expression of revulsion and the darkness of the

17

kitchen erased her blonde curls and replaced it with a hoary grey mane. The gurgle came from deep within the chest of the thing. One of its pupils was dilated to such an extent that the iris was completely invisible, the other one nothing but a pinprick.

He froze, an ancient fear rising in his gut.

As he looked on, something seemed to release Gertrude's body, making her sink to the floor limply. Blood was gushing from the top of her head, closer to the back than the front. He was confused about how it must have gotten so far up, as he ran to her. How does a person fall down onto the top of her head like that?

A botched backward somersault?

This thought quickly vanished as Gertrude started emitting a high-pitched keen, culminating in a screech. She took gulps of air between screams and continued louder and louder until he reached her. He fell to his knees in order to rest her head in his lap. Her eyes rolled like an animal's and she lapsed into a resigned weeping that broke his heart.

Gillian and Albert also came running out of their room, pale faced.

Once Sam had gotten her up off the floor and lying down on the couch, he asked her what happened.

"I was hungry and wanted to get the fire started so that, when everyone woke up, it would be ready to cook the chicken."

"Okay, but what happened? Did you fall?"

"I don't know. I had gotten the wood, matches and newspaper and got a little fire going. Then, I went into the kitchen to make some snacks."

"And then you fell."

"No, not exactly. I mean, as I walked into the kitchen I just, kind of…lost control of my body."

"How do you mean?"

"Well, in midstride, my spine started bending backwards of its own volition." She stopped talking and wept softly into her hands.

Sam rubbed her hand and encouraged her to go on.

"I heard my head strike the floor, the room was upside down. And, then, you came running down the stairs."

Gertrude's eyes slid towards the dark, walk-in pantry. As he followed her gaze, he thought he saw a dark shape move into the shadows but dismissed it as shock making him see things.

Gertrude looked like she was about to scream.

* * *

2012 – present day

Albert was getting extremely bored listening to his co-worker, Stephen, going on about Gargoyles. The guy was turning pink from lack of oxygen, talking without breathing.

Stephen was an architect by qualification. He had never worked in that field but frequently spoke about what he had learned at varsity. He said there was great symbolism behind some of the historic designs, some beautiful, others terrifying.

The story of the gargoyle was his favourite to recite, the most famous: the gargoyles of Notre-Dame de Paris.

"Architects added them to buildings to fulfil the role of protruding gutters, directing rain water away from the main structure, preventing the masonry from being damaged."

"Uh huh, hmmm," Albert said distractedly.

"The name 'gargoyle' originated from the French verb *gargariser* which means 'to gargle', as well as the noun *gargouille*, which means 'throat'. Don't you find that mystically enchanting?"

Albert found nothing mystical or enchanting about it but felt it would be impolite to verbalise this point of view. He thought gargoyles were ugly and evil looking, contrary to Stephen's ramblings about them "warding off evil" as well as being glorified gutters.

"The whole concept of the gargoyle was derived from an old legend about a malevolent creature, known as Goji, a fire-breathing dragon, hell bent on wiping out humans."

Albert wished Goji was here right now, hell bent on wiping out Stephen.

"But, then, the people killed Goji and tried burning the remains. But, you see, for obvious reasons, the head and neck were fire resistant. So, they decided to mount it above the entrance to the local church to warn off other evil creatures and protect the congregation."

"How anyone could dispute the beauty of the gargoyle, after hearing its amazing heritage is beyond me," Albert said but his sarcasm was lost on the man.

Stephen opened his mouth to continue his rant and Albert's heart sank but, before Stephen could say anything else, his head jerked up as if he was startled by something. Albert watched surprised, as Stephen slightly cocked his head to the side as if listening to a faint sound.

Albert also listened but couldn't hear anything. He decided to make his escape while he still had the chance but, as he stood to leave, he could swear he saw Stephen slightly nodding his head as if acknowledging an invisible person with an inaudible voice, with them in the room.

Aw man, he's finally lost it, Albert thought to himself, quietly slipping out of the office.

* * *

Sam came home from work to find Gertrude still sitting in bed, looking paralysed.

She was whispering again. He was mildly thankful for the whispering rather than the gasps and moans he usually had to endure from her in the evenings and in the dead of night.

"It's time to fight, time to fight, time to fight for Her." Sam wasn't sure that was what she was really whispering but it sure sounded like it.

"Hey sweetie, how are you doing? Is something wrong?"

"I dreamt of a goat last night," she said.

The hair on Sam's arms stood on end at the sound of her voice. She sounded so haunted.

"The goat was chained to a pole in the middle of a village. Black wraiths were floating all around it. Then, a black hole opened up, engulfing everything around it momentarily and then ejected it back into place.

"Except nothing was the same after it had been in there, it had somehow changed."

"It was just a dream, honey."

She finally looked at him and he saw how pale and thin she was.

"I wanted to help the goat, it was the only untouched creature left in the town but the apparitions frightened me and then it was too late." She sagged as she said it.

Sam saw the coffee he had fixed her before leaving for work still standing on the nightstand. It had a white leathery circle drifting on top of it. He thought of the dream she had just told him about and wondered what the goat would come back as.

* * *

Sam was getting extremely bored listening to his friend Albert going on about the apocalypse.

They had become friends because Gertrude and Albert's wife, Gillian, were best friends.

"I'm telling you, Sam, it's not just campfire stories anymore. People are literally killing the planet. There's this new thing called 'fracking' where they use toxic chemicals to draw out oil and stuff from the earth and it's infecting the water. Apparently, Pennsylvania is just about ready to stick a fork in because it is *so* done"

"That's fracked up."

"It's not funny."

"Well, what do you suggest, Al? That we all go live in the forest, wearing fig leaves and eating rocks?"

"Ya, right, as if we'll even *have* forests to go live in. And, anyway, I read about this place called Easter Island where the people really *didn't* have anything but stones to work with but, somehow, they still managed to chop off all the trees and all the people died because the sun-exposed soil got compacted and infertile and they had nothing left to eat."

"I think I already heard all this from Mister Gore in that movie he did and, honestly, I don't give two hoots about the planet, I have real problems to deal with. Besides, I'm not scared of death, death should be scared of me."

"That's arrogant and, FYI, you won't be the only one dying."

"*Oh*, fine, the poor unfortunate children in Africa too. Sorry."

"No, I mean the planet Earth, Mother Nature, will die too."

"So, the Earth and Mother Nature is fracked?"

"I'm not talking to you anymore, you have no respect for what's happening."

"Sorry man, my mind is just elsewhere."

But Sam wasn't really sorry, he was just relieved.

What a depressing subject.

* * *

23 September 2011

Albert and Gillian had just returned from their long trip to Brazil and were elated about spending the long weekend with Sam and Gertrude. They had booked a chalet on a nearby wildlife reserve where there was lots of sun and dust.

Albert was very tired of rain and mud. Brazil had a moody climate.

It had been two months since the foursome had last seen each other.

"This is going to be so awesome, Gill!" he heard Gertrude exclaim through the speaker on Gillian's phone. "I've missed you so much! We are going to swim and drink and tan and listen to music and watch movies and chew bubblegum!"

"Yay, bubblegum!" his wife said with a smile.

Arriving at the reserve and smelling the muskiness of the thatch roof already dropped fifty percent of the stress of the long flight from his shoulders.

Feeling the burn from the first sip of red wine felt like a baptism of sorts. They were home.

Later that night, he woke up to a sound he couldn't quite place.

"Albert, wake up. What was that noise?" Gillian whispered from next to him.

"Yes, I hear it and I have no idea."

It was breathy and rhythmic, so, he decided not to go out of their room until it stopped. He didn't want to walk in on Sam and Gertrude getting busy on the couch. But the next sounds made him and Gillian rocket from their bed: A high-pitched squeal. Loud footsteps coming down the stairs. Sam yelling. And, somewhere, Gertrude started crying loudly.

As they walked out of their downstairs room and into the kitchen, they found Sam cradling Gertrude's head in his lap, shock and confusion written all over his face.

Blood was spilling onto him and the floor.

2012 – present day

Sam was on the verge of a panic attack. Gertrude had been in for blood tests, an ECG, EEG and now an MRI.

He had to leave the room – for his own safety – with Gertrude lying in a big plastic tube with a big plastic needle in her arm.

It's taking too long.

It'd been twenty minutes but it felt like an hour, at least. He felt helpless and incompetent. Gertrude had had a lot of weird symptoms over the last couple of months (and year, he despairingly reminded himself) and if Sam hadn't been so practical, he might have thought of demonic possession. Or, maybe, he's just seen The Exorcist one too many times.

On the bright side, at least, we're on a good medical aid plan, he thought.

The tests were outrageously expensive and would have killed them financially if they weren't so well supported.

The doctor had told them that the seizures, auditory hallucinations and night terrors could very well be attributed to a psychiatric disorder but that he intended to rule out all other possibilities first.

He also mentioned Central Nervous System Lymphoma.

Cancer.

Sam took out his phone and started playing solitaire.

That night, Sam was petrified as he watched Gertrude wrestle with the sheets. She was wet with perspiration, her hair matted and dark with sweat. She was murmuring gibberish into the night. Her eyes were wide open and not their usual blue-green but pitch black.

Is it happening again?

* * *

November 2011

Albert, Gillian, Sam and Gertrude had met at a work function. Strangely enough, Sam and Albert had worked there for at least a year and knew about each other but hadn't really bothered to strike up a conversation. Especially since Gillian and Albert were married and spent lunch together most days, away from the office.

Gertrude was the only one not working at the firm.

The women had clicked instantly, the way soul mates are rumoured to, and they quickly became inseparable.

It was not very long after that that the couples decided to go see a band together at the Dome but, at the last minute, Sam had to work and Albert had to leave town on business. So, Gertrude and Gillian went together. A girls' night.

That night, something happened that would bind them together forever.

Sam sat next to a badly shaken and bruised Gertrude at the police station the next morning, wanting to bang his fist through a wall.

"Okay, let's start at the beginning," said the officer, pen poised over a notepad.

"There were thousands of people there and Gillian and I had to hold hands not to lose each other in the crowd," Gertrude began. "As we exited the building, there was a huge cloudburst and the crowd turned into a bunch of skittering animals." Gertrude was getting visibly more distressed.

"Someone bumped me from behind, I looked over my shoulder for a moment and, when I looked back, Gill was gone. When I saw her again, a big man had her by the arm and was ushering her into the dark."

As he listened, Sam couldn't believe this happened in front of so many people. The way nobody had noticed made him feel nauseous.

"I ran to the dark spot where Gillian and the man had disappeared and found a van. Inside the van was a group of scared girls…and Gill." A fat tear rolled over Gertrude's cheek as she said this.

"I yelled for the big man to let my friend go. He was about to get into the van."

Sam's stomach twisted in terror as she spoke. If only he had gone with them.

"Was Gillian already in the van with the other girls at this point?" asked the officer.

"Yes, she was in the passenger seat and looked like she had been manhandled. Her hair was tangled and dirty. I think she must have fallen into a puddle of water."

"Then what happened?"

"The man reached inside the van and took out a baton. I lost my mind and grabbed for it but he pushed me down and started hitting me with it."

Sam knew it was a miracle that she had not been struck in the head. He also knew that if she had been, and had lost consciousness, the man would have probably abducted her too.

As it were, he "luckily" got her mainly in the back and kidneys.

"While I was down, Gillian had gotten out of the van and was hammering on the man with her fists. The man swung around with his baton and struck Gillian in her side and it looked like it knocked the breath out of her."

"Good, just take your time and think what happened next," said the officer.

"Gillian fell down next to me.

"I was trying to get up but stopped when I made eye contact with Gillian and saw her slightly shaking her head telling me to stay down."

"And then the man just got into the van and drove off?"

"Yes. We were starting to attract attention."

"How many other girls did you see in the van?"

"At least five. What will happen to them?"

"In my experience, they will disappear forever. But we are still trying to find them. What is the world coming to? Maybe we deserve to die out as a species," the officer muttered cynically.

Sam had to leave the room to quietly vomit into a bin outside the door.

* * *

2012 – present day

Albert had had a terrible nightmare the previous night.

He was in a hospital where seemingly no one could see him. It seemed like everyone there was busy with their own thing and strangely hostile towards him whenever he tried to make contact. He had a needle in his arm but it was not connected to a drip. He kept trying to leave but he couldn't get any of the nurses to help remove the drip tube from his arm and it was plastered right in there.

Suddenly, he realised that there may not be a drip connected to his arm but that there was something in the air of the place, filtering into his veins. Something sinister.

The next day, he was sitting at his desk thinking about how he had woken up with a start, sweat running into his eyes or were they tears, when the phone rang.

"Hello, Albert speaking."

"Albert, I need you. There…there is someone in my office."

He was on his feet before the phone beeped off.

Gillian's department was oddly empty. He found her sitting at her desk, looking frozen.

"What's the matter?" he asked.

"I want you to sit down and listen to me very carefully."

He did as she asked.

"There is something…someone… else in my head." She pointed to her temple with a shaking hand.

If he hadn't seen the state of her, he would have thought she was joking.

"What do you mean? Like a tumour or something?"

"No…a voice spoke to me… it's quiet now but I still feel it."

"Well, what did the voice say?"

"It said-" Gillian paused to swallow. "'She is deep in thought.'"

"Is that it?"

"No. When I lifted my head to see who was speaking, it said: 'She lifted her head.'"

"I don't quite understand," Albert said.

"Like…it reminded me of when my brother was little and he kept repeating everything I said until I had to pound on him. Except, this time, it was more like a narration of what I was doing."

"And then?"

"And then…" Gillian had to swallow again.

He could see she was fighting back tears.

"It said: 'She is thinking about her brother…Donnie.'"

"What? It said Donnie's name?"

"Yes. Then, I said: 'Hey, who said that? How do you know my brother's name?!'"

Albert was starting to get nervous. There *was* something different to her. He scanned her face. He could swear her brown eyes had a reddish tint to them but, when she blinked again, they were normal.

"Let's get you to a doctor."

* * *

"Toxoplasmosis."

"Toxa-what?"

They had expected the worst, AKA lymphoma. They had seen movies where characters had lymphoma and they never had happy endings.

"Have you ever owned cats?"

"We currently have three cats, doctor," Sam said because he could see that Gertrude was stunned into silence.

"Well, the toxoplasmosis parasite is usually contracted from cats. Do they use a litter box?"

"N...n...n...no doctor." Gertie sounded a bit like Rain Man and Sam had to stifle a hysterical guffaw. "They have been going outside since they were old enough. We only used a box when they were kittens."

"Well, the toxo parasite spreads by means of cat faeces, so, I would assume that's how you contracted it."

"But what about me, doctor? I was there too. I helped clean those litter boxes. And Gertie washes her hands thirty times a day, how come I don't have it?!"

"I have to admit, this is irregular. Almost half the cats in this city harbour the parasite, thus, almost half the people in the city too. But, mostly, the parasite lies dormant. I've only seen acute symptoms like this in severely immune-depressed patients. "

"But Gertie is not immune depressed! She's just...depressed!"

Sam knew he was trying to bargain with the doctor but he just couldn't help himself.

"Like I said, it's highly irregular. But medically possible, certainly. It seems Gertrude has been exposed to toxo at some point in her life, as were you, by all odds, but, now, the parasite has been activated. 'Awakened', if you may."

"Wait...are you calling me a crazy cat lady?" Gertrude hadn't spoken in ten minutes and both the doctor and Sam started.

Sam's head spun like a wheel.

He bizarrely thought about how the cats had been bringing

home a lot of live mice. He had a soft spot for mice. Gertrude was scared of them, so, she only tried saving the birds. The job of saving the rodents inevitably fell to him.

Gertrude had rescued countless pigeons from their cats but they had always died, even though she fed them watery ProNutro and cooed sweet nothings into their little faces.

Sam couldn't help resenting the little creatures for making his girlfriend cry. But the mice he liked. Their hematite eyes, their agility and the fact that they were just seemingly more determined to live. They fought harder than any of the other creatures the cats had ever caught.

One of them had once effectively used his body as a makeshift ladder to escape them.

That morning, he had woken up to a strange rattling sound and found all three of their cats trying to coax a field-mouse from behind the bathroom bin. He had shuffled all three out of the toilet cubicle, closed the door and hunched down to catch the mouse in order to set it free.

The mouse had other plans, though. As Sam had reached out to it, the mouse circumnavigated him, jumped at lightning speed onto his butt and raced up his spine, onto his head and straight out the window.

He didn't even have time to stand up straight.

Give that mouse a Bells, he had thought to himself.

Of course, the mouse had been brought back, in the mouth of their best little hunter.

He had managed to corner the pride of cats once again but it was seemingly too late. He found the mouse lying on its side, completely stiff, with its mouth slightly open showing its cartoony front teeth.

But, astonishingly, as he picked it up by the tail, it miraculously recovered and made a break for freedom once again.

Why would the mouse just lie there waiting to be chowed down by cats?

It had taken some effort to catch it once more to finally free it into the neighbours' garden. But that was only the first of many.

He couldn't find any nests in the garden and no reason why the mice would flock to the house. He and Gertrude usually scavenged left-over cheese and bread for supper and, therefore, there was normally not a crumb untouched that could lure them.

The cats rarely left the premises. Their prey was usually easily accessible. Their cats were well fed and lazy. They would only hunt if it was made easy for them. And, then, only for sports.

However, these days they were *eating* the mice. Not the birds or the lizards. Just the mice.

The thought of suicidal, death-wish mice occurred to Sam more than once but certainly that would be against nature?

As he listened vaguely to the doctor going on about toxoplasmosis, Sam looked into Gertrude's eyes and thought of the goat she had dreamt of. He thought of how much a goat's eyes looked like the devil's.

And how much Gertrude looked possessed.

* * *

That night, it was Sam's turn to dream and he dreamed of the ocean again.

He dreamt of the ocean at least once a week. The most frustrating part of this recurring theme was that he never got to see the beach. There was always something withholding him and, before he knew it, the holiday was over and he had to return home.

Plus, he somehow never reached home in the dreams either. He either got lost driving back or held up at the airport or drowned in a tidal wave. *At least I got to swim in those dreams*, he thought.

This ocean dream was a little different, though.

It was supposed to be a holiday with friends but something was happening that made people disappear. So, it was just him and Gertrude in a crummy little ground-floor apartment. When they arrived, the ocean was visible but, as the dream continued, it disappeared systematically.

He knew it was still there but it seemed like ten thousand miles away.

It was Christmas Eve. A feeling of impending doom lingered over him. Why? Christmas was their favourite time of the year.

All three the cats were there with them and they seemed happy but Gertrude was anxious that they would disappear too, along with the other people and the ocean view.

She seemed troubled in the dream but Sam didn't know if it was because of the cats or just another mood swing.

He wanted to do something nice. Maybe go out for Christmas dinner. He felt lonely in the nameless coastal town but Gertrude said that she wasn't feeling well and went to bed, leaving him feeling depressed and disappointed.

After making sure all their cats were alive and kicking, he decided to join her in bed. But, suddenly, the flat was not on the ground floor anymore. He started climbing the stairs to the first floor but then another floor spawned on top of it.

Bizarrely, he could not remember their flat number. All the doors were open but nobody was home. He spent the whole of Christmas Eve looking for their apartment and Gertrude – in a frenzy of panic and anxiety.

Then, daylight. It was Christmas Day.

They were back in the original flat, the patio led onto a little garden with a big tree in the middle. As he walked outside, he felt afraid. Very afraid.

Something was wrong.

As he looked up, the tree was full of dead mice, entangled in the leaves and twigs. One of the bigger branches had a shoe on it. And there was a foot in the shoe. And a leg attached to the foot. But he could only see up to the knee because of the foliage.

"Hey!" he shouted.

And, then, they were gone – the mice, the shoe, the foot and the leg.

He could hear someone laughing softly. What kind of a sick joke was this? He flew around and tried to call for Gertrude but he had gone completely mute. As he glanced back to the tree, the dead mice were back.

He blinked and, when he opened his eyes again, they were gone once more. He turned back to the house and saw that the roof was littered with dead rats. Sam knew he was losing his mind.

In a moment of pure horror, he remembered their cats and whirled back to the garden where he found all three lounging peacefully in the sun.

The youngest came to him and looking up into his eyes she said: "I am tired. I need to have some peace now. It's time to fight."

Sam picked her up and cradled her in his arms like a baby.

* * *

The next day, Sam was back at work. He had been there for four hours, thirty-seven minutes and fourteen seconds. He had a mountain of work to do but continually found his eyes sliding towards the analogue clock, entranced by the long hand's staccato movement.

He wanted to go home to Gertrude. She was not coping well and hadn't brushed her long hair for about a week now.

Sam's desk was right across Stephen's office, so, he clearly saw him pushing back his chair and standing up. He sure hoped he wasn't coming over to his desk to ramble on about architecture again.

As he stepped out of his office, Wendy went up to him with worry written all over her face.

"Are you okay? You look ill," she said.

As Sam looked on incredulously, Stephen simply bent his knees and shoved his forehead hard into Wendy's throat. He could swear he heard cartilage shattering.

She dropped like a stone.

Sam knew she was dead.

He saw movement from the periphery of his eye and turned his head towards the hallway where he saw people running, looking almost comically afraid.

He quickly looked back at Stephen. The man had the look of an injured animal, blood was streaming from his brow but he didn't seem bothered by it. His eyes were full of fear…and fire.

Sam instinctively shot out of his chair and into the passage but Stephen darted in front of him.

Stopping him short, Stephen glared from beneath his messy hair; Sam could hear strange noises coming from somewhere in his face.

He had a split second to realise it was the sound of grinding teeth before Stephen lunged at him, snapping and growling. Sam felt the pain in his hand before realising Stephen was biting down on his thumb. He could hear the tendons tearing as Stephen worked away at it like it was a rack of ribs. He howled in pain and drew closer to Stephen to counter the ripping sound and, as he did,

Stephen lifted his face to his.

His eyes cleared momentarily. "Run," Stephen whispered. "Run, Sam."

So, Sam ran. He had time to look over his shoulder to see Stephen still standing there for a heartbeat, looking sad and crazy and confused.

And, then, the human went out of him and he fell forward onto all fours and started pounding after him, hideously, uncannily animal. As Sam rounded the first corner, he could feel the Stephen-thing snapping at his heels and heard an awful guttural growl coming from his throat.

A door opened in front of Sam and he barrelled through it, grunting and scuffling.

"Sam, are you alright?!"

It was James, he was wild-eyed and perspiring. A handful of his colleagues were huddled around him.

"What the hell was that?!"

"Stephen went berserk. I…I think he killed Wendy."

"And, then, he came after us!" Susan from Sales, as he liked to call her, was visibly trembling.

"Is your hand alright?"

Sam looked down at his hand. The thumb was almost completely torn off along with a chunk of the palm. He didn't feel pain but he couldn't seem to get his cell phone out of his trouser pocket until he realised he had to use his other hand.

The one with the opposable digit.

* * *

March 2012

The second time it happened was the next year.

Sam and Gertrude hadn't had a date night in what seemed like forever. So, when Sam found out about a 1980's theme party at a nearby club, he immediately asked Gertrude if she would like to join him for a nice dinner and then go dancing and, of course, Gertrude was elated.

Once you hit thirty, getting to dress up and go clubbing is like winning a tiny lotto, Sam thought, listening to Gertrude's excited yapping as she was pouring over her wardrobe trying to establish what people in the 80's wore and how she could concoct something resembling it from her eclectic collection.

Once she came up with a 'fabulous' outfit, they were on their way to dinner at their favourite restaurant where people wouldn't think twice about her 80's-inspired outfit.

"How do you think other people will be dressed?" she asked Sam, who refused to dress up as anything. "Don't you think we're too late? What if there's no one left."

"No, we should make a fashionably late entrance."

"Oh my word, what if I'm the only one who 'dressed for success' and end up looking like a clown?!"

* * *

Sam was only half aware of her chattering as he thought about how tender the rump was that he had just eaten. And how good the baked potato felt, settling in his stomach.

Once they arrived, they stood on the curb holding hands, Gertude exasperatedly looking at the non-clowns, walking in and out of the club.

"Let's leave," Gertrude whispered loudly into Sam's ear.

"No, we came all this way...you with teased hair... Just one drink."

They went in after about five minutes of arguing and were instantly welcomed by a bunch of swerving middle-aged men.

Well, they're welcoming Gertrude, actually, thought Sam.

"Seems like this party was actually meant for people who were in high school in the 80's, not born in the 80's," said Gertrude as a balding man drunkenly offered her a drink, igniting a tiny spark of jealousy in Sam. "Ah, but so sweet the glory of being the youngest woman in a club again!" Gertrude continued, smiling sweetly at him.

He didn't tell her how much he secretly enjoyed showing her off; he considered it a compliment to him when she turned heads. *That's my girlfriend there.*

He also failed to mention to her how happy it made him when she smiled up at him like that, happy and care-free.

They stayed well into the night, dancing and joking like teenagers, before finally going home with aching feet.

Then, they spent the rest of the night on their couch; chatting, drinking beer shandies and watching silly movies that made them laugh until the sun came up. Just like the good old days.

Sam had a meeting later that day, so, at some point he got up and took a shower. The warm water felt good on his skin but he felt a little sad about washing off such a splendid evening.

But, when he emerged from the shower, all his good spirit vanished as he saw Gertrude's legs protruding horizontally from the toilet cubicle across from the bathroom. They were shaking.

Sam ran slipping and sliding to his girlfriend's side.

Gertrude was lying face-down on the tiles, beside the toilet. She was shivering and moaning. Blood was rapidly pooling underneath her chin.

Sam yelled out her name but, after getting no response, he grabbed Gertrude's legs and yanked her out of the cubicle. Once out of the small space, Gertrude's face was visible. Framed by hair that was no longer blonde but ash with blood highlights.

She stared unseeingly at Sam, stuttering like a machine from deep in her chest, eyes black as coal.

Sam didn't know what was happening. But he had seen it before.

* * *

Present day

She finally picked up after five rings.

"Gertrude, I'm at work. Something weird happened to Stephen. I think he's gone crazy. He…he bit me!"

"Oh dear," she responded to the news like it was a commercial for diet coke.

"I have to get to a doctor but I'll be home as soon as possible."

"Okay," Gertrude said sounding distracted.

"Time to fight," he thought he heard her whisper before breaking the connection.

After driving around for what seemed like an eternity, desperately trying to reach a doctor, Sam was overcome by a strong feeling of unrest. As he swung into their driveway, he saw that Gertrude was standing outside, waiting for him.

"I couldn't find one open surgery! Where has everyone gone?!"

"I heard on the radio that there has been an alert. People are killing each other. They say it might be an infection of sorts. They said we should go to the nearest hotel. There will be security. I have to phone Gillian. Oh, look at your poor hand! Let's get that cleaned up first."

Sam felt uncomfortable with the way Gertrude said this. She had a brisk businesslike attitude to her as she spoke. *Is this the end of days?*

"I think this might be the end of days, Sam," Gertrude said, frightening the hell out of him.

Did she just read my mind?

Gertrude turned her face to his and smiled with teeth like a cat's.

* * *

As Albert ushered Gillian towards his car, a strange calm came over him. *Things are going to be okay. Just fine.*

He suddenly heard a snarl echoing from somewhere close by and stopped short, tugging at Gillian's arm.

A man emerged from behind a sedan to the left of them. He started scrambling on hands and feet towards them, accelerating with a look of dark murder painted on his face.

As Albert started moving protectively in front of Gillian, the man saw her and froze. His legs straightened and he stood up, looking her dead in the eyes. Albert thought he detected an immense internal struggle in his expression but, as they looked at him, he rearranged his face into a lop-sided smile and nodded courteously at Gillian. He walked away without a word.

"What the hell was that?" Albert muttered, rattled by the man's behaviour.

"Cull the scourge," Gillian whispered thoughtfully.

Albert walked faster, almost dragging his wife behind him.

Once they arrived home, Albert tried phoning the doctor's office to make an appointment for Gillian but the line was busy. He tried four other practices, both GPs and psychiatrists were all occupied.

As he looked out the window, he saw Gillian talking to the gardener. He didn't think he'd ever seen her speak to him. She probably didn't even know his name. *What* is *his name?*

Suddenly, the gardener dropped his shovel and walked briskly out of the yard. Albert saw him walking down the street with a sense of urgency.

"Where did he go?" he asked when Gillian came back inside.

"I asked him to run an errand for me, quickly. I don't think he'll make it back, today."

"All the doctors in the world seem to be extremely busy; we'll have to go to the ER."

The hospital was a place of mayhem. The waiting room was packed so full that people were milling around trying to fit in somewhere. Lots of them were bleeding and crying. Others were just sitting there, pale and obviously in shock. The receptionist seemed on the verge of a nervous breakdown and nurses and doctors were scurrying around like rats in a panic.

Gillian's phone rang; she picked it up and listened intently without saying a word. Then, she hung up.

"Who was that?"

She paused for a moment as if considering the question before replying. "Gertrude. We have to go there immediately. She says people are going mad all around the city."

As Albert turned to hurry out of the madhouse, he noticed Gillian make eye contact with a buff guy standing by the entrance. She cocked her head towards the rest of the waiting room, her eyes never leaving his.

"What was that?"

"Never mind, we need to go now."

Albert thought he heard screaming as they power-walked to the car but, when he tried to look over his shoulder, Gillian took his arm and marched him to the car.

She's much stronger than she looks, he thought.

Arriving at Sam and Gertrude's house, he felt strangely jumpy. The streets were very quiet on the way there but the air seemed cleaner somehow.

They rang the bell and a haggard-looking Sam opened for them. When Sam saw Gillian, he looked at her face for a full minute before saying anything.

"Oh, sorry, how rude of me! Hi, you guys, please come in! Gill, did you change your hair or something?"

"Or something," a deadpanned Gillian replied.

Albert was scared. Something very peculiar was happening to his wife.

But, when he saw Gertrude, his heart almost stopped. Obviously, something very peculiar was happening to her too because her green eyes were almost completely black and, he thought, he saw a crimson light in them but decided it must be the red rug in the sitting room reflecting off them. Her hair had streaks of grey in it as if she had dumped the contents of a full ashtray onto her head.

Albert vaguely noticed that the rug didn't seem to be doing the same thing to Sam's eyes, though...

They stood around staring at each other for a while. He felt awkward, so, he decided to break the silence. "So, how have you guys been?"

Sam started at the sound of Albert's voice. He had been looking at the women, standing face-to-face, seemingly oblivious to the men's presence.

"Things have gotten really weird, really quickly," Sam said lifting his hand, bandaged into a ball. But Albert wasn't listening, he had also noticed the girls' behaviour. The funny thing was that they seemed to be communicating. Gertrude would nod her head slightly from time to time as Gillian's eyes bore into hers and vice versa.

"Sam, you want to join me for a chat on the patio?" Albert said quietly.

As the two men went outside, the women didn't seem to notice. Albert closed the sliding door behind him as they exited the room.

"Dude, what the hell?!" he asked Sam.

"Erm...I got nothing," he replied.

"How long has she been like this?"

"Who? Gertrude? Well, she's always been a little weird but, now, she's either going crazy or dying from this parasite the doctor found in her head."

There is something in my head, Gillian's words floated back to Albert. "What? What parasite?"

37

"The doctor said it's something you can get from handling cat litter."

"What, toxoplasmosis?"

"Yeah, that's it. Toxoplasmosis."

"But that's rare, isn't it?"

"Well, the doctor seems to think it was triggered somehow but he's clueless as to what it could have been. Apparently, lots of people get it but they're okay. He asked Gertrude if she's HIV positive or diabetic," Sam said.

"What are her symptoms?"

Sam thought about it for a second and said: "She's had two seizures in the last year but that could have been from her medication and, about six months ago, she started having night-terrors and started talking to herself...sort of arguing with herself. Why do you ask?"

"If Gertrude has toxo and it's been triggered, then, maybe the same thing is happening to Gillian."

"Really? Gillian? She seems fine...isn't she fine?"

"No, she is most definitely not fine. Earlier today, she phoned me from her desk saying she has something or *someone* in her head and she needs my help."

"The doctor told me and Gertrude that the infection can cause hallucinations, both visual and auditory."

"Well, that might explain it. Gillian's had a haunted look on her face for a while now and today just sent her over the edge, it seems."

"We should go back in and check on them."

When they walked in, Sam felt an enormous sense of *déjà vu*. The women were coiled, close to each other on the couch, eyes wide open and staring into different corners of the room. They were whispering something into the air but it was inaudible.

The men stood in the doorway, mouths agape, horrified at the scene but, as their minds raced to find the appropriate response, the women came out of their fugue.

They both looked up at them and smiled.

"What have you boys been doing out there?"

"Talking about us?"

As the men looked at the women, they hardly recognised them. Their faces had changed. They had a sharp look to them. Their noses seemed pointier and their eyes shone like those of black widows. Their hair had somehow dyed into charcoal coloured locks, filigreeing down their necks and backs.

"We should go to the nearest hotel. There will be people there," Gertrude murmured.

"Yes, we should find the people," Gillian repeated after her.

"No, we should stay here and wait. By the sound of it, the world has gone crazy. It would be dangerous to leave." Sam was anxious to keep Gertrude out of harm's way. Or was he anxious to keep 'the people' out of Gertrude's way?

Both Gertrude and Gillian had unwavering smirks lingering on their lips. He thought he saw the faintest glimpse of sharp, yellow teeth and decided not to argue any further.

Albert stood to one side, wild-eyed and semi-catatonic. Sam took a second before he realised what that expression was. His own blind terror, mirrored in Albert's face.

* * *

When they arrived at the nearest Protea Hotel, the women sprang into action like athletes leaping out of the blocks. Sam and Albert were having some difficulty keeping up with them.

Gertrude was basically running, Gillian short on her heels. As they entered the building, the women split up. Gertrude rounded a corner into a dining room and Gillian bounded up the stairs to the first floor, Albert scrambling after her.

As soon as Gertrude entered the room where about twenty people were huddled, she leaned back onto her haunches, hissing. And, as Sam looked on, reality went out the window, making way for the *Twilight Zone* to enter. His sweet, harmless little girlfriend's cheeks pulled away to reveal long, curved fangs and she launched herself at the closest person with the force of an off-road vehicle and the speed of wind, aiming directly for the jugular.

As she tackled the unfortunate man, her granite grey hair stretched all the way down to her waist. Her hands twisted into black talons, tucking themselves into the man's chest. Two giant grey wings sprouted like fountains from between her shoulder blades and she lifted the man about thirty centimetres from the floor as she tore into him.

The other people reacted like wild horses and started piling through the door leading into the next room, screaming like children.

Sam stood frozen as the Gertrude-creature up righted itself and looked at him with nightmare eyes and feral grin. He presumed the man on the floor was dead, judging by his torn neck.

"The Earth has called on me, Sam. She found me in a dream," she said and, as she spoke, her wings folded behind her back, her face plumping back to that of a girl's. He had a moment of doubt about what he had seen. But her hair hung like concrete curtains around her frame and her voice had a scratchy, baritone quality to it that confirmed the horror.

Screams reverberated from the first floor where Gillian and Albert had gone.

People were running down the stairs and he saw Gertrude prepare herself for another lunge, flaring her wings.

Just then, a man charged out of his room, wielding a revolver.

"Don't move!" he cried. "I have phoned the police and they are on their way."

"The police can't help you now, my friend," Gertrude snarled and hurled herself at him, contorting once again into a magnificent dragon-like creature.

Sam turned and ran once again.

* * *

Albert caught up with him, breathing heavily, and Sam found himself peering anxiously into his eyes, looking for the tell-tale glimmer of the monster that took Gertrude.

"Sam, what did the doctor prescribe to Gertrude for her nightmares?"

"A sedative."

"Have you got it here?"

"No, it's still at home on her bedside table."

"It's a long shot but I think you should go get it. I'll stay here with them. Keep your phone with you in case we move."

"I saw her change, man…"

"I know, I also saw…something…where Gillian used to be. But we have to try."

As Sam ran out of the hotel, he caught a whiff of the metallic scent of blood and wondered when, exactly, life had turned into a horror film.

Driving back to the house, the streets were like those of a ghost town. Except for one man walking next to the side of the road, there was no one. As he passed the man he noticed the red glance he gave him and sped up.

Once home, he decided to grab the meds the doctor gave Gertrude for her toxo too.
Maybe this will work, just maybe.

* * *

"Sam, thank God you're back! We have to give them the pills. They've torn everyone in here to shreds!"
"How many pills do you think might work?"
"All of them."
"How the hell are we going to get them to take it?"
Just then, the two women stopped in their tracks, heads cocked to the side as if listening to some far off sound. They slowly turned around and, as their eyes met the eyes of their loved ones, they levelled their beastly gazes at them in perfect unison.
"Gertrude, what are you doing?!" Sam stuttered. She had fixed him with an intense gaze, like the look of a lion about to pounce.
"I'm sorry, Sam, but the Earth has spoken."
Albert and Sam were standing side by side sharing a feeling of absurd surrender.
"Please, we brought you some pills. It might help. You don't really want to kill us too, do you?"

* * *

Let's take the pills, Gill. I love him.
I know, Gertie, me too. But we have to complete the assignment. There is no other way. The Earth needs us...

* * *

41

Later That Same Year

The creatures previously known as Gillian and Gertrude sat perched on a ledge on the Union Buildings, motionlessly peering over their domain.

As the sun set on mankind, it washed the city with golden rays. They watched them retreat and fade into crimson bruises on the horizon.

The Earth rests and so shall we.

Yes, until she calls again.

Yes. And she will. Spring is coming.

Others will come with it.

The Dragon with the Girl Tattoo

♦ Ryhen E Knight ♦

Waking up one unobtrusive morning with aching wing-like appendages on your back would freak out most people of the sane humanoid species. But not Tom. No, Tom took it in his stride like he usually did when life threw him a lemon or one of those cheese filled sausages. He got up out of his bed, inspected the new body accessories and got dressed, awkwardly. With his favourite green shirt on, he had a cup of coffee and left for work.

Tom owned the local TLCFS store in Doolin, which was ironically short for Tom's Lemon and Cheese Filled Sausage store. Once you have enough lemons and cheese filled sausages thrown at you by life, you may as well open a shop selling them. Your stock is free and only slightly used, depending on your ability to catch them before they hit the ground...or your face. And the tourists flocking to Doolin to get good camera views of the neighbouring Cliffs of Moher or trying to find their way to the ancient Celtic site of Burren loved it.

Walking down the small streets, Tom always felt a sense of pride and deep-rooted love for his musical town of birth, geo-somethingly situated on the north-west coast of Ireland. He had no talent for music but he was always the perfect dark-corner-lonely-seat occupant at the pub. Every town needs one and Tom volunteered eagerly, though silently. He lived three blocks away from his store and the pub, and walked there with a friendly gait and an open smile and a ready hand grabbing stock coming in hot from all directions of life.

Today, he had started carrying a lovely knitted mauve bag to transport his daily, randomly delivered stock. Until last night, Tom had not known that mauve was indeed a word, let alone a colour.

Then again, until last night, he had never needed a knitted bag to carry his en route stock acquisitions.

Until last night, Tom had not known what love was.

Tom was a very observant fellow with an eye for detail and incoming flying objects. The other eye went about its own business, mimicking his blue-eyed neighbour's every move.

And, on a fine winter's day, some few days earlier, with the sun cowering behind some aggressive puffy clouds, Tom saw a life-changing apparition of what turned out to be a fake Elvis shadow cast by some enigmatic leaves. But, beneath the enigmatic tree, sat a girl. She was no ordinary girl, for Tom did not observe girls as normal men did. Tom was a black and white person and girls fell into those shades of grey that made Tom uncomfortable.

But not this girl! She had an air of something special about her. After all, she did make Tom ignore the nifty Elvis apparition! Maybe it was the way she showed absolute naïve enjoyment of the world around her. Or the way her twinkling amber eyes lit up as a bird flew overhead. Or the way she twitched her delicate little nose as a wet dog strolled by.

Whatever it was, Tom was smitten the moment he laid his deep blue eyes on her. Never had he seen such absolute beauty personified in a single creature of the opposite sex. Nor did he see the approaching cheese filled sausage that hit him squarely on the forehead.

Normally, a hot sausage on the forehead would hurt but this morning he hardly noticed as the pain skulked away in the presence of the delightful giggle of the girl. Tom duly moved on, embarrassed and in love, averting his eyes towards other incoming flying objects and tracking a flighty, smitten heart.

Over the next few days, after the initial introduction that included no communication or exchange of names or contact information, Tom's mind was often found wandering back to the park and the tree. And the girl. That girl.

Tom started to feel a growing emptiness during the days following his encounter in the park. He returned to the park to seek out the tree and the girl only to find the tree and the branch and the leaves. And a squirrel that started to wave at him suggestively after the third visit.

It was not until the previous night that an Elvis-tree-like

incident happened again to Tom. Only, this time there was no tree or sunlight to cast images of musical wonders. But there was a girl.

That girl.

Tom was walking back home from his nightly dark corner occupation at the pub when he passed a dark alley and heard a noise that suggested life other than the feline type. He stopped and peered into the darkness, detecting vague shapes of boxes hiding in the gloom.

Just as he was about to move on, he heard a slight whimper. This was followed by that awkward silence that follows when you have been caught in an embarrassing situation and do not know if you must say something or try to hide it. Tom froze with his left foot mid-air. His head turned slowly back towards the alluring silence that dressed the dark alley.

Dark silence. The worst kind.

Like dark matter, dark silence is the opposite of normal silence. Not the exact opposite but almost, for it bore more weight. In fact, dark silence was 1.13205 times heavier than normal silence and almost had its own movie, until they decided to rather go with Silence of the Black Sheep.

Tom stared some more while his size-nine left foot slowly descended down towards earth in a beautifully artistic slow motion arch.

The awkward, dark silence deepened to at least 1.24327 times normal silence.

"Hullo?" Tom ventured a verbal disruption of the inconspicuous voiceless gloom.

The gloom answered his bold venture with some humble muteness.

"Somebody there?" Tom boldly pursued his adventurous investigation from the safety of the lit street.

The silence grew in stature. So did Tom's now solid stance and transfixed stare, both ready to bolt at the first sign of anything.

"Please move on," a soft, almost terrified voice crawled out of the boxed-in darkness.

Tom's mind heard the message but his lack of intelligent thought translated this verbal note into statue-like motion, commonly mistaken as a fighting stance.

"Please!" the whisper grew in intensity if not in volume.

"Sorry," Tom eventually replied, sensing no immediate threat to his life or his claim to his feet-occupied land. "Can I help you with something?"

"No… Maybe."

By now, Tom had deduced through methods of elimination that the voice belonged to a member of the female species. He had heard them speak at his shop and considered himself an expert on female voices pronouncing 'grilled cheese sausage, please'.

"Are you all right, Miss?"

"Yes. No. Maybe." Her voice stalked uncertainly towards him in a way that turns every man into a chivalrous knight. "Do you maybe have an extra jacket with you?"

It sounded like a rather odd request in the middle of the night, coming from a dark alley, conveyed by a timid, vulnerable and yet unidentified female voice.

"Hmmm, okay, yes. I think so." Tom silently cursed himself for he was indeed the proud owner of the jacket that he was currently wearing. He slowly took off his jacket. He had not planned on providing textile protection this morning when he left his apartment, so the jacket contained an adventurous odour of sausage. And, for some reason, he felt embarrassed by the malodorous fact as if that would be the main concern of some cold and/or naked woman in a dark alley.

Nervously, Tom left the safety of the light and ventured into the dark alley, bracing himself for the worst. A few seconds later, his feet followed his imagination as he edged forward. It took him a while to adjust his eyes to the darkness and eventually he saw movement behind the dumpster in the deepest corner of the alley. It just had to be the deepest corner. It is never the slightly gloomy, friendly wall with lots of room to run away. No, it is always the deepest and darkest corner.

"The jacket, my lady." He stretched out his hand with the jacket to said dark corner.

A petite hand emerged from behind the dumpster and traversed the air in the general vicinity of the jacket until it landed on target and grabbed it. Tom froze as he tried to figure what the gentlemanly procedure would be from here on. He had offered the jacket, smell and all, lived to tell the tale and was now starting to feel why he had worn the jacket as the night chill encircled him.

Does he leave her now? How would he get his jacket back? Does he offer her coffee and a biscuit and hope she comes up with a jacket-exchange solution that will result in his jacket hanger being occupied again and her nakedness not being reengaged?

"Thank you," a less nervous voice softly spoke as a head, hair in halo formation, appeared from behind the dumpster.

Tom squinted, frozen to the spot. Eventually the silent squint and its silent forefathers started to become a thing with its own presence and name. Non-existing observers later fondly referred to 'it' as George.

"Okay. Pleasure. Hope it fits." He was more than a foot taller than her and was worried that the jacket would fit. Tom slapped himself in his mind. It hurt. Luckily the mind-slap stirred up some cohesive thinking. "Can I offer you some other assistance, my lady? Some coffee and biscuits?" Obviously not intelligent thinking!

George briefly returned as the halo considered the odd offer.

"What sort of biscuits do you have?" the halo asked, her stature growing as she started to emerge from behind the dumpster. The jacket seemed quite big for a rather small frame. His hanger possessed more bulk than the current inhabiting shoulders.

Tom took a step back towards the light, partly to give his occupied jacket some more safe space to emerge in, partly because his mind eventually recovered from the slap and registered his mortal danger: A woman was seemingly interested in coming to his place!

"Some shortbread, my lady."

The shape began to exhibit legs and feet that moved in his direction. Tom retreated until his feet touched lighted pavement and he could nervously look up and down the street for help. All clear. When he looked back, an angel was slowly emerging from the darkness.

"I am not your lady, silly." Her voice began to relax and enthral Tom. "My name is Elyan."

Tom had never heard such a name before but it seemed to fit the frail, angelic apparition in front of him perfectly. Light finally fell on her and Tom almost gasped. Moonlight-white skin covered the parts of her body not covered by a smelly jacket or the halo of tangled red hair. Slender legs emerged from the borrowed clothing

49

and ended in bare feet. Small feet. Tom had never noticed that women had feet – small, beautiful feet. Embarrassed, he looked up and into her green, amber trimmed eyes as he realised she had spoken and asked him his name.

"Tom, I think. Yes, Tom," he stammered as he mind-slapped himself again.

"Do you live nearby, Tom-I-think?" She smiled at him, her eyes laughed in innocent joy. "I am rather cold and some coffee and biscuits would be really nice." She was hugging the jacket tightly, as if trying to squeeze out some extra heat through fierce cuddling.

"Yes," Tom answered and felt rather pleased that he knew the right answer. It took another mind-slap before he realised that she was hoping for an invite to some warmer enclosures. "Hmmm. Right this way!"

Tom led the way to his humble abode. There were few people in the streets of Doolin at that time of night, mostly the alcohol enriched type, so they paid scant notice to Tom awkwardly leading a shivering little lady, wearing only a jacket, down the street.

But someone did. Dark, concealed eyes followed them as they walked down the street. To be factually correct, two eyes followed them. A third eye was eyeing an alley cat rather deliciously, whom in turn became uncomfortably aware of being checked out for culinary compatibility from some unseen shadow. The cat skulked away nervously, looking fretfully over its feline shoulder until it was sure that cat-tartar was no longer on the menu. The shadow also moved on, gliding from darkness to darkness. The gliding stopped when it got tired and then it just walked casually behind the odd couple at a safe following distance.

Tom and Elyan arrived at Tom's apartment without being any the wiser about the out-of-breath darkness stalking behind them. They hardly spoke a word along the way. He did venture a brisk "We're here" when they arrived at his front door. Elyan, naked legs and bare feet, smiled back at him hardly showing any signs of the cold on her kitchen appliance white skin.

A brief moment of panic flashed through Tom's mind as he opened the door and revealed a prehistoric man-cave, lived in by a single guy with little social aptitude or friends and a lot of alone time. Elyan slid in once the door was open and stood there, studying the pizza box and magazine covered apartment, eyes darting from one corner to the other, taking in all the glorious symbolism of bachelorhood. Or maybe looking for any sign of civilisation. Or a vacuum cleaner!

"You live here alone?" she asked innocently.

If Tom understood the concept of sarcasm he may have answered differently. Instead, he smiled sheepishly and nodded. He started to scurry around, touching here and there, grabbing stuff only to let it fall while darting off to the next pile of eye-catching something. In his travels around his cave-world, he started to take more notice of the girl (yes, a girl!) in his apartment. She had some wild, long, dark red hair that flowed over her slender shoulders to some undetermined point on her back. Her eyes were big green, amber trimmed dream catchers that could ensnare a carnivorous dinosaur. Her flawless skin covered a face that contained the cutest nose and prettiest lips known to mankind. Pale, delicate legs provided a stairway from an oversized jacket to her delectable green-tinged feet.

In short, like her height, she was the most amazing thing to have ever crossed into his Tom-cave. She was even better than his XBox. Tom did not know it yet, but a small cluster of cupids suspected it: Tom was smitten!

She took up a seat less littered than the other one and crossed her legs underneath her. This seating position was a trick that women learned in the dark ages to look both seductively cute while hiding hairy legs. Elyan did not seem to have a need to hide hairiness on her smooth legs. Tom could, however, just about make out a tattoo that seemed to be crawling up her thigh. A blue tail of some sort protruded from beneath his jacket.

"May I be so bold as to ask for that coffee and biscuits now?" her angelic voice pierced Tom's ensnared thoughts.

"What? Yes, of course. Where are my manners?" he stammered as he set out to rectify his oversight and to go look for his manners in the open plan kitchen. He could still see her from where he started to spoon coffee into less dirty cups. "Sugar?"

"Yes, please. Three spoons." She smiled in his direction while her eyes continued to canvass the cave for clues as to how a species could survive in this habitat.

He eventually produced the biscuits and steamy hot coffee on a tray in front of her. Elyan helped herself to some coffee and a biscuit. Then another biscuit. And another. And another. After she emptied the plate, she looked up sheepishly at the doting Tom.

"Sorry, Tom. I was feeling a bit peckish."

She could have eaten his leg for all he cared. Seeing her red lips open and close and chew was utterly mesmerising. Even a stray crumb on her lip seemed to be worthy of a whole sermon on the virtues of all things wonderful.

He caught sight of her blue-printed upper leg and bare feet. As far as Tom could see, she had no clothes on beneath the jacket.

"Can I offer you some more clothing? I do not have woman's clothing that will fit you but I may find a few things that will cover you against the cold."

She smiled at him as if he had said something funny. Tom's ego just stared at her beautiful smile.

"That would be very kind, Tom. Thank you."

Tom got up and disappeared into the bedroom on his quest to find something a woman (in his apartment!) half his size could fit into. Eventually, he decided that his old skinny black jeans may fit, along with some purple tennis shoes some client's kid once left in his store.

He found her in exactly the same spot, legs still curled underneath her. She got up and took the clothes happily from Tom's hands. As she stood in front of him and the jeans slid effortlessly up her shapely legs, he could get a better view of the blue tattoo. It seemed to have scales along a tail that went up way beyond her legs and over her hips. Where it went to from there Tom had no idea because he had never really thought about women and what was hidden behind their sweaters or blouses. Tonight, Tom thought about the mystery. Mother had never explained that part to Tom.

"Perfect fit!" Elyan stated excitedly and jumped over to Tom's side and gave him a hug.

Tom suddenly thought of a whole lot of things he had never thought of before but instinctively knew were something he should not be thinking about. Unlike the Tom of old, who had disappeared about forty-five minutes ago, he acted impulsively. He hugged her back.

"May I ask you a question, my lady?" the words blurted out when their bodies parted.

"Yes, my lord," she replied mockingly, which went way over Tom's level of wit.

"You seemed to be rather misplaced and slightly underdressed," Tom pressed on bravely. "Why were you alone in the alley?"

"I got lost," Elyan answered, somewhat hesitantly, hoping that the answer was enough.

Luckily for her, it was and Tom moved on in this inquisition.

"And the bare feet?"

"I must have lost my shoes somewhere."

Again, Tom seemed quite happy not to question the answer and probe the sense behind it. In general, sense was far less common with Tom than one might have expected.

"Ok. Maybe I can help you go look for it tomorrow," Tom offered sincerely.

Elyan smiled relieved at the offer and the absence of deeper, more probing questions.

"More coffee?" was the only question that followed in the Tom-ish Inquisition.

Elyan nodded and smiled as she glanced up at the clock mounted on Tom's wall. The wall was surprisingly clear of anything, unlike the rest of the apartment that seemed to have collected everything the world did not want.

"Tom, do you perhaps have a car or something? I really need to go somewhere right now."

He stopped pouring the water into the kettle and considered the question. He had 'something' that would serve as an answer to her question. That something might not be 'the' answer to her question for he was the proud owner of his hippie father's old Vespa. One that he had painstakingly ignored in his garage until tonight.

"I have a Vespa that may not be ideal but it will get you where you want to go!" Tom declared chivalrously, praying silently that the gods have mercy on his poor girl-less soul and grant him a scooter that would run irrespective of his disinterest, care or license. "Where do you have to go?"

"The big gateway dolmen!" Elyan sounded relieved at her fortune of finding both a warm jacket and source of transportation on this rather strange night.

"The dolmen at the Burren?" Tom sounded less relieved. He was kind of hoping that she needed to get to a pub and that he may fake drive her there. The Burren was almost an hour away on a small, winding road. It was dark outside!

"Yes, that is the place. We need to go right now, please!" She jumped up, briefly displaying a part of a white upper buttocks and lower back as she swirled towards the door.

Tom only saw what he guessed to be a continuation of the tail of something, tattooed over the revealed bodily area.

"Let's go!" He opened the door and paused. It was a dramatic pause, as far as pauses go with an adult male clutching a key on a Hello Kitty key ring. "I will meet you up front. Just need to go and get the scooter from the garage."

Tom sped off. A daring plan had begun to form in his head. It involved a lot of praying that the Vespa would start. And, failing that, breaking into the neighbour's garage and stealing the little girl's bicycle, which led to some more fervent praying!

Tom's garage was a dark place with many boxes and stuff that belonged to his dead parents. And behind all the clutter was a sheet-covered Vespa. Tom dramatically removed the sheet and beheld his pride and joy, and symbol of his manhood and independence: his father's Vespa. He boldly mounted it and slotted in the key. It was the right key! Confidence soaring, Tom turned the key. Then, he turned it clockwise. A small miracle happened: A droning sound erupted from between his legs and the Vespa came to life.

He quickly drove his scooter out of the garage and found an awaiting Elyan outside. She hopped on behind Tom and snaked her arms around him. A warm feeling enveloped him as his brain registered the fact that the most beautiful woman he had ever met in real life was holding on to him. Pain also followed as a lemon struck him on his arm. He did not really notice or care as he revved up the Vespa and sped off at a very sensible and safe speed for this time of night.

Tom silently cursed as the cold struck him for he had not replaced his borrowed jacket and, with no helmets or any face protection whatsoever, that proved to be a rather poor choice in retrospect. The single light from the Vespa in the middle of the night seemed to draw insects in numbers that any boy band could only dream of. If not for the cold-clenched mouth, Tom may well have learned what bugs taste like. He felt a little bit sad about it.

He was hungry and Elyan had eaten all the biscuits. Her enfolding embrace made up for most of it but not for taking the last biscuit!

They arrived at the Burren just before twelve. It was closed to the public, much as Tom had suspected, since it was a bit after office hours. Luckily, it was not a fenced off area and access was not really a problem. Elyan let go of Tom and Tom let go of the coldest and happiest hour of his life.

"Thank you, Tom." Elyan looked him deep in his eyes and his head swam dizzily as he stared back into her eyes. The amber trimming her eyes seemed to sparkle in the full moon's light. He was willing to drown in those eyes. He wanted to say something of value or romantic. Instead, he nodded like an imbecilic idiot, even when she leaned forward and kissed him lightly on his lips. She turned around and headed into the Burren.

Tom looked after her as she disappeared into the night. He instinctively knew she was not only disappearing into the dark but also from his life. A few hours ago, he had been happily meandering back to his empty apartment with a liver full of ale, oblivious to women and insects. Now, he had the taste of woman's kiss on his lips and the taste of a moth next to it. His heart was pounding and he wanted more. Not so much the moth but more of her.

His legs began to revolt against his addled, slow mind and started to run after her into the Burren. She had said something about the dolmen, so, he headed in that direction over the natural pavement stones that covered this area. As he came over the hill, he could see the big gateway dolmen in the distance. Tom could just make out the form of the love of his life bending down to walk into the massive flat rock archway that made up this supposed gateway. Tom wondered why she would want to walk through it, but the night had been pretty strange so far, so, he did not let logic interrupt him now. He expected to see her crawl out on the other side any moment as he walked towards the dolmen.

She did not.

Nor was she inside it when he got to the entrance. It was empty all the way through to the tapered-down other side. Totally baffled and more than a little bit concerned, Tom stood there scratching his head through his thick brown hair. Impossible! He looked around for signs of her elsewhere and found nothing except a cat skulking around nervously.

Instinct drove him on as he bowed his head and entered the dolmen. It seemed to be both large and narrow at the same time as he shuffled into it. After two small steps he had to go down on his knees to continue. The dolmen was literally about four steps in length but the more he crawled, the longer it seemed to grow. The pavement stones ahead of him also appeared to be glowing. Tom crawled and crawled until at last he reached the exit. He was even out of breath as he exited and stood up.

Tom looked around him. A feeling of unease settled over him in the same way as when you accidently walk into the wrong bathroom and realise it way too late and the girls start screaming at you. He was standing on pavement stones, similar to the ones at the Burren, but these felt different. The stones glowing in the dark should have been the first clue. The spritely tree walking by should have been the second. And yet, Tom still could not put his finger on it as he waved at the tree. His mind was operating in overdrive. It was a new speed for his mind and he was getting used to it very slowly.

Tom tried to make sense of what just happened. He had entered the dolmen many times as a kid but this time it was different. The paving stones had never glowed back then. The stars had not shone, mostly because it was usually daytime. And there were no trees strolling down the path, humming Queen's Bohemian Rhapsody. Tom liked that song and gave the tree a thumbs-up as he hummed along.

His surroundings looked similar but appeared totally different. The usually random pavement stones now had a very 'pathy' feel to it, with two lanes and a warning sign for potential trolls crossings. He looked back towards the dolmen and it was the same one, with some nifty Celtic graffiti on it. He could make out a normal skyline and non-glowing stones on the other side. His side, Tom realised. Where he was standing now was not his side. This was some other side that belonged to walking trees, dangerous troll crossings and Basil, the town's tattoo artist, bar owner and reigning champion chicken tosser.

"Hi, Tom," "Hi, Basil," they greeted as Basil moved along. Tom had never noticed his pointy ears before. Must have been because he had never seen him without a hat or beanie until today.

So, what to do now? Elyan had gone down this path, of that he was sure. Basil had gone down this path. Even the humming tree had gone this way. Tom was great at conforming and disappearing in a herd and being a real team player. Except the team never knew he was there apart from the extra water bottle being used.

So, he did what nature intended him to do: He conformed, made a little sheepish noise and turned his gaze towards the path. With Queen's words in his head and the easy come, easy go music moving his feet, Tom started to walk. He even caught a fresh cheese sausage. Different world, same stock. And he was hungry, so, he ate it not worrying about the potential loss of earning from eating his merchandise.

In his world, the Burren pavement stones meandered through a rather boring grassy field and ended against a big tar road. In this world it seemed to continue forever and a day, with enough distance to provide a supply of two chest-high flying cheese sausages. It went up hills and down hills, a little high, little low, with some trees walking and others standing still, having a refreshing drink. There were trolls running randomly across the road, often chased by gesturing blue wildlings. Birds and fairies chattered overhead and an old dwarf sat on his mushroom, puffing his pipe and checking out the staring tourist.

Tom could not help but stare at what was going on around him, chewing slowly on his sausages. It was night and the stars were all bright and shiny, which made it a pretty strange experience here in Ireland where clouds and rain were more common than Englishmen and logic. Everything had a surreal feel to it. Even the word surreal felt surreal since Tom had never known the word until it had popped into his head just now.

He came to the top of a hill that turned out to be the top of a cliff that overlooked giant hexagonal-shaped stone-pipes sprouting from the sea. Tom stood amazed, looking down at the Giant's Causeway that was supposedly miles away from Doolin, yet, he had covered the distance in less than an hour. A giant was walking onto the causeway, carrying a pack on his back that looked a lot like an old Beetle backseat. It also looked a lot like Elyan sitting on the car seat on the giant's back that was fast approaching the sea.

Tom wanted to shout out and stop them as they would surely drown but the wind blew his words away and a small fairy, back into his mouth. He looked around embarrassed and then swallowed. At least, the wind was still normal Irish wind, cold and tasting of weak ale and pixie dust. He looked on in utter dismay. Miraculously, the giant did not disappear below the waves. Instead, the sea reached up to his knees and, then, eventually his hips and no deeper as he waded into it. Eventually, they disappeared into a thick mist that was hanging around nonchalantly over the water.

A dark shadow passed over Tom and flew off into the direction the giant took. Tom's first thought was that it was a plane passing over but that seemed less likely in this land of strange things. He did not hear the drone of engines or see any lights flashing. Instead he heard what sounded like a flapping noise with a distinct, yet menacing, out of breath-ness to it. It was big whatever it was and it was heading in the direction of his lady. And his jacket!

Tom looked around for a way down from his paved stone walkway and found that the stone-pipes of the causeway made a staircase all the way from the sea up to the cliff's edge. He ran down the natural stairway to the ocean's edge and stopped. The water looked very cold and deep. Tom turned around when he heard some big feet marching in his direction. Another giant was approaching, carrying a sofa on his back.

"Excuse me sir, could you–" was all Tom could say before the giant brushed past him, nearly knocking him off the stones. As the giant disappeared into the mist, Tom could hear him muttering something about outlanders. Tom looked around frantically for another giant without any luck. He bravely took off his shoes and rolled up his pants, venturing a toe into the cold water. He shuddered but bravely stepped into the water onto a submerged rock. The rock promptly slid deeper into the water, almost causing Tom to topple forward into the water. All that saved him was a firm hand grabbing him from behind.

"Stand down, sonny. Theres be no point strolling over these stones, matey."

Tom spun around to find himself looking into the eye of what was, most likely, a pirate. He had the pirate garb and mannerisms that was part of the pirate trademark, copyright protected and all. What was slightly disturbing was looking into his one centre eye while the other two eyes were covered in patches that looked like they had been bought at a costume shop selling toy pirate outfits.

"Why not go there, sir?" Tom ventured politely, trying hard not to look awkwardly at the eye and the kiddie-patches.

"Theres be giants' stones and only giants can take someone across. Us rest shall only steps them deeper into the seas. And thems giants that shall not like to stroll through the yonder seas with scrawny outlanders likes you." He winked at Tom, or so Tom guessed. How do one-eyed people wink at people without it looking like a blink?

"I need to follow that young lady that just taxied on the giant to... Where does this causeway go?" Tom gestured and asked, focussing his gaze on the pirate's forehead to avoid the odd third eye. But, no matter where he looked, the eye seemed to move to follow his gaze's focus point.

"Sorry, sonny, but thats be the Kingdom on the other side of the causeway."

"The Kingdom on the other side of the causeway? Really? Was that the best name you could come up with?" Tom was slightly angry for some odd reason and marginally more frightened at the prospect that he would not see Elyan again. And the not-so-distant memory of the huge, menacing flying shadow ignited his timid chivalry into fearful wrath.

"So it be called since the dawn of Saturday two weeks past, young sir." The pirate's expression changed. "Why seek the stony path through the sea, I seek to know?"

"Hmmm..." Tom had a strange feeling about this pirate chap, apart from the three-eye thing and wagging tail. "She has my jacket."

A plausible excuse that was the truth, if not all of the truth. Tom did not lie. He did not have the face for it, nor a devious enough mind or intellect to deceive others.

"A superb jacket it surely be. Splendidly fortuitous for you, laddie, I be a sailing sort of pirate." The pirate seemed to accept the one-quarter truth. Tom was not sure what other kind of pirates there were, but he happily accepted the pirate's acceptance of his ruse. "My ship can sail you to yonder shores…for a sufficiently succulent price of course."

Tom did not have his wallet on him since he had not really planned the whole night in advance. Nor did he think that money would be of much worth here in this odd, almost-Ireland world.

"What can I offer you, sir? I do not have my wallet with me," Tom replied honestly, hoping it would not scare of his only possible lift.

"Sausages! Cheese sausages for a month! I be tired of thems cats."

Tom was surprised beyond measure. Sausages he could supply – and save some cats. "Yes. Sure!" he exclaimed in relief.

"Super! Shall we go set sail to yonder shores?" he asked but headed off without waiting for an answer. Tom followed until the pirate suddenly stopped, spun around and held out his hand to shake Tom's hand. "Sorry, I say, for my seeming rudeness. I'd be the Pepparidge Pirate. Pleased to serve you!"

"Like the American cold drink?"

"Nay, I say, thats be Dr. Peppers."

"Oh." Tom thought a bit as they walked on. "Like the American biscuits?"

The Pepparidge Pirate stopped, shoulder tensing. To his credit, he turned around and forced a convincing smile. "Surprisingly not the same. Thats be Pepperidge Farm Biscuits." He turned around a stumped off down the path, clearly inviting no further comparative name-calling.

At last, they came to a small rowboat tied near to the Causeway. It was not quite what Tom had in mind. All the books always showed pirates in big ships with lots of sails and cannons. This one had a slightly less pirate feel to it with no sail, no cannons and just two small benches.

"This is your boat?" Tom asked the obvious, hoping to be proven not right.

"She'd be my spunky beauty," Pepparidge spoke lovingly of her. "Speedy she can be and stable as a stone!"

Tom did not wish to argue the point or spell out his fear of deep water and small boats and the scientific theory that stones tend to sink in water. No, he was out on a mission. He climbed into the rowboat and took the seat at the front. Pepparidge followed him and took the seat at the back. Then, the boat started to move without any input from either Tom or the pirate. Giant's Causeway quickly dropped into the sea beside them and they skimmed across the water at an alarming speed for such a small floating endeavour. The lacklustre mist soon swallowed them up and the cliffs disappeared into nothingness. Tom had no idea what lay ahead in the Kingdom on the other side of the causeway. All he knew was that Elyan would be there and he wanted to be there with her.

Like most things in this other world, the 'sail' across the sea was a lot shorter than expected. A few short minutes of trying to plug his ears against Pepparidge's less than lovely rendition of 'Somebody to love' was enough to see them cross the waters to where the Causeway appeared again from the ocean. Tom was very relieved. His ears were even more so. Even his teeth chattered happily when the rendition stopped.

"Safe and sound she'd be sailing, I said," Pepparidge crooned.

Tom was convinced the boat sailed speedily to get her captain to stop singing. He was sure he could hear the boat sigh with relief when the gentle lapping of water against rock replaced Pepparidge's voice, which had sounded very similar to the diabolic grinding of a thousand whale carcasses against rock.

"Thank you, sir." Tom gratefully got out of the boat and stepped onto a slippery hexagon stone. "Any time you want your sausages, just come by my shop and I will give your payment gladly."

Just then, a giant passed them by and looked slightly angry at them. Maybe he had heard the singing spawning across the water. Pepparidge eyed him back suspiciously with his left eye squinting aggressively.

"Excuse me, sir giant," Tom ventured. "Have you perhaps seen a petite red-haired girl in an oversized jacket that smelled like old sausage come this way?"

The giant stopped, for a short moment contemplating politely answering this intruder or smashing his skull in with his bare hands. Fortunately, he chose the first option.

"Mine eyes beheld such a beauty thou art questing for, young lord," the giant answered in a lovely tenor voice. "I carried the fine little lady myself and she graciously ascended the pathway hence." His big hand pointed towards a stony path leading up a green hill.

"You do not, by chance, know her destination?"

The giant looked suspiciously at Tom.

"She has my jacket," Tom offered.

"Oh." His face softened. "A fine jacket indeed, sir. She mentioned something about seeking the Wise One. He lives yonder and beyond in the Castle Rocks. Just follow the path 'till you get to the Red Bicycle. Turn right, continue on the path and then you will see it. Good day to you, sir." With that, he turned and moved onto the Causeway, meandering into the sea and the hanging misty curtains.

Tom moved up the Causeway towards the rocky road and up the hill. He stopped when he realised he was alone and that the pirate had not followed him. When he turned around, the shore was empty. The boat and pirate were gone and Tom felt guilty for not saying goodbye. The guilt got kidnapped by a sense of relief that there would be no more singing and no more whales committing suicide to save themselves from the torture.

He kept to the path, wondering what this new place would be like. It was similar to the world on the other end of the Giant's Causeway, with bright stars above and a surreal, dreamy feel to the landscape. He was rather pleased that he had remembered the word 'surreal'.

There were not many creatures moving about and all the trees seemed to be of the kind that did not move at all. A one-horned white badger did pop out of a hole once but quickly flew away when he saw Tom looking at him. Or her? Tom did not know how to tell the difference in gender with one-horned flying badgers.

After a while he reached a red bicycle with a sign hanging over it: 'Here be the Red Bicycle'. Tom assumed that this was the point where he was supposed to turn right. So, he turned right and stopped after a few steps. A goblin was blocking the path. It was not a particularly pretty goblin as far as ugly goblins go. It looked at him. Tom looked back at him. The silence grew until it formed a George. George stood between them and looked shyly at its feet.

"Here!" the goblin said, dismissing the awkward George.

Tom looked down at what the goblin was offering. It was bag of some colour that looked like a sick purple. He stretched out his hand and took the bag, afraid of offending the goblin.

"Thank you?" Tom offered in return. "May I ask why you are giving me this… bag?"

"It is part of my rehabilitation. I knitted it myself. And, now, I have to give it to a needy peasant. You look needy."

"Thanks, I think." He slung the bag over his shoulder and grabbed an incoming lemon. He slid it into the bag and it fell comfortably to the bottom. "Nice!"

"My pleasure." The goblin smiled, stone teeth not-glowing in the moonlight.

"May I bother you with another question?" Tom asked, pushing past the urge to admire his nifty new knitted bag and vomiting from the sight of the goblin.

"You may," the goblin answered, smiling handsomely.

"What colour is this?"

"It is called mauve. It fits in well with other pastel colours. The other lady that came by here a few minutes ago also liked hers as it looked very good with her very nice, oversized jacket. I really liked her jacket!"

A blood curdling screech of a scream vibrated through the air, interrupting the jacket appreciation moment and setting the hair on the back of Tom's neck all straight and neat. The goblin scurried away looking fearfully over his shoulder towards the unseen nightmarish source of the shriek. Tom gaped a bit as realisation struck home in some sensitive areas, including his memory.

"Girl! Jacket! Scream!" Tom let the bag go and ran up the path. Another lemon flung itself at him and he caught it expertly and bagged it in one smooth motion. As he ran, he began to see what looked like a gigantic castle made from humongous rocks. A feeling of claustrophobia began to wiggle its way up his spine as the rocks around him started to grow and become more sheer, totally engulfing him. The castle looked dark and daunting every time Tom laid eyes on it through gaps in the walls. Dead tree roots protruded from the walls, scraping at Tom's body and tearing at his clothes.

He did not dare to stop or slow down, so, he took the punishment that the walls dished out, vowing to come back with a big chainsaw and show the roots who's the boss! Over boulders and beneath roots he dove until another howl of dreadful proportion emanated from the approaching castle, which resulted in Tom speeding up. He was not a brave man in any traditional sense of the word or any other sources of descriptive literature but the thought of losing the girl, and his jacket, drove him beyond literature and down the path towards the possible mauling jaws of danger.

Panting heavily, mostly due to absolute athletic ineptitude, and bleeding from dozens of small cuts and bruises, Tom suddenly exited into a clearing, leaving behind the narrow tunnel and a whimpering claustrophobia. He looked round in amazement at a big clearing with a shaded parking area and a shiny new pay point. Tom's eyes canvassed the empty parking area all the way to the other end and locked onto the big castle. The height of the sheer black walls would dwarf a giant – and Tom was no giant. Tom guessed the massive size of the gate to easily accept a couple of big trucks through it. It could accept five big trucks on top of each other! Tom considered himself quite a fundi on truck dimensions.

For the first time tonight, Tom felt a shiver of fear tingling down his back. It tickled a bit but, mostly, it felt very cold. He gripped his new nifty bag tightly and gathered his courage that was hiding beneath some lemons, lifted his chin and marched forward, wishing he had a really big something to arm himself with. Then again, no matter the size of his weapon, whatever lived in there would have a significant size advantage. Up ahead, in that dark place of untold horrors, behind the Information desk, his girl and jacket were in the presence of a beast. He thought back to the massive shadow that had flown over him earlier and shivered anew.

He entered the gates like a sheep into a slaughterhouse. He had the same sensation as when he first went to kindergarten and all the mean-looking babies had stared down at him. Something was watching him and it was not pleased. Inside the entrance, a big hall sprawled out in front of him. Enormous pillars held up the rock roof and many doorways exited the hall on all sides. Even the doorways inside were more than large enough to allow an elephant through. Tom hoped there were no elephants. They were creepy!

Tom bent down to examine the dirt covered ground. He could make out small shoeprints that went straight ahead into the gloom of the castle. Large window-like holes placed high up on the sheer walls allowed the moonlight to filter in bravely and light his path slightly as he ventured forward. At the end of the big hall, there was door. A man-sized door. It was slightly ajar and Tom pushed it to see if it would not kill him. It did not and, instead, silently slid open. Tom peered nervously into the room beyond. It was mostly empty, except for a bed and table and a pair of small purple tennis shoes. She had been here! He went in to see if there was more to this room but found nothing except the skinny pants. Panic started to rise. No jacket!

Movement outside peaked his sense of danger and reflex to scream. His scream got choked a bit by a fairy-wing that had somehow got stuck in his throat. He blushed and then turned around towards the great hall. He gasped.

Outside the door, in the gloomy light, was the naked figure of a beautiful woman, red hair flowing down her body. Her female curves were something Tom could write poetry about – if only he knew how. It also made him feel a little bit uncomfortable in parts he had not known could feel uncomfortable, except when the bathroom was far, far away. She seemed to be hovering slightly in the air but nothing phased Tom anymore.

"Elyan?" he asked nervously.

He jumped back in fear as a dark, scaled form whooshed by, Elyan disappearing in one smooth brutal motion.

"No!" Tom screamed and charged out the room.

A giant lizard shape merged into the darkness of the hall's corners. Tom charged after it bravely, not really contemplating what he would do should the large lizard thing, that had just in one smooth motion captured Elyan, turned on him. Luckily, he did not have long to not contemplate the possible horror.

As he came towards the dark corner where the lizard had disappeared, a large dragon head materialised out of the gloom. The jaws of the blue dragon were big enough to grab a horse, or four Toms! The teeth that smiled at Tom were the length of swords. The yellow eyes burned with infinite hunger for all things flesh. Steam blew from flaring nostrils. A clawed foot stepped out of the dark, talons scraping across the stone floor. Sparks flew for extra dramatic effect.

Tom stopped dead. His spirit kept on running in the opposite direction, screaming hysterically. His eyes did not really notice all the finer details of the dragon's huge form. It focussed more on the imminent death staring at him.

"Who dares enter my home?" the dragon's voice boomed, searing through Tom's body and mind.

Tom clutched his mauve bag like a little girl. He dared not speak but felt compelled to revenge Elyan's demise in whatever little way he could.

"You killed her!" he whispered boldly.

The dragon took a giant step towards Tom. Tom stepped back. His step size did not quite match the dragon's, the net effect being that the dragon was only a foot away from his face. The warm breath pouring out of the dragon's nostrils felt warm enough to roast a small pig. Tom felt like a very small pig about to be an appetiser, with some fresh lemon juice squeezed all over his roasting body.

Tom's mauve bag nearly got sucked up as the dragon took a deep smell of the intruder in front of him. He grabbed the bag protectively.

"You may have my body, but not my bag!" Tom screamed defiantly.

"So be it!" the dragon roared as it reared up onto his hind legs, massive mouth opening, revealing a double row of sharp, long teeth more than capable of cutting down trees in one bite.

Tom closed his eyes and went into a reflexive crouch, whimpering a final word of farewell to his dead parents, Elyan and his lost jacket. The dragon's open mouth came crashing down towards Tom.

"Stop it, Dorian!" a woman's voice screamed.

The dragon stopped inches away from Tom's appetiser body. Tom pried open an eye, seeing himself reflected in one of the white fangs close to his face. The other eye eventually opened up to see Elyan standing to one side of the dragon. She was in one piece! And was holding his jacket.

"Tom?" she asked after a Georgian silence came knocking at the door. "What are you doing here?"

"You know him?" Dorian, the dragon, asked looking a bit sheepish in a dragonly way.

"Yes. He gave me this jacket when I needed it tonight."

"Borrowed," Tom chipped in.

Elyan and the dragon looked at him.

"Borrowed the jacket."

Elyan and the dragon stared blankly at him.

"Which does not really matter, all things considered…" Tom realised a bit too late that now was not the ideal time to bring up his jacket-return policy.

"You came all this way, into our world, to get your jacket back?" Dorian asked, seeing the dismay and slight hurt on Elyan's face.

"Yes." Wrong answer, but Tom was rather stupidly insensitive to such matters. "And to make sure Elyan is safe." Right answer, and Elyan smiled warmly.

She ran to his cowering body and gave him a hug and kiss on his cheek.

"What are you doing here, Elyan? You gave me a big fright. I thought I lost you." Tom hugged her back fiercely. For the first time he realised something, as he held her: The jacket felt really good on her and he would not mind if she kept it.

"I came looking for Basil. He was busy finishing the blue dragon tattoo on my back and then ran out saying he had to come and finish the girl tattoo on Dorian's neck."

Tom looked up to see the red haired girl tattooed on Dorian's neck.

"And you being naked in the alleyway?"

"I wanted to get dressed and leave but opened the wrong door and ended up in the alley. The door closed and locked behind me and I was stuck. 'Till you came along."

She kissed him on his lips. All kinds of bells chimed in Tom's body and head.

"And you being naked here?" Tom stammered out the words. The kissing, hugging and frequent female nudity were starting to take its toll on him.

"I am the model for Dorian, The Wise One's, tattoo. I arrived in this part of the world a few days ago to assist Basil and to get my own tattoo done. That's when I first saw you in the park."

Tom looked up at Dorian and the girl tattoo. It did look like a life-size mirror image of Elyan. The tattoo artist was really good, Tom thought.

Jealousy was a new emotion that Tom suddenly discovered at the thought of sharing Elyan's image with another male, albeit a dragon. It felt wrong. He held her a bit tighter, claiming her back from the dragon. Dorian did not notice.

"And the wild savage screams I heard on my way here?"

"It's a tattoo! It hurts," Dorian answered defiantly with a pout, his ego slightly hurt but not as much as his neck.

"Who's next for a tat?" Basil's voice pierced the happy gathering as he entered the hall, oblivious to the near death of Tom and the happy reunion of girl, boy and jacket.

"I am," Tom said impulsively. If the dragon was going to have an image of his girl on his neck, then, Tom would have something on his body! And he would show the dragon that he could stand the pain more manfully! "I would like some dragon wings on my back," Tom declared boldly. At no stage did he think about this. Tom had discovered love and being stupid for the sake of a woman, all in one night.

"You sure?" Elyan asked, looking worriedly into his eyes.

He smiled contently, drowning happily and deeply in her eyes. This was an ideal opportunity for Tom to visit the think-room in his brain. Unfortunately, it was locked and hidden behind a thick piece of furniture.

"Dragons and tattoos brought me here, to a new world. And to you. So, yes, I am sure," Tom stated bravely, smirking at the dragon.

She kissed him again, this time even more passionately. Tom's head began to swim again as time, and the world in general, slowed down to a speed where progression could be measured with glorious love-struck heartbeats.

Until Basil started to take off his shirt.

For the next two hours, Tom screamed like a little girl until he passed out and woke up in his bed in his world. His back was burning with his new wings, yet, his only concern was where Elyan was. He sat up quickly, cursing loudly at the pain. The sight of her sleeping in his bed next to him calmed him down and made his heart burst with joy.

He looked at her sleeping body for a long time, smiling sheepishly in love. She smelled of wet grass after the first rains. Her long red hair flowed perfectly over the cushion. Her delicate white skin looked fragile and inviting to adore. His jacket hung contently over a chair. Could life be more perfect than this?

He got out of bed, got dressed in his favourite green shirt, had some coffee, slung his nifty mauve bag over his shoulder and headed off to the shop.

His smile was different.

His walk was different.

Tom was different.

He had grown wings!

The Phoenix Syndrome

♦ H J Kruger ♦

Phase 1

Jessica awoke screaming from a horrifying dream: charring flesh, her arms and hands on fire and a handsome young man dying at her feet, blood streaming from his head as she looked on helplessly. She sat up unable to go back to sleep but, as flashes of the dream still raced through her mind, she reached for her night lamp. A sharp sudden pain surged up her arm and came to a rest on her left shoulder blade, shaking her to full consciousness.

Slowly, she reached with her hand to inspect the pain and her finger came to rest on a small bump at the base of her shoulder blade. She jumped up, searching for a mirror to inspect the growth and rushed into her bathroom.

She turned on the light while taking off her shirt and whirled around in front of the mirror. She suddenly went cold. At the base of each of her shoulder blades were two inflamed red pustules, like two red eyes glaring back at her.

She gently touched one of the boils and it burst open, spilling blood and puss down her back. Jessica grabbed hold of a toilet roll, unrolling some onto her hand and moistening the pad before she hastily cleaned the blood from her back while peering over her shoulder.

The young man from her dreams haunted her, the look on his face as he stared helplessly up at her and she shook her head, focusing on cleaning up the blood. She looked up and noticed a young man standing in the doorway behind her, looking at her in curious understanding. Jessica stopped in fright, it felt like she were dreaming with her eyes open. Quickly, she turned around, but the man was nowhere to be seen.

She hastily covered her back and rushed down the passage to look for him but the house was dark and the passage empty. Only the sound of her mother's soft snoring and the suburban barking of a dog far away broke the silence of the night. She checked the front door and the back one but both were locked and all the windows were closed.

She silently opened her mom's bedroom door a crack to peer inside. No one was in there either. Just her mother lying sprawled across the large double bed. Finally satisfied that the house was empty, she returned to the bathroom and poured some antiseptic liquid into the sink, she doused a cotton bud in the mixture and carefully started to clean the open sores on her back.

On closer inspection, she saw a piece of bone that looked like a finger, protruding from the centre of the open sore. After placing antiseptic ointment on the wound, she grabbed hold of a bandage and criss-crossed it over her shoulders before unrolling the rest around her chest.

She finished cleaning up, walked back into her bedroom and came to a standstill in front of her window, looking out over the sleeping landscape of Capital Park. The first rays of the sun slowly crept over the horizon, turning the dark night sky into the hue of the deepest blue and, for a moment, Jessica didn't feel afraid.

Then the slow throbbing in her back reminded her of the wounds there and she turned away from the window. She grabbed her iPad from her desk and sat down on her bed. Googling the key words 'back sores', 'skin ulcers' and 'bone growths', the top three hits were a medical thesis entitled 'Patterson Syndrome – New genetic mutations and a case study of Werner Human, a conspiracy page titled *The Naked Truth*, and a blog dedicated to the Indian god Garuda, a colourful winged god, half-man half-bird with a beak and talons.

She clicked on the medical thesis scrolling through the article filled with medical jargon that she barely understood. Then, at the sight of the first photo, Jessica gasped. It was of a young man's back showing the same growths that she had on her back! Jessica read the caption: 'The bone protrusions at one week'. She looked up and saw the same man she that she had seen in the mirror only minutes ago. He was standing outside her window looking in but, when she blinked, he was gone.

* * *

General Rupert Eksteen walked through the foyer of the 'Department of Patterson Syndrome Control', a large underground facility. In the centre of the room stood a cryogenic tube covered in a thin layer of dust. He paused for a moment as he passed the tube and peered through the dust at the contents: a man with large brown feathered wings. This was his trophy. The subject was named Werner. He had originally volunteered during the first outbreak about nine years ago so that the scientists could study the extent of the syndrome. Now, all that remained of him was this body, frozen in eternal slumber.

It had started with boils at the base of each shoulder blade that quickly erupted to expose new bone growth. These 'fingers' kept growing and, by the third carpel, the structure became clear A *carpometacarpus* – a bony structure similar to that of a bird's wing.

While the wings grew, the individuals became progressively stronger. After about a month, a fever gripped the individual as the *pollex* – a small bone protrusion – became exposed. Up to this point, the bone appeared totally bare but, after the fever subsided, the radius and ulna began to grow rapidly and became covered by a thin layer of skin.

Then one night, by a stroke of luck, he was called to Pretoria to report on their findings when the call came through. The 'Department of Patterson Syndrome Research' had burnt to the ground, killing everyone inside except for Werner who was found naked at the heart of the building.

After a big struggle, Werner got away and a manhunt ensued that involved half the army's forces but, finally, they caught him and the order was given to place him in permanent suspension. General Eksteen finally convinced the President to fund his operation and give him military backing to do so. But then the outbreaks stopped and, for several years, there had been no reported accounts of PS syndrome. This left him without funding, confined to this small, dusty bunker in the middle of nowhere.

Unceremoniously, as if the thought of the past quickly bored him, he turned from the tube and he swiftly walked away without looking back.

He entered the operations room and it was buzzing with activity. A young soldier saluted him and handed him a report sealed in a big brown envelope. The soldier stood in salute but didn't move, making General Eksteen ask: "Is there something else, private?"

The nervous young soldier cleared his throat. "A new outbreak of the PS syndrome has been reported, General, and all observers have been put on high alert, Sir."

He tried to contain his glee at these words. This might just turn out to be a good day after all, he thought.

"Thank you, private. Keep me posted on all new reports." He dismissed the soldier and returned to the report in his hand as he walked to his office and closed the door behind him. He sat down at his desk and opened the report. The title read: 'Universal rise of twenty percent in Patterson Syndrome cases.'

He looked up at a picture standing on his desk. His wife, beautiful Ellen, had been killed in an accident after she had tried to help a Patterson-infected man during the first outbreak. He remembered that day like it was yesterday. She had been a nurse at the military base where he was stationed at the time.

A young man had been escorted in by two guards and handed over to Rupert's care when he had still been a major. He was taking the young man to a facility for testing and he relished the opportunity to see his wife. He had let his guard down for a moment when the man ran for the window and burst through it.

Then, everything slowed down. His wife stumbled backwards and fell five stories to her death. Rupert still remembered rushing to try and catch her, then, looking down at her lifeless body lying on the sidewalk a moment later. The young man stood over her looking down before he turned and ran away without looking back.

Rupert was consumed by his grief. After that day, he had made it his personal mission to capture these people. He became obsessed with pacifying. He had promised himself that he wouldn't rest until he had rid the world of the Phoenixes. He picked up the photo and looked at her face with sad determination.

* * *

Eric sat at his desk doused in the dim light of a computer screen, listening to 'It's the end of the world as we know it' by R.E.M on his earphones as he updated his blog: a conspiracy page about all kinds of mystical and occult accounts, called *The Naked Truth*.

His apartment was a small student flat close to the local university that he attended during the day. At night, he pursued his other passions: exposing hoaxes for what they were and giving merit where merit was due.

Every day, he posted new articles, new rumours and supposed sightings of anything from aliens to mermaids. Recently, he'd been bombarded by images of people growing strange bone protrusions on their backs, resembling premature wing bones.

According to some medical journals that he had been able to get a hold of, these protrusions were classified as a genetic mutation called Patterson Syndrome, also called PS, so named after a Dr Blake Patterson, who first documented the syndrome in nineteen ninety-four, in South Africa.

It didn't take long before people on his forum started referring to PS as Phoenix Syndrome and it quickly stuck. Eric browsed the Net every day. He hacked into the CCTV archives and searched for new research from the Centre of Disease Control to feed the curiosity of his loyal readers. For the past four days, however, he had barely been able to recover any publishable information.

Having worked in this industry for four years now, he was able to tell instantly which conspiracy theories held truth and which were just bogus paranoia but, here, he definitely sensed a cover-up. It was half past three in the morning and, after a lot of searches, he finally found a new statistical document stating that there was a twenty percent increase in PS cases all over the world.

He was uploading the post to his site when a soft 'ping' alerted him to an incoming email. He opened the message but it was blank and the only thing in the message was a video file attachment. Quickly, he downloaded the file and pressed play.

He was looking at amateur cell phone footage of a young man, his shoulders bleeding, rushing down a crowded street somewhere in London. People parted way for the man. As a police officer approached the man, he resisted and pushed the officer away, sending him flying several meters through the air before the officer crashed into a storefront window.

The man and the officer looked equally shocked before the man turned and ran in the opposite direction. The video ended.

Eric sat back, taking his glasses from his face and rubbing the two-day stubble on his chin. *"Scheiße."*

* * *

Jessica jumped as her bedroom door opened and her mother, Sandy, walked in with her morning cup of coffee.

"You're up already? Bad dreams again?"

Jessica tightened the charley around her shoulders and nodded.

"It's freezing in here," her mom said as she walked to the window, closing the open pane. She turned and sat down at the foot-end of the bed, handing Jessica her coffee.

"What time do you fly out today, mom?" Jessica asked her.

Her mom was a sales-rep and, on occasion, she had to fly away on business for a week or so and this was one of those times.

"At nine. I will be back the day after tomorrow around eight. You have Ms Simpson's number and I will always have my phone on me, so, if there are any problems, give me a ring. Any time."

Her mom always got like that, all dramatic and overprotective, and usually it annoyed the crap out of Jessica, but not this time. This time she honestly wished her mom was staying but she kept telling herself that she would be fine.

"Stop stressing about me, Mom, this is not the first time I had to spend a night or two alone. I can take care of myself."

Her mom smiled and reached out, lovingly caressing her face. "Sometimes I forget how independent you've become." She leaned in and gave Jessica a kiss on the forehead then whispered: "Love you."

She picked up her bag standing in the doorway and looked back at Jessica.

"Don't be late for school! Rachel will pick you up at seven. See you in two days." She blew a kiss and turned around and left.

Jessica reluctantly got out of bed and slowly walked to the mirror. Her hands trembled as she unwound the bandages around her chest. Fearful of what she would see, she turned around slowly and inspected the two red dots on her back.

There was still some minor bleeding but the bones that were just below the surface last night had now grown to a full centimetre from her back. In a panic, she covered them up again and hurriedly dressed. After picking the largest jersey in her closet, she draped it loosely over her shoulders before inspecting her profile in the mirror.

She looked okay and she exhaled, letting all the tension and worry fall from her shoulders. A car horn broke her train of thought and shook her to action. She quickly finished dressing, downing her remaining coffee and tying up her hair. She grabbed her bag, ran out of the house and forgot her keys on the coffee table.

* * *

Jessica was sitting lost in thought in a classroom, her mind occupied with flames and feathers, when an eraser hit her on the head, shaking her back to reality.

"Jessica, pay attention!" screamed her grade twelve science teacher, Mister Rick, a large, bald, disgruntled middle age man with the posture of a burlap sack. It was no wonder that everyone called him Mister Dick and, today, he deserved his nickname, she thought.

"Welcome back to reality, Miss Mons," he sneered. 'Glad to see that your exams are so important to you. Next time, if I don't bore you too much, try to stay awake."

Luckily, she was saved by the school bell announcing recess. She grabbed her bag, got up and disappeared into the chaos of the school halls before Mister Rick could call her back.

Dodging the kids in the halls, she quickly made her way outside seeking both solitude and comfort. She felt like she was losing her sanity and needed to be alone, so, she took the back route and ended up underneath a tree on the far end of the school grounds.

"You look terrible girl, what's up?" said her best friend Miriam as she plunked down on the grassy embankment next to Jessica. "You okay?"

Jessica looked up into her friend's familiar smile, relishing the opportunity for some non-judgmental company. "I didn't sleep much last night. Terrible…awful dreams of people burning and screaming in pain.”

“Yikes, that's some messed up stuff! Your mom away on business again?”

“Yes, but only until tomorrow night.”

“You okay to be alone at home?”

“Yes, I'll be fine.”

“Okay. Now, you have to see this.” From her pocket she got her iPhone and opened YouTube searching for the title 'Superhuman man pushes cop in London'.

Hopeful to get her mind of her problems, Jessica leaned closer and watched the video.

A young man was rushing down a busy city street and, as the video continued, her eyes grew wider and wider. It was the same man who had died in her dream, the same man who appeared to her last night.

A police constable tried to assist him but he was clearly confused and disoriented. He lightly pushed the cop away in a gesture that suggested he want to be left alone. The impact sent the cop flying ten meters down the street, where he slammed through a department store window.

She noticed the fear and surprise on his face as he turned and ran down the street. The video ended and Jessica looked up while contemplating the video. Then, she saw him shimmering into view right in front of her as he rushed across the rugby field.

Uncertain of whether she could trust her eyes, Jessica scrambled backwards in shock. He paused in front of her and smiled. As their eyes met, a stream of emotions – fear, loneliness, hunger and curiosity – streamed from him, enveloping her like an avalanche. Jessica gasped for breath and reeled back onto the grass with the sheer force of emotion.

Just as she thought she couldn't take it anymore, he faded back into nothing. She opened her eyes and looked up to the sky, taking a large gulp of air.

Miriam stared at her, worry now clearly written on her face. “Dude, WTF? You look like you've seen a ghost!”

Jessica sat up again and looked around as children stared at her in open curiosity. When people's attention returned to whatever they had been busy with before, she picked up her bag and turned to Miriam.

"I think you're right, Em. I shouldn't go home alone. Would you come with me?"

Miriam nodded and without another moment of hesitation they snuck off the school grounds, heading towards her house.

* * *

Peter ran down the streets of a shanty town in Mamelodi, followed by a police car in close pursuit. He knew these streets well and ducked into an alley. The officers set chase on foot. Overcome with fever, Peter's sight was severely blurred. He took a wrong turn somewhere and ended up in a dead end.

The police advanced on him and he turned to the wall, grabbing hold of the corrugated sheeting. He pulled it like paper from the side of the small family dwelling, throwing it at the police officers before he turned and rushed into the shack. Inside were three kids and a mother, staring at him from where they sat on the bed. Before they could even react, he was out of the door on the other side.

About a kilometre later, he stopped by the side of the new Mamelodi Mall construction site and looked around, expecting someone behind him. There was no one on his trail for once. His shoulders were killing him and the strange bones were now poking out further through the holes in his t-shirt. He couldn't hide them anymore.

He pulled a loaf of bread from his bag and hungrily took a bite. Then suddenly, she appeared – the crying girl. She always looked so sad when he saw her but he couldn't talk to her. Instead, he received so many feelings of disgust and self loathing. Slowly, more and more of the others appeared and, in an effort to block them out, Peter grabbed his earphones and blasted his music at full volume while closing his eyes.

As he opened his eyes again, he saw the blue lights of a police car speeding towards him. Peter barely had time to react and, as the car screeched to a halt, its dust trail enveloped the car, giving Peter just enough cover to get a good head start.

A shot rang out and a searing pain in his left leg brought him to a halt. He looked down and saw the blood flowing freely from his leg. A second shot sounded out, this time the bullet found its mark as it ripped through Peter's chest.

As he fell to the ground, the screams of a thousand different voices filled his ears. His body began to feel hot. Within seconds the cops were on top of him but, as soon as one of them touched Peter, he screamed in pain and quickly retracted his hand, shaking it fiercely.

"He burned me!" the man screamed in agony as the skin on his hand formed huge blisters.

Peter gave one final piercing scream and instantly burst into flame. The cops looked on in horror as Peter got to his feet and stumbled towards them. They instinctively grabbed their guns and unloaded their rounds into Peter's body without effect. One cop took aim and fired a head shot and the fire abruptly went out. Peter's body fell lifelessly to the ground.

* * *

Jessica searched desperately through her bag for her keys as Miriam stood next to her at front of the door of her house. She looked through the window and noticed the keys lying on the coffee table in the foyer. She laughed at herself as she realised her mistake.

Then, unexpectedly, another searing stream of emotions enveloped her as she saw the young man struggling to protect himself from the attack of several people who were hitting him with clubs. He looked up. Seeing her, he nodded and, as abruptly as it started, the vision ended in a flash of searing pain.

When Jessica finally opened her eyes, she found herself lying on the grass in front of her house with Miriam crouching over her with a very concerned look on her face.

"I think you should sleep at my house."

"I... I'm sorry, Em, I don't know what happened."

With Miriam's assistance, she slowly got to her feet. Her head throbbed like she had been hit repeatedly with a sledgehammer. She walked back to the patio and grabbed hold of the door handle, shaking it in her frustration, pulling it right off the door.

Miriam stared at her with eyes wide. Jessica stood with the door handle in her hand and looked back at the door, seeing the mangled remains of the lock mechanism, shredded metal and splintered wood.

"Shit, how do I explain this to my mom?"

She tried to fit the broken handle back on the opened door and looked back at Miriam. "Please don't tell anyone."

"That's your secret! You're one of them... It's okay," said Miriam in quiet awe and gently took hold of Jess's trembling hand. "I won't tell a soul."

* * *

Peter's dead body lay on a metal gurney surrounded by other dead bodies underneath white sheets. Only their toes and tags were exposed to the glaring florescent light flooding the otherwise empty morgue. A coroner walked in and wheeled Peter's body into the autopsy room where two medical doctors began their investigation. One was speaking into a recording device.

"Subject: John Doe. Cause of death seems to be a bullet wound to the head. There are signs of extreme charring. Strange, this shouldn't be here! The subject has ten-inch bone protrusions from his shoulder blades, new skin growth and- Are those feathers?"

Suddenly, a group of men wearing dark suits accompanied by armed guards walked into the autopsy room and started confiscating all the evidence. While zipping up the corpse in a body bag, one of the men handed the doctor a piece of paper, demanding full cooperation in the collection of dangerous assets.

"This never happened. Thank you for your corporation," said one of the men and, before the doctor could react, the John Doe was gone and the autopsy room was left eerily empty.

* * *

Eric casually walked down the street, listening to his classic rock album on his iPod on his way home after he had attended his classes at the local University in Bielefeld. He noticed his friend Kate skating down the street towards him and she screeched to a halt in front of him.

"So, how does it feel to go viral?"

Eric stopped and looked at her with a raised eyebrow, utterly confused.

"Don't tell me you don't know! For goodness' sake Eric, just go online!"

Eric reached for his phone and opened his YouTube app. His video was top of the day, with one million hits in less than eight hours. A ping notified him of a mail and he immediately noticed that it was from the same sender as the last video.

'Thought you might like to see this' read the subject and, without even a glance at Kate, he turned and rushed home, leaving her standing alone by the side of the road.

"Hey! Wait for me!" she screamed and sped to his side, barely managing to enter behind Eric before he slammed shut the door of his apartment.

"What's up?"

* * *

Jessica sat on the couch browsing through a few hundred videos and news inserts about PS-positive people being prosecuted and arrested all over the world. She watched in horror as the President declared PS-positive people as national threats on the breaking news.

"In light of the new international treat, I, President Mokoda, declare PS-positive individuals threats to national health and security, and request all South African citizens to co-operate in locating these individuals. We grant asylum to PS-positive individuals who willingly turn themselves in."

After Miriam had helped her repair the door, she had to leave. As they said goodbye, both Jessica and her best friend knew that it might be for the last time. She was certain that she couldn't return to school and her chances of being discovered were growing by the minute. Subconsciously, her hand reached for the knobs on her back, trying to push the bones back into her body.

"I never thought I'd live to see this kind of thing happen in my lifetime," said her mom who entered as Jessica sat deep in thought.

Jessica had been so lost in her own thoughts that she did not even notice her mother's presence until she placed her hand on Jessica's shoulder. Startled by the touch, Jessica snapped out of her daydream. She grabbed the arm of her invisible assailant and flung her mother over her shoulder with such force that she slammed into the coffee table in front of her.

Luckily, the table's legs broke and halved the force of the impact. Jessica stared down in horror at her mother's frightened face.

"Honey, it's me, Mom!"

Jessica jumped up as her mom looked back at her in fear and confusion. Unable to explain what just happened, she rushed out of the house into the streets and just kept on running into the night without looking back.

* * *

An hour later, she stopped and noticed that she was still not tired. She also realised that the pain from her shoulders was more manageable, although the bones had grown another centimetre. It soon would be impossible to hide them.

Finally, at around four o'clock that morning, Jessica snuck back into the house, finding her mother asleep on the couch in front of the TV. A newscaster brought 'breaking news' and cut to another amateur snippet of a PS man throwing a boulder close to thirty metres across a field, followed by a decree by the secretary of PS Control, General Rupert Eksteen:

"These individuals pose a risk to our safety and the public is urged to report any individuals who show the following symptoms: Bone-like protrusions growing from their shoulder blades, aloof and reclusive behaviour, and abnormal strength. These individuals have been classified as dangerous and might pose a threat to national health and security. They should not be confronted alone. If anyone knows of the whereabouts of anybody fitting this description, please notify the police on our emergency number immediately."

Jessica picked up the remote and switched off the TV before she gently woke her mother from her sleep. "I'm sorry mom. I don't know what came over me."

Her mom propped herself upright on the couch and took Jessica's hand. "Why didn't you tell me earlier?"

Jessica looked down, fully aware of the controlling effect she could enforce on others using her eyes, and replied: "It started the morning you left and I didn't want to frighten you."

She took off her jersey and unwrapped her bandages, revealing the bony stumps growing from her shoulder blades. Concerned, Sandy reached out to touch her daughter's back.

"Does it hurt a lot?"

Jessica nodded.

"You have to learn how to control your strength, Jessica. You have to hide it from everyone! I don't want you to get arrested and end up in some detention camp! Whatever this is, they will figure it out and then everything will go back to normal. But, until then, you have to stay hidden."

* * *

That evening, Jessica was awoken by the sound of police sirens and flashing red and blue lights. Her mother rushed into her room.

"We have to get you out of here! Now!"

Crouching towards the window, Jessica parted the curtains just enough to peek through the gap. The cops were raiding their neighbour's house and slowly led the neighbour's son, a young lad called Richard, out of his house and into the street as his mother rushed after the police, pleading with them not to take her son.

It was no use, however, and Jessica looked on helplessly as Richard was escorted into the paddy wagon and the doors were locked behind him. Jessica stared at Richard as the van drove by and unexpectedly his eyes focused on her, begging, pleading for her to help but the wagon turned the corner and sped away. Jessica felt powerless standing alone at the window.

Her mom pulled her away from the window and sighed in relief but Jessica grabbed her mom by the shoulders.

"That could have been me, Mom. I can't stay here. I can't hide my stumps anymore and I'm only putting your life in danger by staying."

Sandy looked outside as the last police car drove off down the street. Slowly, the neighbourhood spectators who were spying out of their windows or lurking behind their fences returned to their houses and the suburb returned to its slumber. Sandy faced her daughter with a look of pensive fear and nodded in agreement.

"Pack your bags, Jess. We're leaving within the hour."

Phase 2

General Eksteen sat in the Parliament waiting for his chance to address the house. He was no stranger to pressure and this certainly wasn't the first time that he had addressed the congregation but, this time, he was nervous.

He had come to ask them for a substantial cut of the military budget and these politicians were more interested in enriching themselves than spending money where it should be spent. He had a strategy however: *fear*. It had worked before but he had to lay it on thick this time if he was going to get the funding he needed.

Finally, he got his chance and got up, walking slowly to the speaker's podium. He cleared his throat and began.

"Honourable speaker and members of parliament, we have all heard the accounts from across the globe, we've seen the videos on YouTube. We have seen people throwing trees and boulders thirty meters far, running through walls and ripping doors out of frames like someone taking off a bandage.

"These individuals are dangerous on their own but if they were to mobilise... There are eight thousand reported accounts of PS in Gauteng alone and we need to detain these dangerous individuals before they realise there is strength in numbers. That's why I'm requesting ten billion rand from the defence budget to build a concentration camp strong enough to isolate these individuals from the general public."

There was a sudden uproar from some of the members but the speaker brought everyone to order and put the notion to a vote. The notion was passed with an unprecedented seventy-five percent and

General Eksteen turned around, taking his leave as his heart swelled with satisfaction.

* * *

Jessica and Sandy were driving out of the city, heading down Route 25 out of Johannesburg on their way south. Then, just outside of Alberton, they drove into a roadblock. Sandy looked for a turnoff but couldn't find one and they drove straight into it, unable to find an alternative route.

Sandy gripped the steering wheel with one blanched hand while she groped around in her handbag, searching for her driver's license with the other. Jessica gave her mother one look and she relaxed just as the officer walked up to her open window.

"License please, ma'am. Where are you travelling to?" asked the officer as Sandy handed him her license.

He leaned in closer to inspect the passenger and the contents of the car. Then, he looked into Jessica's eyes and stopped in his tracks. Without another word, he handed Sandy her driver's license and stepped back from the car, letting them drive on.

Sandy sighed with relief as they drove away but, before they were safe, they had to drive past several other cops. Jessica sat back in her seat, pressing her stumps into the foamy seat, avoiding all eye contact with any of the other cops. She didn't want to show her mom how frightened she was and, after they had cleared the blockade, she finally allowed herself to relax properly, taking a deep breath.

* * *

As the new day broke and the sun rose over the profile of the Drakensberg, they drove into Clarence. The town was just waking up when they drove into Aunt Melody's driveway. Melody, her mother's sister, had been a freedom fighter back in the Apartheid years and her mother knew that it would be the safest place for Jessica right now. Melody came rushing out of the house still in her night robe and, before they came to a full standstill, she was crouching at the driver's window.

"I'm sorry, Sandy, it's too dangerous for her here. There is a rumour of a sanctuary that has sprung up in the mountains. I think it might be best for Jessica to seek them out. Keep on Route 711 out of town and stop at the viewpoint halfway up the mountain. Continue by foot until you reach the summit where, I hope, you will find the others."

"Thank you, Sis," murmured Sandy.

"No time, just get her to safety!"

She leaned into the car and lovingly touched Jessica's shoulder.

"The sanctuary is the safest place for you now my dear. Stay safe. Now, go! There are spies everywhere nowadays."

* * *

General Eksteen was sitting in the passenger seat of an armoured SUV being driven down a dusty Freestate road. As they drove over the crest of a small hill, a large construction site rolled into view.

The driver, a young sergeant named Swart, slowed down at the security booth and handed his identity card to the two military soldiers at the gate. After peering inside, the soldiers saluted the general and handed Sergeant Swart back his identification.

"Construction is right on schedule, General, and Mister Kotze is expecting your arrival."

Slowly, the gates opened and they headed straight for the operations office while dodging all sorts of large construction vehicles that were crawling all over the busy site.

After they came to a halt in front of the site office, General Eksteen hastily got out and entered an empty office. The plans for the 'Detention Centre' were unrolled on the operation table, marked all over with notes and tags but Mister Kotze wasn't there. He grabbed a hardhat and exited the small office, heading out onto the site.

The foreman, Ben Kotze, a nervous mountain of a man, rushed to welcome the general onto the site and started to lead him through the large concrete bunker.

"We are on track, General. The completion date will be within this month, as expected."

"And have all the others arrived?"

"Yes, General, they are all assembled in the demonstration

room."

"And the package?"

"It arrived early this morn. As instructed, it was stored under guard in the demonstration room."

"Thank you, Mister Kotze, that will be all, I can find my way from here."

General Eksteen turned and walked into the depths of the already completed subterranean section of the detention centre.

* * *

He walked into the demonstration room, where several of his high ranking officers and some Presidential representatives waited for his arrival.

"Good afternoon, gentlemen. You were called here to see the fruits of your investment firsthand. Recently, confiscated evidence gave us new insight into these creatures' physiology."

He pressed a button on the control console and a screen on the one wall slid into the ceiling, revealing a window that looked into a standard detention module. Inside, Werner stood naked and disorientated in the foreign concrete cell. His wings were clamped to his back with a metal breast plate and his hands and feet were chained to the walls.

General Eksteen placed his hand on the glass and the one way mirror polarized and became clear. Inside, Werner was rapidly becoming aware of his audience and covered his nakedness with his hands. As he glared through the lights, he recognised the General and tried to move forward, straining his chains.

"At last, someone who will listen, Major Eksteen. Where am I?" asked Werner angrily but his voice was muffled by the glass.

General Eksteen looked down at Werner like a man would look down at an ant, not even acknowledging his question or, at the very least, his rights as a living being. Instead, he removed his hand from the window and the one way mirror returned.

Werner tugged at the chain that creaked and clanged against the strain but he was still weak and his attempt proved futile to all who observed him. General Eksteen smiled self confidently and continued his demonstration.

"Constructed from the strongest concrete and reinforced with the strongest steel, this new method of controlling Phoenix Syndrome has proven to be the most effective. Our subject has been chronically suspended for several years and has recently been transported to this facility. From a central control room, the temperature, oxygen and humidity can be controlled, enabling the centre to function with minimal staff once operational."

An abrupt thud interrupted the General and everyone's attention returned to the captive Werner. He had managed to break one of the chains and was trying to break the glass using the chain as a whip. Fearfully, the observers recoiled as the second impact hit the glass. General Eksteen approached the control panel, confidently pressed the button marked 'subdue' and returned to the group. A stream of smoke bellowed in from all sides and Werner fell to his knees, gasping for breath as he desperately struggled against the cold.

"What long-term costs are there for maintaining these 'specimens'?" asked the President's military advisor, Major Kubai, a cocky, shifty-eyed man whom the general disliked immensely.

"The cost will be kept minimal once we detain the individuals. Temperature control keeps them in a state of sentience but keeps the body frozen so that they won't need long term maintenance for as long as the system is maintained."

He pressed a button on the control console and the room froze over. Werner was frozen where he stood, forever frozen in mid-struggle.

"Any further questions, gentlemen?"

* * *

Jessica embraced her mother for what felt like the last time as they stood by the side of the road. "I will let you know where I end up as soon as I'm safe."

Her mother grabbed her and hugged her. Jessica gave her a quick kiss on the cheek and lifted her backpack to her shoulder.

"You better," Sandy said as she got back into the car, then she drove off as she tried to hide a tear running down her face.

Jessica turned towards the mountain and started climbing. Exposed to nature and unrestricted abundance, she started to feel fulfilled, content and reinvigorated. She climbed and scaled the small hill within half an hour.

On the summit, she stopped and breathed deeply and, with every breath, she felt lighter. She looked around, soaking up the beauty of her surroundings. All around her the sandstone cliffs of the northern Drakensberg stretched on and on for as far as the eye could see.

She looked around in search of signs of life but there wasn't even the faintest trace of a structure. Jessica was standing at a crossroads and left with three possible routes to choose from. For a moment, she contemplated which she should take.

The first led down the far side of the hill into a forested valley; the second road led along the escarpment towards the sandstone cliffs; and the last road led through a small stone gulley up a crack in the mountain face, leading to the escarpment far above. After short contemplation, she decided on the small stone gulley up the mountain and started walking.

* * *

Eric sat on the edge of his seat as he waited for Kate to finish reading the anonymous e-mail that he had received. Kate was glued to the computer screen in the dim gloom of the living room.

She finished reading and turned to Eric. "If this is real, we must go."

"We? I can't take you with me, Kate. South Africa is known for its PS-intolerant policies and I don't want to be responsible for you too."

Kate gave him a look of such ferocious intensity that Eric backed away a few steps and sat on his bed.

"I just meant-"

"I know what you meant, Eric, but I have long been able to make my own decisions and there is nothing I would rather do than go with you. I can be responsible for myself! I've got some savings and will buy my own ticket. When did you want to depart?"

Eric smiled and leaned forward. He retrieved a printed page from the dark depths of his desk drawer. "I've already booked our tickets. We're leaving in the morning."

He laughed out loud as Kate recovered from the shock and leaned in closer, punching him as hard as she could manage on the shoulder.

"You bastard."

"I figured that I would never hear the end of it if I went alone. I just needed to make sure you were up for it…"

* * *

After about half a day's climb, Jessica finally reached the summit and noticed a sprawling tented city some distance away. She quickened her pace and, with solemn joy, she walked into the Sanctuary. Jessica was home.

All around her she saw Phoenixes going about their routine business, their wings in different stages of development. As if summoned, everyone turned around as she approached to acknowledge the new-comer.

A young woman walked up to her and grabbed her hand in greeting. "My name is Ansie, who are you?"

"I'm Jessica."

"Welcome to the sanctuary, Jessica." Ansie turned, took her by the arm and started to lead her into the city of tents. "Where are you from?"

"Pretoria and you?"

"Dundee… Small towns aren't very tolerant to change and, once the President declared us as a threat, I packed my bags in search of a place where I could hide. This is the safest place for our kind now. Let's go and find you a spot to set up camp."

Jessica stopped and looked around. Strangely, everyone felt familiar and she was elated. A place she could be herself, where she could explore and experiment without fearing discovery.

"All a bit much at first but there is nothing to fear here, we are all here because we have nothing left but each other," said Ansie smiling at Jessica and then continued leading Jessica deep into the heart of the sanctuary. Jessica couldn't help but notice the simplicity, the unity and calm that hung over the place like a dense fog. At the centre of the 'city' was a large open square.

Jessica paused to watch as two young Phoenix men sparred off against one another. The one threw a punch and landed a blow on the other's chest, sending him flying backwards. With one quick leap, the seemingly defeated man jumped back, clearing ten metres easily and connected his foot on the first man's shoulder.

"That's my friend Kunene. This is where Phoenixes can challenge one another and test their strengths," said Ansie over Jessica's shoulder, making her jump for a moment. "Come on, this way."

Finally, Ansie led her to a small group of tents arranged in a circle around a small fire pit. To the right there was an open space and she dropped her backpack on the ground. She started to unpack her tent in the clearing with Ansie's assistance. A brown-haired man emerged from one of the tents to inspect the ruckus and, as he locked eyes with Jessica, she immediately recognised him and froze in bewildered disbelief. What were the odds of meeting her hallucination in the flesh? And here he stood right in front of her.

Ansie noticed their awkward stare and cleared her throat. "Brendan, this is Jessica."

Jessica snapped out of her bewilderment and, immediately, Brendan walked to her and, without warning, embraced her. "I was waiting for you!"

After he finally let go of her, Brendan looked her up and down until Ansie slapped him behind the head. To hide his embarrassment, he jumped into work and, within minutes, the tent was set and Jessica's backpack was safely stored inside.

After the work was done, Brendan walked up to Jessica and took her by the arm. "Come, take a walk with me."

Excited to finally get some time alone with him, Jessica follow Brendan and, together, they walked through the tents and people. Jessica looked around and marvelled once again at the simple tranquillity that reigned over the camp, as if these people weren't strangers but family. Brendan came to the edge of the escarpment and looked out over the large expansive landscape with no sign of human life.

"We are linked, you and I. It seems that there are groups of us who are linked to one another and who are able to appear to each other, like we did."

Jessica knew this to be true. She felt that she knew Brendan intimately, not physically, but emotionally. Since their first meeting, she had immediately known how he felt and that bond gave her a sense of belonging, as if she and Brendan had always known one another.

"I can't believe how peaceful things are here. It's bad out there, Brendan. There are police blockades all over the place, parents turning in their own children, neighbours turning on one another. The noose is tightening and I'm afraid that it's just a matter of time before they find us," Jessica said as she faced him.

"The Government can't control us, so, they fear us. We're being hunted but we have nowhere else to go at this point, Jess."

"So, what are we going to do?"

"I don't know. If we were strong enough I would say that we should disperse into smaller groups all across the escarpment but a new fever has weakened almost half of us. It is a risk we will have to take for the moment."

Jessica turned and looked across the rolling domes of a thousand tents. "Can I ask you something?"

"I've been wondering when you would finally ask about our 'gifts'. Not everyone has the same gift. I'm an empath. I feel other people's emotions and am also able to mediate understanding between people. And you?"

Jessica didn't even need to think about it. "I can persuade people to do things by simply looking at them. It's very strange but I've been able to do it for as long as I can remember. I've always been able to get out of any trouble."

Brendan looked at her with an interested smile. "Cool…"

* * *

Eric and Kate claimed their bags from a luggage carousel at OR Tambo International Airport in Johannesburg after an extremely invasive screening at customs. Feeling somewhat violated, they just wanted to get out of the building. Finally, they walked through the doors of the arrival hall and were bombarded with anti-PS propaganda everywhere they looked.

Searching through the hundreds of nameplates being held up, Eric noticed the small name board in the far back with his name on it. After dodging the crowd, they reached Bongani, a friend he had made while travelling through India two years before.

"Eric! Welcome to South Africa! And you must be Kate, so nice to meet you. Let's get out of here. I'm sure you would agree that this place is a bit too fascist for our tastes."

Eric smiled with sarcastic consent and nodded as Bongani guided him and Kate directly towards the exit. The automated doors opened and an icy wind blew past them. Bongani lifted his collar to the wind.

"Hope you bought your jackets. We had no autumn this year, it just went straight from summer to winter."

As they finally drove out of the airport onto the highway Eric turned to Bongani. "We must set out for a place named Clarence immediately. Something terrible is about to happen there."

* * *

General Eksteen looked at a satellite photo of the Drakensberg on a large screen as he stood alone in a large war room in the detention centre. On the screen was a kaleidoscope of dots on the mountain: the Phoenix sanctuary. The screen showed the layout of the camp and estimated the inhabitants of the sanctuary to be in the thousands. A young lieutenant walked in and saluted the general.

"Sir, the troops are ready to depart."

He thanked the soldier and, after taking one last look and inspecting the finest details of the city's layout, he turned and walked out of the empty war room.

As he finally walked into the aviation hanger, he saw a dozen helicopters with seventy-two armed men who waited for him to lead them. Quickly, he made his way down to his helicopter and, before he boarded, he turned to the soldiers.

"Men, tonight we execute operation 'Dark Moon'. Remember, these creatures are stronger than we are and can survive several torso hits, so, aim for the head if it can't be helped. Remember the goal of our operation, however: to detain, not kill. Now, let's go catch some Phoenixes!"

Within seconds, the twelve helicopters were boarded. As the sun set over the arid desert surrounding the detention centre, they all took flight, rapidly disappearing over the horizon into the dusk.

* * *

That evening, Jessica and Brendan lay outside their tents next to their small fire while watching the stars. The fever had spread across more than half of camp and now hung over the sanctuary like a silent heat.

Abruptly, a heavy hum echoed up the valley, steadily growing louder as panic spread across camp as the sound of helicopters broke the silence of the night. Ansie stumbled out of her tent and stared into the darkness.

"They've found us," said Ansie anxiously and hastily rushed off.

"What should we do? Surrender or fight?" asked Jessica in a panic.

"If we are to have any chance of survival, we need to pack up now and leave," Brendan said quietly.

Jessica knew he was right. She felt the fever growing deep in her chest and she could see the beads of sweat growing on Brendan's forehead as well. Several of the others were almost confined entirely to their beds and unable to move, not to mention fight.

She felt weak and vulnerable, and Brendan felt the same. Suddenly, the fact that they were all concentrated together like this seemed to be a really bad idea.

"Jessica, we have to leave, now!"

Brendan struggled to get up and helped Jessica to her feet. Every muscle in her body ached, her joints were stiff and she could feel the bones on her back throbbing with pain.

"But where would we go?"

"Anywhere but here right now. If we leave now, we can disappear into the darkness before the helicopters arrive."

She nodded and, as quickly as she was able, she walked to her tent to gather up her things.

At that moment, Ansie and her friend Kunene rushed towards her and Brendan.

"Are you abandoning us?" asked Ansie with fearful concern.

Jessica nodded as she struggled to get her backpack over her folded wings.

"But what about the others?" asked Ansie.

"We cannot help them now, we need to live to fight another day," Brendan said. He turned to Jessica and placed his backpack on the ground. "And, if we are to succeed, we need to at least try diplomacy... I will stay and be our eyes inside."

Jessica started to protest but Brendan looked deep into her eyes and an understanding fell over her.

"We need you to be out there, Jess. You need to plead for our cause by using your 'gift' to get through to the President. I'm sure he would listen if you could only talk to him. That's why you need to get away. When the time is right, I will always be at your side. Now, go!"

Jessica grabbed her bag and, as the others prepared to surrender, she slipped into the dark shadows of the escarpment as the helicopters approached. She looked back at Brendan for a sign of encouragement and he nodded to her as she disappeared into the cover of darkness.

* * *

Eric rushed after the military helicopters that swept past them up towards the escarpment. They needed to move quickly or risk missing the event that he and Kate had travelled halfway across the world to film. He frantically ran ahead with Kate and Bongani at his side. They were gasping for breath, barely managing to keep up.

Finally, the tented Phoenix city rose into view on the opposite mountain and Eric grinded to a halt. *Best to avoid being seen*, he thought. He saw a large boulder some way ahead and quickly ran towards it. Taking cover behind it, he slowly peered over it and formed a frame by touching his thumbs and index fingers together.

This is perfect, he thought and turned to Kate indicating for her to quicken her pace. She swiftly pulled the camera out of the bag that had been on her shoulders and handed it to Eric. He placed it on top of a sturdy tripod and pressed record as the last helicopter landed on the escarpment.

A regiment of foot soldiers streamed out of the helicopters and quickly surrounded the city. Armed with AK47s, they held the perimeter of the city but didn't advance.

* * *

General Eksteen climbed out of a helicopter that had landed in the city square. Accompanied by foot soldiers, he walked towards the scared, feverish Phoenix crowd who had collected around the square in hope of evading the soldiers.

He lifted a megaphone to his mouth and, as the spinning blades of the helicopters settled, he started speaking. "By order of the Government of South Africa, we are here to arrest you all and take you to the detention centre for processing. No harm will come to you if you surrender peacefully."

The troops pushed into the town and started to raid the tents, apprehending whoever they could find. Suddenly, a soldier cried out from somewhere and a single gunshot echoed across the mountain. Panic swept over the soldiers like a wildfire in the savannas and several other shots rang out in quick succession…

After a short but fierce battle, several Phoenixes lay dead on the ground and the rest were huddled in fear, hands lifted in surrender. A Phoenix, who identified himself as Brendan, struggled forward, carrying a white flag which he handed to the general.

"We surrender."

* * *

Snow crunched underfoot as Jessica walked across the deserted mountains towards a small hut built as a hikers' retreat on Mount-Aux-Sources. Since the raid, she had an almost constant connection with Brendan but it had faded gradually until she could barely feel him at all unless she focused on him. But even that was muddled and all she could really get from him was fear and cold…a bitter cold.

She slumped down on the porch exhausted and looked around. Jessica unwrapped her wings. They had grown to about forty centimetres and the final bone had begun to develop.

She could feel Brendan's fear but the fever muddled their connection, making everything merge together. She closed her eyes and focused on Brendan and, after a bit of a struggle, she finally managed to see through his eyes.

He and the others were huddled together, slowly making their way into a large room somewhere in the detention centre.

"Brendan, are you okay?" she whispered to him.

"Jessica, leave now! I feel an ominous dread hanging over this place."

Abruptly, her ears were filled with the screaming of a thousand Phoenixes. The sound grew so intensely that it threatened to split her head open. She grabbed hold of her head, fell forward onto her knees and passed out on the snow.

* * *

Eric stood amidst the tents in the abandoned Phoenix sanctuary, filming the abandoned campsite. During the night, a soft dusting of snow had covered the mountains, turning the rolling hills into an immaculate wonderland. The snow gave the sanctuary a haunted feeling in the diffused, early morning sun.

Bongani and Kate were scouting through the empty tents for signs of life but the military had done an excellent job of sweeping the tents clean, leaving only the empty tents as evidence that there were ever people there.

Eric sat down at an abandoned fire pit where the smouldering embers still burned. Crouching close to the fire to get warm, he scrolled through the video footage of last night. He pressed play on the first file and noticed a woman rushing into the darkness on the far side of the camp. He called Kate and Bongani and they watched the footage in shock.

"We have to go and find her," Kate said with fierce conviction.

Eric rewinded the footage and pinpointed the direction that the unknown woman had disappeared to. Once he was sure, he flung his backpack over his shoulder and took the lead as Kate and Bongani followed him higher into the mountains.

* * *

In the heart of the desert stood the newly completed "Phoenix Detention Centre'. General Eksteen walked down a dark passageway lined with detention cells. From here, he could observe each prisoner individually and, by dropping the temperature to minus twenty Celsius, they could subdue the subjects relatively securely. He came to a standstill in front of one cell and turned to face Brendan, the leader of the remaining Phoenixes.

Brendan was sitting cross-legged on the floor of reinforced

concrete cell, shivering from the cold. His wing bones were clamped to his back with a metal breast plate and his legs were chained to the floor. He looked up as if he sensed the general's presence and stared directly at him through the one-way window.

General Eksteen placed his hand to the mirror and it polarised into clear glass. He just stood there looking down at Brendan in disgust.

Brendan struggled to his feet as he looked up at him and began to speak: "General Eksteen, what are your plans with us now that you've got us all detained?"

General Eksteen remained unmoved, staring down at him and turned to press the freeze button.

Brendan moved forward with his palms up in surrender. "What is it about all of us that frightens you so badly? What have any of us ever done to deserve this?"

"You threaten my happiness and you pose a threat to everyone you touch. You need to be destroyed."

Brendan walked to the window, reaching out with his palm to touch the glass but Rupert recoiled and the moment his hand left the glass it returned to its one-way mirror stasis.

"We are just as much human as you, General!" screamed Brendan to the mirror and his muffled words echoed the voice of the general's wife. In fact, those were almost the exact words Ellen had spoken mere minutes before her death.

He stood there for a moment, hesitating whether or not to place his hand back on the glass. He didn't have to explain himself to these people. He pressed the bottom and Brendan was frozen where he stood. A messenger rushed down the corridor and saluted him as he came to a halt.

"The President has summoned you, General. Apparently, there was a reporter on the mountain during the raid and the video has caused an outcry from the public."

Phase 3

Jessica slowly opened her eyes and the light of the early morning sun blinded her until her eyes became accustomed to the light. A shadow fell across her face and she tried to speak but her mouth was so dry that no words would come out.

"Are you okay?" asked a voice in a heavy German accent.

She quickly snapped to full consciousness and began to focus, shading her eyes from the glare of the early morning sun. Over her knelt a young man with dark hair and black-rimmed glasses. He stared at her with an intense look in his eyes. Behind him stood two others, a young skater girl and a fashionable young man, carrying heavy backpacks.

The German extended his hand with a smile and she reached weakly for his hand. Slowly, she was hoisted to her feet but the fever that had crept over her like a midsummer sweat had weakened her more than she had realised and she almost toppled over again.

He grabbed hold of her and the other young man jumped closer to grab her other shoulder. They walked her carefully towards the hut and seated her on the edge of the hut's timber deck.

Jessica tried to speak but her mouth was just so dry. It felt as if she was trying to talk through cotton. The girl handed her a water flask and she drank greedily. After regaining some strength and clarity, she handed the flask back with a simple: "Thank you."

The girl smiled and they all looked down at her like she was a trophy or a rare oddity.

"You know what I am and you're not afraid of me?"

"No, you're wonderful, just wonderful!" exclaimed the German. "We saw what happened last night und came to find you, und here you are. My name is Eric und this is Kate und Bongani."

He quickly turned to his friends who jumped into action, setting up their equipment.

Eric turned back to her with a sly smile. "Would you mind if I tape an interview with you? It'll give you an opportunity to tell your story!"

Jessica looked at him with curiosity, though she was still shivering lightly from the fever. "So, you're, what, a conspiracy theorist and some kind of sympathiser?"

"Of sorts. I have this blog called *The Naked Truth.*"

* * *

Jessica walked at the front of the small group of travellers, making their way down the precariously steep mountainside under the dim light of a crescent moon.

Since she had recovered from her fever, Jessica had experienced odd changes. Her senses were much keener, her sight near perfect and she was astonished that, even by the dim light of the moon, she could see in perfect detail. Her human companions, on the other hand, were not so lucky and struggled down the steep mountain slope.

Eric had decided that it would be best to travel under the cover of darkness in an attempt to avoid Jessica being detected, since her wings were now almost fully grown. Even folded they protruded about thirty centimetres from her back and, when extended, reached about a meter and a half. It had seemed like a good plan at the time but the shifty stones and patches of mountain gravel on the upper slopes were dangerous even in daylight. It was borderline suicidal to walk there at night.

Jessica reached the bottom of a particularly precarious area and looked back. Bongani was making his way down on his bum while Kate, a few paces behind him, had a different strategy. She was taking small steps down the gravel-filled incline, supporting herself with her arms. Eric was not as successful and he was clearly fatigued, struggling under the weight of this backpack.

He slipped on some loose mountain gravel and started to slide downhill. Desperately scrambling to stop his momentum, he caused a landslide and the shifting stones gave way beneath Kate. It dragged her along with him down the incline towards a ledge some way down the hill.

Bongani reached for them as they slid past him but missed Kate's hand by mere inches. Desperately, they tried to grab hold of anything that could stop the increasing speed of their fall but it seemed useless as the ledge came closer and closer.

Jessica knew she had to do something or they would surely die. She timed her approach, running on top of the sliding gravel and grabbing hold of the frantic Eric and Kate, inches from the edge of the abyss. She dragged them back to safety and they fell onto the rock, trying desperately to catch their breaths.

Bongani carefully made his way down and reached them just as Eric finally got his breath back. He looked up at Jessica.

"Thank you," he breathed. "I am indebted to you. Whatever I can do, just let me know."

She smiled reassuringly at him. "You need to be more careful. From here on, we walk at arms' length and I will tell you what I think you can't see."

After a long walk, they finally arrived at the place where Bongani's City Golf stood parked. Exhausted by the effort and still shaken by their near-death experience, Eric and Kate collapsed onto the soft mountain grass next to the road.

"Are you all okay?" asked Jessica and, one by one, Eric, Kate and Bongani nodded in confirmation.

A tense silence fell over the travellers as they thought of what they all had to do. They would be lucky if they made it to Pretoria undetected. Bongani quickly got up and started to pack the car. There was no time to waste if they wanted to remain undiscovered and make it to Johannesburg before sunrise.

* * *

Sandy sat down at the Fida Café at Lanseria Airport. She was on her way to George for an important meeting that could possibly lead to the biggest sale she had ever made. She ordered a double espresso and she retrieved her sales figures and quotes in preparation for her meeting from her bag.

A TV screen showed anti-Phoenix propaganda and she placed her earphones in her ears to block it all out. At that exact moment, her phone alerted her of a new message. Desperate for news from Jessica, she quickly checked her notifications.

It was an e-mail from Miriam, Jessica's best friend, with the heading 'Thought you might want to see this'. She opened the attached link and a YouTube video popped up with the title 'The story of Phoenix Jessica'. Sandy's heart skipped a beat and she quickly pressed play.

The video clip began with footage of the apprehension and capture of a large assembly of Phoenixes by the military. Helicopters descended on a large tented city – the sanctuary high in the mountains – and Sandy's blood froze when gunfire erupted on the scene. Moments later, a white flag was raised in surrender and a young man with dark hair stepped forward. The video cut to the young reporter standing in the abandoned sanctuary surrounded by eerily empty tents.

"Then, we discovered Jessica, a refugee from the 'Sanctuary'. We gave her the opportunity to tell her story," said the narrator.

Jessica appeared, sitting on a timber deck in a rolling landscape blanketed with snow. Sandy uttered a short shriek of relief at the sight of her daughter. It'd been almost three weeks since she had had to drop Jessica off somewhere in the Drakensburg. Jessica looked well but frightened and vulnerable with her bones exposed for all to see.

"My name is Jessica and I have Patterson Syndrome. About three months ago, I woke with a fever and discovered to my horror that two bumps had appeared on my back. After a quick search, I realised that this might not simply be some skin disease. I researched it on the Internet and realised that it was Patterson, a rare genetic mutation that is not well understood or documented. Limited research keeps the public in the dark about the realities of this mutation and there are authorities that wish to exploit this. They want for you not to understand. They want for you to fear us and help them to destroy us.

"We used to be your neighbours, your friends, your brothers and sisters, your children and all it took was fear to turn on your loved ones.

"We were brutally and fiercely removed from society. The

military would have you believe that they are protecting you from us because we are capable of dangerous acts. They would have you believe that you are in danger of contracting our disease. However, Patterson is not a disease, it's a syndrome! It's a mutation with a specific genetic marker, like Down's Syndrome. You can't catch Patterson unless you were born with it. All the military is doing is to destroy lives and keep the public in the dark so you won't question their actions.

"We were stumbling through a transformation period and were still struggling to understand it ourselves. We had to hide it from everyone. Is it really so surprising that some of us snapped under the cropped-up emotion we each contained within us? That some of us reacted violently when they were attacking us? Unfortunately, this didn't help our cause and panic spread across the globe.

"I had to flee my city and only with the help of my family and friends was I able to make it to safety – to the Sanctuary. It was the only place where we, for the briefest moment, could be free. We were safe and, while we were learning how to control ourselves, you were safe from us. For the first time, we could discover the changes that were happening to all of us without fear.

"Finally, we embraced the changes that were happening to our bodies and came to understand our condition. We realised that we could control our strength. Then, we were discovered and were persecuted once again. The military raided our sanctuary and everyone I knew and loved was taken from me for the second time.

"I managed to get away only because the others decided to stay. If we had all run, the prosecution would simply continue and we would never be free. I was tasked to bring you this message: We are not your enemy. We do not wish to hurt anybody. All we want is our freedom..."

Unexpectedly, Sandy's attention was diverted to an announcement over the airport intercom: "Final call for passenger Sandy Hirsch aboard Mango flight 813 to George, final boarding call for passenger Sandy Hirsch."

She grabbed her bag and ran through her tears for the boarding gate. She handed her boarding pass and ID document to the sour-looking stewardess waiting at the gate, her mind swam with Jessica's words. She paused, distracted by an announcement on the

TV about the upcoming Freedom Day celebrations at the Union Buildings.

"Ma'am, you really need to board now."

Sandy looked at the impatient stewardess handing her back her boarding pass and ID and she took it from the woman. "No, I don't. Sorry!" she uttered and turned around, running for the exit.

* * *

Jessica had been hiding in the boot of the car since before Johannesburg. She had insisted on it because she could control someone better when they didn't expect it. Above everything, she didn't want to endanger her new friends who had so selflessly risked everything to help her.

She heard a tap followed by Eric's voice. "We are close. Bongani says it's only about fifteen minutes to his house."

"I have a bad feeling," Jessica said.

Then, a message alert broke the monotonous hum of the road. Jessica heard Kate's voice.

"I think we have to listen to her. It's from your mother, Bongani. She says: 'Don't come home. We are being watched'."

"Take the Lynwood exit. I know where we can hide out," replied Jessica.

Without hesitation, they drove past the turn-off where they saw a police blockade searching all of the cars that were getting off the highway.

* * *

General Eksteen walked restlessly back and forth in front of the presidential residence in Pretoria. He had been summoned to a private session with the President to discuss his radical document: 'The detention and permanent incarceration of PS-positive individuals in South Africa'.

After the previous night's raid, there had been a huge outcry from the public when a blog called *The Naked Truth* had leaked footage of the massacre onto the Net. In only one day, it had gone viral and the outcry from the international community had been quite severe, threatening sanctions if this line of action were to continue.

He felt tense, knowing that the President didn't invite him here to congratulate him. The doors opened and the presidential secretary indicated for him to enter.

He walked inside and noticed that the President's desk was littered with law books and red pages of his document. President Mokoda was standing by the window, holding a glass of whisky. He turned to greet him.

"General Eksteen. Thank you for coming at such short notice. We have much to talk about. Please, sit down. May I offer you a glass of whisky?"

Rupert sat down, accepting the President's invitation.

"In the light of last night's raid, we have to re-evaluate our strategy in dealing with these people. With Freedom Day tomorrow, I want to give the public something good. I've taken the liberty of editing and suggesting a few changes in dealing with the Phoenix threat."

* * *

Jessica awoke in the early morning hours in the spare bedroom in Miriam's small apartment. It had been almost three months since she had to start running and Miriam, having been able to finish her matric year, had moved on to study psychology at the University of Pretoria.

She heard the sound of voices and slowly made her way to the living room where everyone was already awake, sitting on the balcony, discussing their plan for filming the day, lost in their own world. As she entered, Miriam was the first to notice her.

"Morning, Jess. Coffee?"

Jessica faked a smile and nodded in thanks but, in fact, her mind was running away with all the possible outcomes to the day's events. She felt feverish but did not want to put more stress on her new companions who were already sitting on the balcony discussing their plans, so, she joined Miriam in the kitchen.

"Are you sure you're okay, Jess? I know that look and it has never led to anything good," said Miriam as she poured Jessica a cup of coffee. "You don't have to do this! You can run away, find a secluded place and…"

"And just live there on my own? I don't think I ever had a choice, Em…but I am afraid. I'm afraid for myself and even more afraid of the consequences of doing nothing. The problem is that I don't know what I'm supposed to do."

Jessica took a sip of her coffee as Miriam stumbled to find the right words of inspiration.

Finally, she simply said: "Just be you. At the end of the day, that's all any of us can do, right?"

Jessica looked out towards the balcony as the sun rose over the city in the distance. Sighing deeply, she nodded and Miriam placed her hand on Jessica's shoulder. Together they walked into the living room and joined the others sitting on the balcony.

* * *

Colonel Rupert Eksteen was seeing to crowd control for the Freedom Day celebrations and was running over the action plan with a group of his sergeants, going through every eventuality in case of the worst case scenario.

After his demotion, he had been reassigned but it was just a minor setback. Once the final stages began to set in and manifest, they would come crawling back to him. Besides, his men were loyal to him and, just for today, he needed to play this part. He ran through the strategy for the last time, got up and dismissed them. His team saluted him and dispersed to take their posts leaving him standing alone in the briefing room.

Staff Sergeant Swartz knocked at the door and entered, bearing a sealed envelope. He handed it to the colonel and, before Rupert could thank him, he turned and walked away. Quickly, he opened it and read a typed message from Sergeant Kabula, the foreman of the Phoenix detention Centre, with news from within. A new disease had spread through the centre, affecting all the Phoenixes…

"Most have thawed out of their cryonic confinement but are so weak that they can barely stand. Doctor Nell says it's not viral or bacterial and that there is nothing wrong with them physically. The most distressing of all is that Nell doesn't understand how they could still be alive, since some of them are running temperatures as high as eighty degrees. Major Kubai is unable to maintain control and seeks your advice."

Colonel Eksteen looked around the empty boardroom and smiled with smug satisfaction. He took his lighter from his pocket, quickly setting the letter alight and dropping it into the metal dustbin. He stood there, looking down as the message was quickly reduced to ash and the flame burned itself out. Suddenly, there was another knock at the door and Sergeant Blake entered.

"Everything is ready, Colonel, the men have been deployed according to your plan. We are expecting the arrival of the President within the hour."

He nodded, thanking the sergeant and, then, dismissed him. He quickly gathered his papers and left the boardroom.

* * *

Jessica sat in the back of a small pickup truck, wearing a hoody and a large pair of shades. She needed to blend in and disappear into the crowd at the Freedom Day celebrations and then, somehow, reach the presidential podium to get the President's attention. It seemed like a near impossible task and she felt the tension building in her chest.

"Brendan, can you hear me? Please be there. I need strength…"

Desperately, she searched for him but couldn't find him. Instead, she found a void. There was nothing and she jolted back to reality as the van came to a halt.

Eric found a parking spot in a small alley close to the Union Buildings and he, Kate and Bongani climbed into the back of the van.

"This is as close as we can get you to the stage. We will trail you and, if you carry a camera, most people tend to ignore you."

"Thank you, Eric, but this is where we will have to go our separate ways. Eric, Kate, Bongani, without you I would never have been able to make it this far."

"What are you planning to do?" asked Kate.

"Whatever I can."

Jessica shivered and she felt her temperature rising. This wouldn't be easy but she only had one chance and it was now or never. She opened the back of the van and stepped out into the crisp winter sun.

* * *

Colonel Eksteen walked onto the presidential podium, doing a final sweep before the President was set to deliver his speech. He looked out over the crowd and noticed the security forces scanning the crowd for suspicious activity.

He scanned the protesters' faces. They had collected like screaming parasites in front of the podium, carrying their banners demanding 'Equal rights to all citizens'; 'Stop the slaughter'; and 'Vote NO to the Phoenix Act!". If it had been up to him, they would have been apprehended immediately but he had to lay low until the President begged him to take action.

Soon. It was only a matter of time but, for now, he just ordered that they be closely watched. He received the all-clear and notified the presidential guard that everything was ready.

* * *

Jessica made her way through the crowd towards the Phoenix supporters huddling in front of the podium, awaiting the President's speech. It seemed like a safe place to hide and it had the added bonus of being close to the podium. Now, all she had to do was wait until the President delivered his speech. For a moment, she relaxed.

So far so good, she thought but the fever made her unsteady on her feet and she stumbled, bumping into a protester.

"I'm sorry," muttered Jessica. As she looked up into the woman's face, she recognised her mother.

"Jessica! What are you doing here?" Sandy squealed and then quickly tried to contain her excitement.

* * *

President Mokoda was surrounded by a small group of guards and assistants.

His personal assistant handed him his speech. "It's time, Mister President."

Slowly, and almost reluctantly, he got up and made his way to the speaker's podium. People cheered as he appeared and the band quieted down. All eyes fell on him.

"My fellow South Africans, on this Freedom Day we celebrate the dawn of a new era. Over the past year, a new disease has swept across the world and a decision was taken to contain the threat before it could spread. With the help and co-operation of all of you, we have succeeded but, in the light of recent information and new medical studies, we now know more about these people…"

* * *

Jessica felt the fever rising and she turned to her mother. "Get away from me, Mom. Go, now!"

Sandy took a step forward trying to assist Jessica who looked up and peered deep into her mother's eyes.

"Mom, you can't be of any help here anymore. Please, go!"

Reluctantly, her mom stepped back and disappeared into the crowd.

The crowd around her scattered abruptly as Jessica took off her hoody and exposed her fully grown wing bones to the crowd. She stood alone in front of the President. She knelt down on one knee and lifted her head, looking deeply into the President's eyes.

President Mokoda stopped his speech and looked down at Jessica. The moment that she had made herself known, a group of armed soldiers swept in from all sides and surrounded Jessica. One soldier approached her when President Mokoda lifted his hand, holding the soldier back and giving Jessica a chance to speak.

"I am Jessica. You have all heard my story and I am here to plead our case with the President. We are not your enemy and we are not diseased. We are your sons and your daughters. Your advisers would have you believe that we are something to fear, Mister President, that there is something wrong with us and that we are dangerous.

"We never meant to do any harm but bad things have happened. But we have learned how to control our strengths. All we want is to be allowed to live where we want, to love who we want, the same as everyone else and the same as each and every one of you out there! Mister President, ask yourself what would you have done if I were your daughter?"

She struggled as her temperature spiked violently and her clothes were scorched by the heat emitted from her body. The guards retreated as the heat intensified and Jessica fell to her knees, screaming as she burst into flame.

People desperately rushed from the podium scrambling to get away but, as she got to her feet, her wings were complete with the flame streaming from her back. She gave the President a look of such serenity that he was transfixed and looked down at her in shocked horror as she crumbled to ash.

As the flames subsided, everyone paused and looked on morbidly to see what remained. A pillar of smoke obscured the body from sight when, unexpectedly, a large wing blew the smoke away and Jessica rose smouldering from the ashes. She shielded her naked body with her new brown wings.

* * *

Brendan was still smouldering, lying naked on the floor. Together, the fever and the fire had freed him from his frozen bonds and he slowly got to his feet, relishing the freedom of not being chained. He spread his newly acquired wings and he could barely contain his delight. He felt light and free. The detention centre was all up in arms and he could hear people rushing around through different passages throughout the complex.

He focused his senses and, one by one, he singled out the smallest details: the silent cracking of drying wood, a jackal scurrying across the desert a mile away…

For a moment, he felt overwhelmed by the new sensory input but he took a deep breath and became aware of the others in cells all around him. In his mind, he reached out for Jessica and found her without difficulty as she was kneeling before the President.

But something was wrong! As the gun shot rang through the air, he opened his eyes, folded his wings around his body and ran at the one way glass with all his might, bursting from his cage.

Then, the lights went off and a hailstorm of bullets erupted. Within minutes, Brendan had broken through the concrete bunker's walls and stepped into the sun. He took a deep breath and opened his wings, spreading them wide.

His wings were quite strong and deflected most of the bullets but a few made it through and grazed his shoulder and thigh. With one quick flap of his wings he took flight and flew away from the detention centre as fast as his wings would carry him.

* * *

The girl who called herself Jessica looked down at the bullet wound in her chest and then, slowly, she looked up at Colonel Eksteen where the barrel of his gun still smoked in his hand. His bullet had hit its mark and was imbedded deep inside her chest, right next to her heart. He lifted his gun again and, this time, took aim straight for her forehead and, without any hesitation, he pulled the trigger.

Instantaneously, a winged man swooped down as if out of nowhere and enveloped her in his wings, deflecting his bullet. Jessica stumbled and the man caught her, slowly lowering her to the ground.

The winged man stood up turning to face Colonel Eksteen and disarmed him so skilfully that Rupert barely noticed that the gun had left his hand until it was too late. The man threw the gun to the floor and Rupert stumbled after it in an attempt to get it back, when he was unexpectedly apprehended by a soldier. He looked up at the President who looked down at him in shock and total befuddlement.

"Look at them! Can't you all see it?! These people are dangerous."

Rupert looked around and noticed that his face was on the big screens. He turned towards the crowd but they just looking on in hushed shock as the scene unfolded. He looked at the two Phoenixes in front of him, creatures that should not be! But there they were with the people by their side. Rupert looked around in disbelief.

If this was to be his fate, he would rather die. He jumped into action, elbowed his detainer in the face and grabbed his gun from the ground in front of him. He turned it on himself and closed his eyes he pulled the trigger.

Almost a split second before the shot rang out, he felt a hand pull the gun from beneath his chin and the weapon discharged its lethal payload into the sky. His ears still rang as he opened his eyes seeing chaos in front of him. The winged man lay dead on the ground, blood streaming from the back of his head.

Within seconds, guards rushed in to detain him.

* * *

Jessica knelt at Brendan's side in shock and disbelief, lost in an almost perpetual déjà vu. Slowly she closed his half opened eyes still hopeful that it was just a dream but she knew he was gone. She felt him drain away as she struggled for breath herself. She looked at the President pleadingly. His gaze shifted between her and the colonel. Finally, his gaze settled on Jessica and he nodded at her in agreement. A feeling of peace fell over Jessica and she exhaled with relief.

"Lieutenant, please arrest the colonel."

She picked up Brendan's limp body and wrapped his wings around him like a blanket before she spread her own and slowly took flight. With every flap of her wings she rose higher and higher, leaving everything behind – the chaos, the resentment, the hate.

* * *

Jessica stacked the final stone on top of a large cairn standing on top of the mountains where she had first met Brendan, overlooking the valleys and rolling hills of the Drakensberg. She rested and placed her hand on the grave.

"We did it, Brendan. Now, you can rest in peace. I thought you would like it here, the view always took my breath away."

She ran her hand over the cairn as tears streamed down her cheeks. She shook her head, wiping the tears from her eyes and patted it one more time. Then, she turned and, with a quick flap of her wings, she flew off into the horizon.

* * *

Eric was waiting for an interview with *TIME Magazine* about his exposé: 'The Plight of the Phoenix'. Since he had released his twenty-five minute documentary, it had once again gone viral and swept the world within days.

That day, he and Kate had watched spellbound as the events unfolded on the stage. Eric couldn't have asked for a more riveting series of events. Little did he know that, once he had released this video into the world, there would be such a radical reaction.

Within a month of the publishing date, there had been worldwide support for the Phoenix cause. Now, only two months later, most countries had re-evaluated their policies and ended the prosecution of PS-positive individuals. And, once they had their freedom, they all suddenly disappeared.

A young, red-haired woman walked in and extended her hand in greeting.

"Danny Lebojovic. Nice to meet you, Mister…?"

"Eric, just call me Eric. It's my pleasure to be here."

"Well, let's jump right into the interview. Eric, let's begin with the questions on everybody's lips. Where are the Phoenixes? Where did they go?"

Ifrit

♦ Caldon Mull ♦

She looked up from the dusty culvert, smeared with the mud that had grimed her face. As she lifted the water bottle to her mouth for a quick sip, she saw a spot on the horizon out of the corner of her eye. In the heat of the early morning sun and in the slow, hot, relentless breeze, the mud lost its battle against the elements. As she tilted her head, it slowly resumed its usual form, a desiccated, fine white dust of what used to be ancient loam, then spun off her skin and resumed its inexorable drift northwards, pointing towards the shape on the horizon.

She tightened the cap on the water flask and saw the spot stay where it was, seemingly growing larger by small increments. Her dress flapped and spiralled in the wind, while whoever or whatever it was came closer, and her thoughts abandoned the task she had been attempting in the culvert. She spun out wild and fanciful explanations as to who it might be or what anyone would be doing here, at the edge of nowhere. This place where even water lurked so far under the sand that finding it again was near impossible. A place she had lived all her life without seeing anyone she didn't know, and very little that was really new.

Someone walking over the desert from the north was certainly new. She thought and thought of this ever happening before and couldn't remember anyone even telling her stories about such a thing. Perhaps she should go and tell the others, but then whoever was coming might just disappear and the whole experience would be just another figment of her imagination, a mirage conjured by longing and loneliness, spun by the wind and called out to by the dust for a brief moment, while she had toiled to find where the water had run to, where her lost lover had gone to these last two years, in a culvert at the edge of her world. Warren would have followed the water; if she could find it, she could find him, she had reasoned.

She took another sip from her water flask and watched the figure move closer with each long step. The shape was wrong, she realised. Almost as if the legs moving the shape were added onto it as an afterthought, like twigs on an orange, but it didn't scare her. With all of humanity on the edge of extinction, fear of the unknown simply didn't register against any fear of the certainty in her current existence.

The closer it got, the better she saw that it was someone carrying something. It couldn't have been too heavy but it looked big. Big things were usually heavy...unless it was tumbleweed. A tumbleweed looked big but wasn't, so, that was easy to explain away. Soon enough, the figure stood before her, draped in some odd-looking, form-fitting cloth with shoulder straps securing the large round shape to its back. For once, she was curious about something other than the water, or Warren...something new.

The face was covered with a cloth of some sort, a mask creating a smooth shape too general to make out any features, with some dark glass covering the eyes. The shoulders were broad and square, so, she decided the stranger must be male. All the books she had ever read from Mams's library-doc about all the polite human and neo-human interaction were useless if she didn't know whom she was dealing with in the first instance. She decided on the easiest and most direct entry.

She cleared her throat: "Afrique? Panglish?"

The figure shook its head; "Nay. No...oo-oort-spek? новыйрусскийязык?"

The muffled baritone voice was quite pleasant. Male, she decided. Definitely, male.

She raced through her thin memories of what the house library had exposed her to; she wished she had paid more attention. "Teangacórais?"

The figure bobbed his head. "Teangacórais!"

"Why are you here?" she asked in Teangacórais. It was mostly a machine-interface language but, despite the tendency to be light on emotional nuances and heavy on information transfer and information exchange, everyone at home would be able to communicate freely in it, even if awkwardly.

"I don't know," the figure responded. "Why are you here?" He shrugged.

"I live here," she replied, cocking her head slightly as the stranger began unclipping the front portion of his face mask slowly. "But you don't, so, why are you here?"

"At this moment, it would be to speak to you. In awhile, it will be for something else, tomorrow? Tomorrow, I am not sure because tomorrow has not come yet." The stranger finished unfastening the mask and slid it slowly upwards, revealing a square jaw covered in straggly brown scruff, mouth, nose, cheekbones...then a pair of pale blue eyes that almost took her breath away.

"Oh." She frowned, not expecting an answer quite like that.

"Yes." He grinned at her. "So, there are many answers to your question, I'm still not sure which one would suit you. I am probably here because of an incorrect calibration."

"No-one comes here but you have." She set her jaw, determined to get an answer to her first, carefully considered question...which turned out to be disappointing when it was answered. "So, why are you here?" she asked a third time.

"Hmmm..." He pondered, screwing up his nose and scratching at the scruff along his jaw while he thought. She saw that he looked much younger when he did that, older than her by no more than a few years in her revised opinion. "Well, I'm here to do something that no-one else has done, somewhere close to here, because it's my job to do it, in places like the one I need to do it in. I am not doing it at present because I am unable to but don't know why I can't. Not yet."

"I suppose that explains almost everything." She shrugged.

"My name is Wash." He grinned. "So, who are you?"

She blinked, that was going to be her next question.

"They call me Ruth."

"So, Ruth, could I get some water, some shade and a safe place to put this down for awhile?" He shrugged his shoulder straps and his parcel twitched. "It's not heavy, but I do need to take it off for a bit and clean out the inside of my suit. Perhaps that would help."

Ruth thought for a bit. All of her reading had not prepared her for this encounter with Wash. His question was simple enough, even though she had to admit to herself she couldn't make head or tail of his delivery or his responses to her questions, and his pronunciation of some words was quite odd to her. She quickly realised she only had her intuition left to guide her decision. Ruth grimaced, she should have paid more attention to her books, just like Mams had scolded her to. So, she said, "Sure, follow me."

"Thanks." His long legs took one step for every two of hers. "It looks like this part of the world can get very hot."

"Yes." Ruth glanced sideways at him. His forehead and nose carried on the same line at the same angle, she had never seen anything like that before. "We live under the ground, where it's cooler and the water is easier to get to." Ruth did a quick double-take. "What do you mean 'this part of the world'? I mean, I know you are from somewhere else but what do you mean by 'world'? Are you from the other worlds?"

"Well, it's all about perspective." Wash grinned at her again. Ruth noticed one side of his mouth crinkled higher than the other. "Your world might not be a big as my world. In fact, I could say this to be true."

"You sure do like to talk a lot." Ruth smiled inwardly, his lopsided grin meant he was not perfect, no matter her first impression. "I'm sure you'll be sick of questions before the next sunrise."

"I've been walking for a long time." Wash sighed, looking down at his feet quickly as if to check if they were still there, "So, I'd be happy to speak with your kin."

"Oh, we're not kin...we're just...just all that's left." Ruth felt a sadness welling up inside her, unbidden, unexpected. "My parents have both been dead for some time, since I was a little girl. Mams has been here since there was grass up to the horizon. We are staying in one of her burrowed earth ships. Shane and his brother, Warren, joined us when the southern run dried up about five years ago, and Warren must have died sometime last year. He wanted to track the new course of the runnels and headed south into the interior to find more water. He...never came back."

"I'm sorry to hear that." Wash glanced at Ruth as she related her brief summation of the last few years of her life, saw her face harden, her shoulders set and the dust cloud up fractionally higher around her feet as she walked.

"There are more that meet up every week or so, they come through to Mams for some extra water, we have something to eat and swap some news. About a dozen or so...fewer each year, it seems. The last few years they have been moving off what is left of their places and into the places that Mams and her mother had built specifically to conserve water and grow plants inside the buildings themselves. I suppose she's their landlord more than anything else." Ruth sighed. "Here we are – Mams' place."

"Ummm, where?" Wash looked around. "There's just a mountain of gravel. What is this place?"

"I suppose I should show you, rather than explain." Ruth picked up a rock, "Take one of these and follow me, it's not far."

Wash shrugged off his parcel, grabbed another white-speckled dark grey rock and followed Ruth around the Talus mound.

"Careful, now stand here and throw the rock, like this." Ruth flung her rock and it arced overhead in the high sunlight and fell...and vanished without a sound. "You try."

Wash nodded, took a step and flung his stone in the same direction. It was an exact repetition of Ruth's throw. "I don't...where..." Wash's brow burrowed in confusion.

"Do this like I do," Ruth lay on her belly on the ground and inched forward "I'm not sure the ground is all that solid anymore." Wash stretched out next to her and leopard-crawled forward with her until they both stopped on the lip of a gigantic crater.

"Wow..." Wash's low whistle of surprise echoed out of the hole. "What is that?"

"It used to be a mine, a couple of hundred years ago. They found diamonds and followed it into the ground. But then they hit water and they had to abandon it."

"The water...you're living off the water..." Wash shook his head in amazement.

"It was the first part of a bigger mine, so there are subsidiary shafts and tunnels. When all the surface water dried up and the big rivers stopped flowing, this was the only water left, apart from some very deep wells. Then, those dried up and the Eye in the south dried up, now this water is all that is left. Our group, Mams's community, is all those who stayed when the dust won out. It just got hotter and drier, though." Ruth inched back from the lip.

Wash followed suit. "It's huge, the hole. You say you've been down there for awhile? I really didn't think people would still be here, there's nothing for a half-a-thousand kilometres in any direction except dust, rocks and that dry wind. I passed many places that looked like they used to be cities, except that everything has been blown over and covered in dust."

"This used to be a city, a couple hundred years ago, you can still see some foundation stones up to a few hours' walk in any direction. Many of Mams's tenants' forefathers have been here for a thousand years, which is why some stayed when everyone else started north. I suppose they expected things to get better but they got worse. Well, there won't be many for much longer, at any rate."

Ruth shrugged. "Certainly two less if we don't get into shade soon, the sun is starting to heat everything up. You're going to have to bring your what's-it along, the wind picks up something fierce around noon, so you can't leave it." Ruth walked back to the side of the hill where Wash's parcel lay wedged into the talus. "There's enough space to carry it down, if that's what you're concerned about."

"No..." Wash hesitated before slinging the package back onto his shoulders "I'm just wondering what I would find down there, is all."

"Oh, I didn't think." Ruth's forehead wrinkled. "I suppose you would want to be careful, considering we are complete strangers and you wouldn't have any idea of what danger might be down there for you. I'm sure you'll be quite safe, even if you don't trust us."

Wash grinned his lopsided grin "No, I'm an explorer and I'm not concerned about that too much. I'm just worried about how much time I would spend down there. I really do have something I need to do, and soon."

"Well, I was thinking you could share your news, clean up, then decide next where to go and what to do. I'm not going to find any water today, that window has passed until tomorrow. Besides which, it's only me, Mams and Shane down there for the next few days, so, there's plenty of space and you won't feel crowded or pressured, I'm sure."

Wash grinned and shrugged the parcel into place. He raised his eyebrows quizzically and Ruth took that as a sign he was ready.

She pressed a button on her dress and a section of the Talus slope slid up to reveal a cool passage, big enough for a large transport to fit through. Ruth entered and Wash followed. The passage door slid back into place behind them. Soft LED lights glowed at foot level a few metres before and behind them.

They walked side-by-side down a gentle incline for awhile before Ruth spoke again. "So, what exactly do you have to do, and do soon?"

"Oh, I'm releasing drones at a series of geonodes over this part of the continent." Wash shrugged the parcel on its straps. "It is part of the project to re-establish terrestrial communications after the EarthGov Central crash. Less smart and much more distributed this time around. This should be the last one before I head back."

"I have no idea what you are talking about." Ruth smiled. "But it does sound important." Mentally, Ruth kicked herself again for not paying more attention to Mams's books.

"The geonode is close, nearby here. My suit will tell me exactly where in a little while." Wash looked at Ruth walking alongside him. "You mean about the EarthGov crash, or geonodes?"

"I know what geonodes are." Ruth stopped at an intersection and pointed to her left, Wash nodded and followed her into the tunnel; it was smaller and narrower than the main servitude but still wide enough for the two to walk abreast. "But I don't know about EarthGov. Perhaps Mams will know something about that. She's never mentioned it before, though. Not that I can ever remember."

"Oh." Wash shook his head in disbelief. "Okay?"

They walked a long while in silence, the walk becoming progressively more difficult. The branching tunnel now descended at a noticeable angle, and Wash observed the LED path had shrunk its coverage to just around them, and the lighting had dimmed to just enough for him to check his footing. His long strides were becoming a disadvantage, jarring on the sparse, loose gravel and threatening his balance with each step. His hamstrings were also beginning to tighten, so, Wash shortened his steps to match Ruth's.

It was starting to get quite humid and he estimated they were about six hundred metres below the surface. His parcel was beginning to catch against the corridor; by comparison to the shafts they had come down through, this was a hallway rather than a causeway. Wash grunted as he bent forward to protect it. The LED path didn't lead them, it only glowed around where they were. Wash reflected on how easy it would be to get lost down here if Ruth wasn't guiding him.

"Not far now, a couple of metres and we're clear of the shafts at this level." Ruth noticed him rubbing the back of his thigh. He probably had a cramp. "There's the exit, where the sunlight streams in."

Wash nodded at her encouragement and shuffled behind her as she disappeared into the light.

"Wow!" Wash exclaimed as he emerged into a lush garden. At the other end of the bottom of the pit was a low building, built into the ground, fronted by a deeply-shaded porch. Soil and plants covered the roof, which would be impossible to detect looking down from the lip of the pit. Fruit trees, leafy herbs and grasses stretched over the rest of the bottom of the pit, a few animals grazed contentedly in the shade, and the long shadows danced with mottled leafy patterns on the sheer side of the pit, reflected from the pool.

The ground had been landscaped into a series of concentric terraces, spiralling down from the house level to a well of clear, azure water about twenty metres in diameter in the centre of the pit. A woven net of some sort of fine mesh had been fixed around the side of the pit, most likely to stop rock fall from above. It looked flimsy, but these days flimsy was a matter of perspective.

"I'm impressed." Wash cleared his throat.

"Warren finished the net just before he left. It was his gift to Mams." Ruth felt a lump rising in her throat as she always did when looking up at it. "Come round to the house." Ruth started towards the building. A stocky youth came out, watched for awhile and then went back inside, re-emerging with another figure. The two stood and watched as Ruth and Wash covered the last few metres of the path.

"Mams, Shane, this is Wash." Ruth waved in Wash's direction, taking out her flask and sipping on it. "I found him in the desert coming from the North."

"Uh, hello." Wash scuffed his feet "Nice to meet you. Nice place you have here."

"Thank you." The older woman watched him with half-lidded

eyes. She appeared to be in her late middle age. "From the North, you say?"

"Yes. I started from the coast about two months ago and moved inland. I have another few days around here and then I start back. It was supposed to be a five month project in total." Wash shrugged the straps off his shoulders and settled the parcel on the ground.

"What's in there?" The youth pointed at the parcel.

"Communication-link drones, and a few other things for my tour." Wash considered his answer, then decided to steer the conversation to safer ground. "I could use some water and a bit of downtime, if you would. My smartsuit needs a bit of repair time."

"I heard of those." Shane looked over the hexagonal weave and dark undulating colour as it shimmered in the partial shade, like dark oil on black water. "It'll be high-sun soon, we should go inside. I guess you'll be bunking with me, boys on the right side of the house. Mams?"

"Sure. Get him settled in, see if something of yours will fit him. He's a long drink of water but the shirts should do." Mams nodded her head.

Ruth stood her ground, finished her water and tapped the last drops onto the ground, tensed for what Mams might say. Mams sighed instead.

"Why did you bring him here?"

"News? Hope?" Ruth kicked off her shoes and scrunched her toes in the cool grass. "Sector 14 looks dry as well. Then he was there, in front of me. How long has it been since someone came through here?"

"A long time, no one has come since before your parents were born." Mams shoulders slumped. "You did the right thing." Mams turned back into the house. "I'll put something on to eat and we can catch up on what's been happening in the world."

Later, Shane led Wash through to join the women in the communal eating room. Wash had left his suit submerged in a basin of water and, with Shane's help, he had moved the basin into a cool, dark space where the household usually kept cleaning implements.

"What's wrong with it?" Shane closed the cupboard door. "What do we do next?"

"I don't know...but we've done everything we can. Now, we just wait." Wash shrugged, looking anxious. "I hope not too long. I've never really waited for anything before."

"You're in the wrong place, then." Shane stood and grinned at Wash "It feels like all I've done my whole life is wait."

After stowing the suit, Shane had taken Wash to an open pool that served as a bath and the two had sat and soaked together for a long while. Shane had warmed to Wash immediately and, after chatting about anything and everything for a few hours, Wash realised that he liked Shane.

As they joined Ruth and Mams at the table, Wash felt a little self conscious as he settled on the bench and tucked his long legs under the table. "I...uh, I've never done this before, so I apologise in advance if I do something wrong."

"Never eaten with other people?" Mams chuckled. "You're serious?"

"Quite serious." Wash nodded, looking down at his hands folded in his lap. "What are the rules?"

"There is fruit, cheese, butter, bread, dried fish and fish paste, honeycomb and leafy salad," Ruth pointed the items out to Wash "You take a portion of what you would like and then you eat it with us. We'll be doing the same." Ruth grinned at the anxious looking man. "Then you can do the same with the juice, water and milk in the beakers."

"Well, be warned," Wash nodded, plucking up courage, "I haven't had any solid food for awhile, so, don't be alarmed if I select items sporadically...and then..."

"Don't worry, we have that all the time." Shane grinned and grabbed a crust of bread "The neighbours fast when they come through, only carrying enough water to bridge the gaps between the earthship oases – the really deep wells that are still left. Take your time, don't rush, we're used to it. If your digestive tract spasms, well...I showed you where the ablutions are already."

"Sure." Wash nodded, sipping on water and placing small portions of each of the items on the wooden trencher in front of him. "Well, I've come from the Northern continent, you call it Arktika. There is a group of us travelling through the global tropics seeding stationary communications relays in the 'uninhabitable zones'. I'm not originally from there...I'm from Out-System stock, but Out-System applied for the heat tolerant genotypes and recruited the template for the project. I guess you could say I was born for the job."

"Ah, I guess that's why you don't have a belly button," Shane mumbled around a piece of fish. "How old are you, Wash?"

"I'm eight of your months old," Wash shrugged. "My template gets to about two hundred years and, from what I've been told by Command, I'm going from here to some of the hot exoplanets nearby after this task is complete and I return to Arktika."

"It seems sad that we're some of the first people you've met." Ruth swirled her milk in a glass. "Almost as sad as you being one of the first people we've met from outside."

"You mentioned to Shane that EarthGov collapsed?" Mams steered the conversation back. "When or how did that happen?"

"Oh, awhile ago." Wash's eyebrows raised in surprise as he tried the fish paste. "This is very good. Salty, just like our journey-protein concentrates. Oh, the main queue cloud was ruptured about fifty years ago. We don't know why or how but the AI was destroyed and the Senate collapsed. Some of the subsidiary AIs provided local support, but essentially all of the Out-System collapsed into balkanised organisations and we essentially lost all contact with Earth until recently."

"That's about when all of our eniacs went offline and our replicators shut down." Mams nodded. "I'd wondered about that...wondered what had happened. You could see some of the big arco-cities lifting off into the sky that time. Their long streaks of light moving off-world, their ion trails sparkling as the first stars twinkled in the first darkness..." Mams trailed off into her own thoughts

"Well, since then, the Out-System has reorganised slowly and is busy establishing some of the newer sub-light communication technology in nodes all through the system. Your eniac should be back online as soon as I'm done with my mission." Wash waited for a few minutes after swallowing some fruit, grimaced and drank some water. "What was that?"

"Pomegranate." Shane grinned, enjoying the sight of Wash nervously picking through the table items.

"Sour, slippery..." Wash shuddered.

"Earth?" Ruth prompted. "What's happened here? Shane and I

spend all our time going through the offline eniac libraries and it all just stops there. The ice all disappears, magnetic inversion, the meteors pepper us, earthquakes, then the heat starts, then...nothing."

"I don't know too much, suit and I don't have too much local data to share but, yes, the interiors of some of the continental masses are almost uninhabitable for human standard templates..." Wash blinked.

"You mean us, don't you Wash?" Shane grinned.

"Um, yes." Wash sighed. "Honestly, I wasn't too keen to spend time here because the last few centuries on earth haven't been too pleasant for...my kind."

"Oh, my boy!" Mams sighed. "We're all different in some or other way. My mother told me to steer clear of EarthGov because it was bad for people, it had become a machine and it was going to try and make anything different conform to its view of what people should be. I suppose it's time for me to let go of everything she was concerned about, and what she believed in, and to start facing the facts about what is going on right here."

"Mams?" Ruth looked up at the faces around the table. Shane, alert but slightly confused; Wash's somewhat apprehensive expression; Mams' anguished look. "What's going on?"

"We're clinging to the edge of extinction, my dear." Mams sighed. "All of the eniac libraries and databases my mother and I scavenged from the city next to us as it started crumbling and before it was buried in the dust, all of it...we haven't adapted to the way the world is changing and now...we're not changing with it. Wash here, his people have changed, and my mother and her belief systems punished him and his kin for a long, long time. She had become so resistant to EarthGov that she was exactly the same as them...the other side of the same coin. Now that EarthGov is finally gone, the Earth has carried on changing the way it was always going to change and everyone is paying for that generation's decisions."

"But, Mams," Shane grumbled, "you always said that there was nothing out there. What are you saying?"

"I'm saying that there is nothing much around here for us either and that Ruth and I have been arguing for a long time about what exactly is out there." Mams looked around the table for something to put on her bread, got up and returned with a jar of preserves. "The world outside this place has become bigger and this place here has become a prison for us."

"Hah!" Shane grunted and left the table suddenly, his stride short and angry.

Ruth started to clear up the empty plates and bowls and Wash began collecting the glasses, while Mams sat and chewed slowly on her bread, lost deep in thought. Ruth lead Wash to the porch outside, the glass door sliding open with a puff of mist as it vented some of the moisture from inside. Shane was a sullen, dark shadow at the far edge of the porch, staring at the stars.

"Now she changes her mind," Shane growled.

"It's not that." Ruth sat Wash down on a woven wicker chair and walked past Shane to get another for herself. "We didn't argue. It's just that she has hope for the present and I have always had hope in the future."

"What do you mean, sis?" Shane sighed. Wash could hear a deep resignation in his tone.

"Every year there is less and less water here. Sure, the deep pipes are flooded and there are lots of the cave fish and some of that new cave grass we found last year but, soon, all of us and the Du Ponts and the Bekkers and the Van Stadens are going to have to move down there, closer to it." Ruth reached out a hand and stroked Shane's head like she had when he was little.

"You know old man Bekker wants you to marry Ansie and bring her here because they've got nothing left."

"I don't want to marry Ansie," Shane growled, "and I don't want them living here."

"And what good will it do them, staying where they are?" Ruth placed the chair next to Wash and sat down "In a few years, this place will be as dry as theirs and everyone will have to move to the caves anyway."

"I don't understand." Wash interrupted. "I know water is important, it's one of the criteria for everyone of my exploration checklist but I don't understand why you are focused on it like you are."

"You're serious?" Shane growled from his dark place "You've..."

Ruth shushed him "Wash, you said you had never shared a meal with people before? How much water do you drink?"

"Not much. Today I've had more than I've ever had. The suit recycles most and infuses ambient moisture to my body." Wash blinked and yawned. "I need about a litre a year."

"What?" Shane yelped from the corner. Ruth nodded as if something had become clear.

"And your suit is faulty, so you stopped to talk to me and ask for help." Ruth's serious face softened as she watched Wash.

"Yes, it had even gone off-line for many hours. I think it was not calibrated for this much solar energy or this much atmospheric desiccation. I think the Mars default settings would have been more appropriate. The mask is an emergency routine...minimum..." Wash yawned again "I'm sorry, I don't know what is happening to me, I can't concentrate and my body feels non-responsive."

"Sis? Is he sick?" Shane's genuine concern drew him from his sulking place to kneel down next to Wash, touched his face and forehead. "He's not feverish."

"No." Ruth grinned suddenly, "He's sleepy. Wash, listen to me. You're fine. You've had food and water and without your smartsuit sustaining you, your body needs to reset itself. It's called sleep. It's natural."

"I'm afraid. I feel like I'm slipping away into nothing." Wash's panicked eyes sought Ruth's in the circle of LED light between the chairs, flicked to Shane's.

"You'll be there when you wake up, all of you. I promise." Ruth held Wash's hand "We'll look after you while you sleep." Wash's eyes closed and his hand relaxed in her clasp.

"Now, there's a thing." Shane shook his head disbelieving, at the sleeping Wash. "An eight-month-old baby that runs on batteries. I mean, he looks like us, except for the belly-button...but, sis, what are they...?"

"They're human beings, made of flesh and blood, for all their DNA tweaking and modifications." Ruth sighed. "They are us, the 'us' of now...and watching him today, sometimes I think they're a better us than we have been. I'm going to bed; you think you can manage him?"

Shane scooped the tall form into his arms, his muscles bunching as he lifted Wash. "He's lighter than I thought. He weighs almost nothing, actually. He'll be no problem; I'll settle him in and watch over him until he wakes."

"Good, I'll catch up with you in the morning." Ruth closed the door behind Shane as he carried his charge into the house.

* * *

Shane dozed in the chair at the foot of the bed, where he had been watching over Wash through the night. The light outside strengthened into daylight and ended his sleep cycle. He napped again for a few minutes and then decided to wake properly and check on Wash. He yawned and stretched and then caught the ice-blue eyes watching him quietly.

"Morning, Wash, did you sleep well?" Shane stretched his upper body and stood up, stretched his legs.

"I'm not sure. My body is energised again and I can think efficiently." Wash moved slowly "It seems like I'm functioning, although, I have some uncomfortable pressures here and there."

"That's all quite normal, you'll need to go there for awhile." Shane pointed to the ablutions. Wash stumbled through to the room, awkward. Shane waited for awhile until Wash was finished, looking out the window at the trees dancing in the wind. He took a deep breath when Wash was back in the room, putting on a robe. "Wash, I'm seventeen years old, Ruth is nineteen and no-one knows how old Mams is. We drink about two litres of water each and every day. We eat produce that each requires a certain amount of water every day. For me, every day for the last seventeen years, I've needed that water."

"Ah." Wash nodded. "Whereas we need water but we have learnt to minimise the quantities we need. It's more efficient than the human standard. We use far more water on other things but not personally, to survive."

"Maybe…Wash, maybe Mams is right and we are on the edge of extinction. I've spent all my life reading, studying all the information in the databases and, although I'm not as smart as Ruth or as learned as Mams, in this house even I have trouble talking to our neighbours when they come through. I know reading bores Ruth and she usually just skimmed through, but I spent the time drumming the information into my head. Our neighbours never read at all, and saw no use in Mams's scavenging the archives, but now...I have as little in common with them as you do with us."

"I don't know that we are that different, Shane. I did not know what was different until I stopped here. I do know that I must finish my task and continue on, and that will not change." Wash shrugged. "As soon as I suit up, I must complete my tasks. This is inevitable."

"Well, let's check on that suit, then." Shane forced a smile he didn't feel. "Then we need to have something to eat and you'll probably need to sleep again. And, then, it will be another day and you'll get to do it all over again."

"Shane, are you...optimal?" Wash watched him with concern. Shane didn't meet his eyes, forced another smile but didn't answer.

"The suit." Shane turned and left the room. Wash shrugged to himself and followed. They arrived at the cupboard and between the two of them manoeuvred the basin out of the tight space.

"It's not as heavy as yesterday." Shane grunted as he scraped his knuckles in the tight space.

"It uses water during the healing process, mostly for the hydrogen. Our economy uses water, we don't, not personally." Wash lifted the lid and hauled it out. Shane's eyebrows lifted in surprise. Instead of the almost-oily black colour, it was translucent, opalescent, and it rolled and folded over Wash's hands almost of its own accord.

"Wow." Shane exclaimed. "Is it working?" In the gloom, Shane could make out the fish-scale pattern of the cold-energy grid infusing it. He touched it, and was amazed that it did not feel like anything.

"Almost. It should be transparent." Wash smiled at the suit. "Normally, you would not be able to tell that I was wearing it."

"So, you walk around naked all the time?" Shane grinned, sensing an opportunity to tease Wash.

"I didn't notice any taboo about nudity with you, since I have been here." Wash looked uncomfortable.

"Nah, it's fine, there's no taboo...I was just messing with you." Shane relented, noticing the relief on Wash' face, Teangacórais was not a language that encouraged teasing. "How much longer do you think the suit needs?"

"Another nine hours? It is a complete restore. We probably have to add another litre of water to be safe." Wash rolled the suit back into the tub.

"I'll bring water through, we'll put it back and we'll go and get breakfast after that." Shane padded off while Wash nestled the suit into place, and shortly returned

"Thanks." Wash accepted the beaker and poured the water evenly over the exposed portions of the suit, replaced the covering and squeezed it back into the cupboard. Shane scraped his knuckles again. They walked through to the kitchen where there was a selection of foods covered with cloth sitting on the table, similar to the supper menu, save for some thick yoghurt.

"Where is everyone? Mams? Ruth?" Wash said between a spoonful of yoghurt and a chunk of pale goat cheese.

"Ruth has gone prospecting for water in Section 10, and Mams is on the south end by the herb garden. They're normally out just after sunrise and back before mid-morning. We've just missed them." Shane shrugged "I'm supposed to go and check up on the sea-grass in the deep tunnel but that's just to keep busy, really. If it's growing now, it'll either keep growing or die and there's not much I could do to change that. Wash?"

"Yes?" Wash looked at Shane, seeing the earnestness in his face.

"You're...you're...not a machine, right? I mean...in your society, where you're from you get to have...personal relationships and have, you know...um...people stuff, friends?" Shane blushed furiously and pushed his salad around on his trencher with a fork.

"Yes, we do all of that and, no, I'm not a machine." Wash snapped "I don't know if all of your 'standards' are full of the same preconceived notions but I have a population of nanites in my bloodstream, they are part of me." Shane flinched, wilted under Wash's retort, but Wash continued. "Their primary function is to make sure my biology is not ripped to pieces by radiation, gravity or extremes in temperature. They heal me, nourish my cells and regulate my energy levels to optimise my efficiency. They provide an interface for yet more devices and tools we would need to survive. They do not make me a machine, any more than the collection of bacteria and fungal colonies you have on, and in you, make you a coral reef!"

Shane sat with his shoulders slumped, not saying anything.

Wash sighed.

"They also make me a colossal idiot sometimes, because that was not what you were asking, was it?" Shane shook his head, silently. "Sometimes, I wish I had friends. Unfortunately, I would probably treat them badly and hurt them without realising it because I have had so little practice."

Shane grinned ruefully and resumed eating. "I think you might have a friend or three that you might not know about. Just saying."

"Do you think we could meet up with Mams in the herb garden? I haven't seen a herb garden before."

Wash sighed inwardly. The suit would have held his anger back, would have given him the time to process the information, would have allowed him to consider the consequences of his retort. He debated briefly, decided on the truth.

"I feel remorse, I should not have taken that tone with you. You don't have to go to the herb garden, I was trying to change the topic. I don't like to be called a machine. My society prizes rationality first and emotion second. Some aspects would be quite strange to you but most others would be identical to your own experience and expectations."

"Thanks, Wash." Shane looked up, smiled "I thought I had made a terrible mistake just then, and insulted you. We should go to the herb garden, Mams will need help bringing in the produce."

* * *

Mams looked up as the men walked along the spiral path towards her. Shane was showing Wash the pool, twenty metres in diameter of clear azure water. It was about a metre deep now. Six hundred years ago, the level was two hundred and fifteen metres higher up the six hundred metres of pit wall, always full to that level. The tide mark was still visible when the sun shone at the right angle. The bottom of the pond was completely impervious kimberlitic rock but the water seepage into the pool from the corner sides of the pit had tapered off drastically as the sands and the dust in the region had driven the water table deeper and deeper underground.

Shane smiled broadly as he waved at Mams and he and Wash started towards the terrace she was standing on. Mams's heart warmed at the smile. Even though they weren't of her own flesh, both Ruth and Shane were dear to her, and their smiles melted her heart, every smile a gem. Sadly, Mams had not seen those smiles often the last few years and far fewer had been aimed in her direction than she would have liked.

Shane waved at a basket and Mams nodded. He hefted the greens with a bunching of his impressive back muscles and started back to the house.

"Wash dear, come sit awhile and keep me company." Mams patted a place beside her on the terrace bulwark. He complied with a folding of his long legs. "You'll be leaving soon, I imagine?"

"Soon," Wash nodded. "The suit is almost rebooted. Tomorrow morning, I think. Then, I'll start searching for the beacon location around here."

"Do an old woman a favour? Take them with you." Mams looked up into Wash's eyes, pleading. "Take them as far as you can, for as long as you want to. I can give you these." Mams opened a large sack next to her, inside glittered thousands of clear, shiny stones. Wash blinked his clear eyes a few times, then laid his hand over hers.

"Mams," Wash said softly, "we make those ourselves, as big as we want as many as we want, in factories. As to taking them with, I'm not sure I want to. It'll be very hard for them, they can't survive out there, between here and the coast. It's hundreds of kilometres of ...nothing."

"Heh." Mams chuckled to herself, stung by his reply. "A kings' ransom in the time my grandmother was alive and, now, just dead weight. You know, now, I think I understand Ruth better than ever. All the things we've stood for, over generations, now...now they are nothing but dead weight. What I thought would be their salvation, this place...wealth beyond measure, a place to grow and thrive, has instead become a cage which will be the end of us." Tears rolled freely down Mams' cheeks.

"Wash, I'm two hundred and eighty-four years old. At the height of EarthGov, when the ice was melting and the seas were rising, there were many responses in the human standard population to this environmental stress. Some developed extended senses, some bloodlines extended their youth, other bloodlines started adapting to form aquatic mutations...and over all those centuries that EarthGov stayed supreme, we hid from them, not daring to reveal ourselves because EarthGov would conscript us and bend us to their will, weaponise us.

"The more repressive EarthGov got, the deeper into hiding we went. When the eniac library docs and replicators went offline, I thought they had found us. I kept a low profile, not daring to do anything and expecting the GovSec agents to pounce at any time. They never did. Now, I know why.

"From what you have said, and from a viewpoint that is nearly three centuries long, it would seem that all EarthGov succeeded in doing was launching humanity into the stars with their oppression, and then providing evolutionary impetus when it collapsed. From a population of billions, how many thousands are we, here on earth?"

"Not more than tens of thousands of standards. All of them in Arktika," Wash spoke past the lump in his throat. "Throughout the whole Out-System, there are only hundreds of thousands, perhaps two million? Mars has three hundred thousand people; they're certainly the biggest group."

"My mother and I were opponents of a system that is no longer relevant. Without that system, we are just as irrelevant. In five or ten years' time, all the water will be gone and, if anyone is still here, they will have to bring it up here from maybe a kilometre down the shafts...or move down there themselves.

"Soon, as things go, anyone living down there won't be very human anymore. I don't want my babies to turn into things like that. It's hard enough seeing them chafe up here, twisting and turning, searching for options where there are none. Wash, please...if you can...please take them with you."

Wash said nothing and, when Shane crested the terrace, he stood, collected a basket of greens and walked with Shane back to the house. Mams watched them go, sipping from her water flask. Then, she stood slowly, her knees wobbling under her and headed slowly towards the house, the sunlight driving her to the shade.

* * *

Ruth closed the door behind her, her shoes neatly placed outside, as was her habit. She doffed her hat and went through to the kitchen, swilled her flask clean and grabbed some yoghurt from the cooler. Mams was sitting in the common room, reading an actual book, and not one of the archive folio screens.

"What's that?" Ruth spooned some of the yoghurt.

"Dickens, *The Mystery of Edwin Drood*. I thought I'd start it." Mams looked up and smiled at her. Ruth found herself smiling back. "There it is, I've missed those."

"I didn't think you ever wanted to read that book, he never finished it, as I recall." Ruth frowned slightly, Mams didn't seem herself. "What's wrong?"

"Nothing dear, I'm just really old and feeling it all of a sudden." Mams sighed, "Besides, I never said I wouldn't read it, I just said that I would like it to be the last book I read. It leaves an open ending where you have to fill in the gaps yourself. I think there are times when you have to train for some things and this would be fitting."

"You've always loved Dickens." Ruth felt a flutter of fear in her chest, inexplicably. "Where's Baby Boy?" Ruth kept her voice level.

"He went to bring in the fish nets." Mams opened the book again, she was only a few pages into it. "Wash is sleeping, he had a light lunch first, though. I think he is coping very well without his suit, all things considered. He is a lot tougher than you'd think."

"Mams...what's wrong?" Ruth pulled up a chair and faced her, gently tugging the book down to Mams' lap. "Please tell me."

"There's a couple of things I've always wanted to say but didn't. I think I should tell you those things now." Mams patted Ruth's hand. "I want things to be good between us."

"Of course, Mams." Ruth sat very still. Mams' hand was cold.

"Warren didn't go and look for water. He was very ill when he got here and, when he left, he went home. He didn't want Shane to think he was being dumped here. He wanted Shane to think this was his home and, when he left, he was leaving to try and make things better for everyone. He made me promise to keep it quiet but I think it's time to clear the air."

"I didn't know he was ill." Ruth sighed. "I thought he was leaving me."

"My poor girl, you were both around the same age." Mams sounded ashamed, "You've been carrying that torch for almost two years, and it made me angry with myself that you would try and follow his dream, and there never was a dream. He didn't abandon you, my dove. He just died."

"Oh, Mams," Ruth sobbed.

Mams drew her in her arms and rocked her like she had when Ruth was a child, shushing her, stroking her hair.

"Dear, you should go with Wash." Mams stood and kissed the crown of Ruth's' head when she had finally stopped crying. "I've always loved you like my own. And I think that's everything I haven't told you that's important. I'm going to lie down now, my dove."

Ruth stared hollowly as Mams slowly paced towards her room, before heading to her own.

* * *

Much later, after sunset, Wash padded through the quiet house and slipped out of the door. The air was cool on his exposed skin. He purposely adjusted his body heat to compensate automatically against the probability it would soon become very cold, as the desert air lost heat so quickly.

Dinner was a dismal affair, Mams had gone to bed early after merely picking at her portion. Ruth sat detached and lost in some internal dialogue that neither Shane nor Wash seemed capable of breaching, had they even been tempted. Ruth had cleared up the cutlery afterwards, almost on automatic, while Shane had dumped the whitebait cave fish into the desiccators. Ruth headed to bed. Shane put the desiccators on a timer and headed to bed himself. Wash had crept out as soon as Shane's breathing had slowed to sleep.

Wash headed for his parcel, tucked away on the porch. As soon as he was sure he was alone, Wash opened the parcel and off-sorted his kit. He pulled out his most prized and most secret possession from a hidden side pocket. A few seconds later, he pulled a small orb from a clip and two slivers of grey powder from another hidden pocket. Satisfied, he did a quick inventory and closed the parcel, sealing it with his thumbprint. Wash stood and started down the spiral path towards the herb garden. As he walked, mist rose from his skin as his internal regulators breached the layer of cold damp air near the pool and swirled in his wake.

Mams had left her sacks of diamonds by the bulwark where they had been sitting. Wash knelt and selected two of the glittering stones, flipping through his ocular magnification range and making sure that the selected gems were without flaws and impurities to specification. His eye muscles throbbed without the suit's assistance but he completed the 100 times magnification scan successfully. Satisfied with the stones, Wash moved stealthily down to the pool and waded to the middle.

He flipped a switch on the orb and dropped it into the centre of the pool. Wash then returned to the side of the pool, submerged the small matter replicator in the water before him and slipped a diamond into the load cell. Six minutes later, he repeated the process. The water in the pool bubbled furiously around the small machine, Wash could actually feel the water draining from his mid-thighs to the tops of his knees while the machine worked.

The hard, impervious kimberlitic rock under his bare feet started to cause Wash discomfort, so he stepped deftly out of the pool and headed back to the building. He stowed his items back in his parcel and headed back to his dorm room. Slipping into bed, as Shane snored softly, Wash grinned with satisfaction before slipping into a deep sleep.

Wash awoke alone in the room shortly before dawn and headed to the cupboard where his suit was stowed. The tub was almost empty of water and slid out of the cupboard easily. Wash lifted the lid, the suit was clear, transparent, and almost slithered out of the tub into his waiting hands. "I've missed you too," Wash murmured to the suit as it stretched over his skin and started to seal. "We've got a big day today, I'm glad you're better."

Wash walked onto the porch, where Ruth and Shane stood by the steps, weighted down with backpacks, external water flasks and heavy sun protection.

"We're tagging along." Ruth looked like she had been crying all night "You'll need a guide to get out of the tunnels."

"I've never seen a geonode and my chores are all done." Shane grinned. "Besides, I wanted to see how your suit looked."

Wash shrugged and started to shoulder his parcel with its familiar straps. Shane watched him move in the thing he had helped tend for the last few hours. The suit was actually quite modest, and was definitely a coverall. While it did conform at skin level to Wash's body, and displayed his musculature, it wasn't transparent on him.

It was more like the suit displayed an approximation of what was beneath it. Squinting carefully, Shane realised that, while Wash looked like he didn't have clothes on, he couldn't see any...details, as he would were Wash actually naked. As Wash settled the straps onto his shoulders, his muscles flexed and bunched under the suit. Shane stole a sideways glance at Ruth and caught her looking with some interest at Wash.

While he was moving, the faintest blue honey-comb glimmer over a moving muscle here and there showed Shane that the suit could probably charge slowly just from the body's electrical impulses.

"Nice!" Shane nodded. "Very fetching."

When Wash was ready, he looked at Ruth and Shane. "You sure?"

Ruth just nodded.

"No, but I'm not going to let a friend down, even if it's only a little way to share a path." Shane forced a smile to hide his anxiety.

"Come, let's go." Wash nodded, letting Ruth lead.

It was still dark when they reached the tunnel system entrance, and Wash's thighs ached from the climb. Ruth and Shane seemed unperturbed by the gradient, not even breathing hard.

"Still short of charge," Wash panted, then opened all the suit's systems to their maximum current capability and turned slowly in a circle. "I have a lock from data retrieval; it's a small hill about fifteen kilometres away, in this direction."

Wash started a steady lope, the first light of dawn casting shadows on the gravel and pebbles for the first few metres of the talus, thereafter, they were in pure, bare dust. As the wind picked up, the eddies and dust devils began to cloud the clear air. Wash slowed to a walk, moving purposefully in a slow, measured stride and, although Ruth's short steps were more rapid, she never faltered. Shane kept pace, uncomplaining.

As they walked, Ruth found herself looking at Wash, his skin appeared to pulse and trail light in bands and different colours. Odd, she determined, while the suit looked transparent, it wasn't actually: At times, it was opalescent, at others clear or opaque.

Before dawn, it had looked like Wash's flesh but, now...Wash looked like he was part of the daylight.

One part of her knew the suit was reconfiguring itself, another part thought it was simply beautiful, as her thoughts dimmed down into the hypnotic routine of walking.

Four hours later, a small hill came into view, its rock face blackened and scoured by wind, its irregular summit looking like knuckles on a fist that had punched through the flat dust plain.

"I know this place..." Shane gasped, "It's my home...was my home."

Wash, Ruth and Shane continued up towards the hillock and saw the small, ruined house at the base of its north face.

"There used to be water behind the house, until the spring dried up." Shane trotted towards the house. "That's when Warren brought me through to the pit. Mom and Dad had died when I was very small, so Warren looked after me until the water went, and then we left." Ruth and Wash followed. At the top of the steps to the patio, Shane froze. "Oh."

Wash looked past Shane at the desiccated corpse sitting on a stone bench, watching the way they had come. The winds must have dried him almost immediately because, apart from being dead, he looked little different than he had when alive, his tattered clothes flapping listlessly in the wind.

Ruth reached out and touched the dead face. "So, you were looking out for us, after all these years. Now, you get to watch over Mams."

Shane looked like someone had punched him in the gut. "Sis, there never was any other water, was there? He never left to find us more, did he?"

"No, baby, there never was." Ruth sighed, looking back to where the pit would be on the horizon. "There never was..."

* * *

Mams woke to an empty house, pulled on a gown and walked through the rooms. Smiling to herself, she slipped out and started down the spiral path to the herb garden. The view from her favourite place was always worth the effort. She knew what was happening to her, she had seen it in her mother. The mutation that massively extended her life and her youth tended to fade away rapidly and all of the effects of aging were going to come all at once. Her mother had lasted three years from this point; Mams was sure it would be the same for her.

Mams looked at the pool and sighed. It couldn't have been more than forty centimetres deep. At most, half of what she remembered. The animals would probably be the first to go. She was sure it wasn't this bad yesterday...or maybe she was just confused. It didn't matter, really. If Ruth and Shane had gone with Wash, then, they would either return...or not. What she did know was that whatever chance they had out there, no matter how difficult it looked, it would be better than here.

Something deep in her heart knew that she had to have hope, have faith in her foster children and trust in herself that she had read the spaceman's character properly. Mams smiled to herself, she used to swim in the pool when she was a girl, nearly three hundred years ago, and now she wondered why she had ever stopped. While she was entertaining the thought, ripples started moving in the precise middle of the pool.

Perplexed, Mams slipped off her seat and moved closer, picking her way down the same spiral paths that she and her mother had dug, following the water as it receded over the decades, each metre they had raked through, disgorging the diamonds that had lain there since time began. Yet, their effort had been made for the water, not for the thousands of gems they had uncovered. Those same gems that Wash had refused as worthless, when Mams had tried to buy a future for her charges from him.

Standing at the edge of the pool, Mams realised it was not her imagination. Something in the centre of the pool was making it ripple, the ripples expanding out in lazy, concentric circles until they lapped at the edge where she was standing. While Mams peered at the pool's centre, the sun breached the top lip of the pit. Just then, the centre of the pool belched violently and a plug of water three centimetres wide shot into the air and fountained back into the pool, spraying Mams with a fine mist as the top of the two-metre column fell back onto the surface.

Mams goggled at the sight. Her brow furrowed then relaxed "What...Wash?" It must be, it could only be...She shrieked with joy, stripping off her clothes and waded into the pool. She splashed amongst the rainbow droplets of her clear, liquid hope. "Wash!" She bubbled with laughter "Wash!"

* * *

Ruth gently turned Shane's head away from what used to be Warren. "Come, Baby Boy, let's stop looking at the present...let's go and see what Wash is doing. We've said goodbye to him in our hearts a long time ago."

Wash had unzipped his parcel and had laid a series of small cylindrical, metallic devices in the dust. A small screen glinted in his hand as he gestured over it, one by one the cylinders cracked open and glittering dust leaked onto the ground. The parcel-covering sheet also crumbled into dust that lay glittering in the dry sand. He opened another small case at hand and unclipped the last orb from its casing. Then, he strode over to Shane. "Show me the spring."

Shane nodded and led Wash to where a clump of dried grass lay forlorn in an alcove of the hillside. Wash nodded and squinted at the orb, then at the dried rock and then the orb again. He clicked the orb and it seemed to shrink to about a centimetre in diameter. He crouched on his haunches and dropped it in the middle of the spring's rock shelf. A dusty, acrid smell drifted from the shelf as the orb disappeared from sight.

It seemed to Shane that Wash's eyes glowed in the sunlight while he was looking purposefully around the site.

"What's that? I told you the spring was dry." Shane shook his head.

"It's a drill." Wash looked up at him, his pupils contracting back to normal, the suit shimmered against his skin. "Water is lazy, it spend millions of years getting to a place by itself. Once you find it, all it needs is an easier route to travel and a small enough aperture to keep doing it. If the aperture is too wide, you don't get the exposed column and the area humidity for optimum e-mote maintenance. It all depends on the pressure of the ocean of water under the sands balancing against the aperture length and radius. If suit and I have our tolerances correct, the water columns would be exposed for thousands of years."

"With all the magnetic lines converging here, whatever signal goes out also has an easier transmission route to the next point." Shane nodded. "I understand now."

"The fusion drill covers about a metre a minute, I tested it on the kimberlitic rock at the pit earlier." Wash stood, "All we need to do is wait...and decide."

"Decide what?" Ruth joined the men.

"If you are to come with me." Wash shrugged. "I didn't think much of the idea when Mams suggested it and then I couldn't think of how that would be possible, but I have worked it out. I think I will try to sleep more often in future. I find some inspiration in subconscious processing."

"Well, I..." Ruth started to say something.

"Yes!" Shane interrupted. "I wasn't sure but, then, I saw Warren. Now, I'm sure." Shane grabbed Ruth's shoulders, "Sis, right now, we *are* Warren. We're sitting on a porch, watching the horizon...Sis, let's not be like Warren anymore, let's just be like us."

"How are we going to get out of here, Wash? It's hundreds of kilometres to anywhere else with virtually nothing in all that space to support the journey."

"Same way as I am." Wash's face beamed. "Exactly the same way, there are suits I made for you. They're difficult to make but I was lucky I had everything I needed at hand." Wash laid two small transparent parcels on the ground, tightly folded rectangular boxes. "But you will also need control nanites for them."

Wash produced two small slivers of a grey dust. "You don't have to like them, you don't even need to listen to them much...but you can't do this without them. It's an all-or-nothing decision." Wash's shoulders slumped. "I'm sorry, but those are the only choices you have. I'd like you to come with me, if that counts for anything. This is the last stop in the project. I leave here empty-handed, everything gets used up in the process. Except you...if you'll come with."

After a few seconds of silence, Shane stepped forward. "I'm coming with you. Show me how."

Wash tapped the grey powder into Shane's water-flask. "They'll activate and map you. It'll take a few minutes for the calibrations to set and, then, you're ready. You'll know when."

Shane downed the water in the flask.

"Here, hold this." Wash handed him a dormant suit.

"Tingly," Shane muttered. The small cube in the palm of his hand sparkled, stretched out thin tendrils to run along the outside of his skin, up his arm. Tiny honeycomb patterns formed, elongated and then smoothed out as the tendrils extruded. Shane cooed quietly and seemed to zone out, staring at the pulsing strands, almost oblivious to the others.

Wash grinned "That's quite normal. The sync process between the nanites, the suit and yourself is like...*a cappella* harmony; you'll find where your refrain fits best and then the harmony is all that's important."

"Ruth?" Wash prompted.

"I loved him," she pointed with her chin at the porch, "and now all of our dreams are dust." Ruth sighed and held up her flask. "I think it's time to make some new ones."

They sat next to the spring until the shadows were at their shortest with the noonday sun, each locked in their own thoughts while they waited. Ruth followed Wash's subtle prompting and found she could actually feel the men near her without having to open her eyes. As far as the suit was concerned, Ruth was surprised at the intensity of feeling her dormant suit exchanged with her.

In her experience, it was similar to the little billy-goat kid that had followed her around at Mams' place one summer, adoring, completely besotted, eager to please. But not quite the same. It was as if the suit had copied the best parts of Ruth and poured back unconditional love as a reward. Ruth felt somehow that the suit had filled the gaps in her, where Mams and Warren had left spaces. In her mental periphery, she felt Shane's intense contentment, signalling a similar process occurring within him.

A pulse from Wash pushed through her ocean of serenity. "It's through." He announced, whether out loud or through a new channel Ruth had not quite discovered yet, he sounded extremely satisfied.

With a belch and a bubble, a metre-tall column of water pushed up gracefully into the air from the spring. The glittering motes from the array of cylinders Wash had laid out began to rise off the ground, drawn to the moisture, sparkling and glittering in the noonday sun as the moisture activated with the stored solar energy.

Everything that Wash had brought with him crumbled into sparkling dust. They rose, facing towards the water; all Wash's baggage gone: his spare face mask, the empty drill containers, the emergency replicator...all consumed by the task.

Swirling and swarming, the crumbled smart dust whisked towards the column of water, rising refreshed, higher and higher into the air. A glittering column of insubstantial sparkles ten metres in diameter, rising...stretching...one hundred, two hundred, three hundred metres high. The tang of ozone draped over the top of the hill as their microscopic fusion cells worked their magic.

"Come, stand here with me, we're on our way." Wash motioned to the others, while their suits activated in the wet spray, closing over them and sealing. "I've set all of them to the amended calibrations, so, we won't have the same trouble I had on the way in. They're ready, but be warned, the activation can be quite...intense."

Shane squirmed. "Dude! You need to give me a little more space there," he muttered to his suit. "Ah...okay. I see why you wouldn't wear anything else, ever."

Shane and Ruth shucked their clothes, dropped their flasks and backpacks. Their suits twinkled at each other and at Wash, all the while sucking in more and more of the spray. Slowly, they started to rise beside the monstrous column of glitter, their suits extruding stabilising wing-nubs and starting a gentle hum that tingled all through their bodies.

"I feel like I am all on fire but it doesn't hurt. Like a dancing flame. I'm a dancing flame above the desert sands!" Ruth laughed joyously.

"We're really high up but it doesn't feel like it matters." Shane chuckled, the vast flat white plain extended in all directions from the hill. "I'm a cloud...part of the sky..."

"Come, let's fly out." Wash called them. "Follow me." He peeled out, the gentle hum surrounding his suit rising in pitch and his wing-nubs extruding as he rose towards the sun, gently banking to the north.

Still laughing delightedly, they followed.

Ifrit

Captive

♦ Natalie Rivener ♦

Chapter 1

Fyhnn blinked in the harsh sunlight. His eyes and nose burned from the salt water he'd just been dragged from. His body spasmed with a cough that sprayed the glistening deck with salty saliva.

The coolness of a shadow fell across him making his water-chilled body shiver. Considering the ocean spent most of its time in the sun, its waters weren't particularly warm. He had really always thought that they would be warm.

A large, calloused hand closed on his upper arm and jostled him roughly onto his now bony knees. Fyhnn winced as they dug sharply into the wet wood. He squinted up, trying to see what was going on around him. Maybe he could make another dash for it.

Besides the crew, who were obviously busy manning their stations around the deck, there were only three others near him. The man holding him up was a burly giant of a man. His sun-bronzed muscles stood out against the fabric of his stained red shirt and the glint of light in Fyhnn's peripheral vision told him that the man also wore a broad ring of gold in his ear. It was this man that had brought him those disgusting, oily biscuits and stale water in the bitter and sour-smelling bilge hold.

The other two were the ship's captain and the woman in red. The captain could have been from Yrthull with his dark skin. It was nearly as dark as Fyhnn's. But the slant of his eyes and the sun-bleached green cast to his hair were absolutely foreign...as were his strange attire – a short dark waistcoat that covered only the top half of his torso and the skirt-like pants that were gathered tightly around the man's calves.

For a second, his eyes settled on the woman. Her skin looked tight and dry where her shoulders peeked out of the flowing sleeves and she was holding onto the ship's rail for balance. Now that he looked at her clothes, they were entirely too clean and dry. Like she wasn't really on the ship with them. Like she hadn't been subject to the constant spray of seawater or the general stains of travel.

His brain grasped for understanding. Maybe, she was some sort of nobility. No. He shook his head. No, that didn't gel. Maybe, she... It slowly dawned on him: She was a mage. That would explain why she had sunburn. She probably hadn't spent much time outside until this sea voyage.

Fyhnn flinched a little as the captain broke into a sudden tirade, making the hand on his shoulder clench a little tighter. The tall man was gesticulating wildly, pointing at Fyhnn, pointing at the choppy green waters beyond the ship's rail, waving his arms about and finally settling them on his hips. Fyhnn could guess at what the man had been saying. He'd caught a word or two in the Beyonder trading tongue, something about "slave" and "ship"... Well, that, combined the fact that Fyhnn had just been hauled out of the water after he had tried to escape, gave him some context.

The woman was now gesturing and talking. Though her voice was softer, her tone was no less vehement. Again, "slave" and...was that "magic"?

He touched the smooth piece of metal that had been snapped around his neck. A shudder ran through his body that had nothing to do with being cold. It took a moment of concentration to stop reaching for magic. He could feel it, though, swirling just out of reach. *Damned collar,* he thought miserably.

He'd been cut off from his power since that day in Kishnee...that day... His mind drifted back, bringing back the memories.

He had been on one of his "little outings", as he called them. The masters went into fits about them. They would harp on about him missing fundamentals and core principles. Like he hadn't covered all of that for how many decades. Being an Alvari student among a bunch of short-lived humans had some demeaning consequences when it came to how time was considered. Just because he would live several times longer, he was forced to work that much longer on things his human counterparts were allowed to finish within a fraction of the time. The apprentice-level classes were stifling and there was so much more out there to discover...

Ever since the Storm had started clearing up, he had been hearing more and more reports about these strange newcomers. In Bish-Ghen, the University was buzzing with outlandish tales about the foreigners from Beyond. Knowing even a handful of words in the Beyonders' trading tongue was considered particularly fashionable. He knew more words in the Beyonder's trade language than the trade language of Kishnee.

Now that his little outing had brought him to the port city of Kishnee, he had to take the chance to sate his curiosity. He wanted to see if they really had red skin; if they truly didn't look like the humans of Yrthull...whether their sailors really wore skirts... He couldn't quite imagine a ship wholly crewed by women.

He was idly watching a seagull swooping by when a cart passed right in front of him, almost bowling him over. It was rushing towards the docks that were just a short way off to his right. From here, he could see people were milling about. In fact, humans and Alvari alike were eagerly pushing closer side by side.

Glancing around, he saw why. Not too far into the deep blue waters off the Kish coast, a dark-sailed ship was coasting in towards the docks. *Beyonders!*

Another cart came rumbling by, also heading to the docks. He almost laughed at their eagerness. Somehow, he had thought that they'd be over the novelty of these strangers by now. Then again, weren't the Beyonders exactly why *he* was here?

The traders from beyond the Serpent Storm brought goods from places Yrthullians were only now learning existed. Among their wares were tools and devices of such wonder that they fetched impossible prices. Only the richest of the rich could afford them.

As he got closer, Fyhnn looked at the press of bodies in dismay. He hated being in such close contact with the uncleansed bodies of the common folk. But...to get close enough to see even the tallest mast of the ship, he'd have to move forward.

Fyhnn felt a tug on his surcoat and he glanced back ready to fend off whatever urchin was about to beg from him. He'd already given away his lunch to another earlier that day.

An alluring woman with copper skin and curly black hair stood right behind him. She wore a layered wine-red gown and she swayed slightly, as if she were a delicate flower caught in a soft breeze.

Fyhnn turned all the way around to face her.

"See ship?" she asked in the trade tongue of Kishnee glancing up over his shoulder at the mast towering over the crowd. Her accent was unlike any he had ever heard before; somehow dark, with emphasis on the last consonant.

He stared at her for a moment. The fabric of her dress shifted around her hips like soft flower petals in a wreath. A slender band of silver encircled her neck, glittering despite being obscured by a diaphanous black scarf. Except for the exotic colouring of her skin, there was also something about the slant of her darkly outlined eyes that proclaimed that she hailed from outside Yrthull.

Though he didn't speak much more than a dozen words of the local trade language himself, at least, he could respond this time. He nodded enthusiastically and said: "Please."

He followed her around the crowd, down to a temporary wooden walkway just below the pier. In only a few moments, they were right by the gangway that had been put up as a bridge to the port platform. As they walked up into the darkwood ship, he glanced around to see the countless faces of the crowd only a few steps away.

Several deckhands were busy lugging out barrels and crates from the open deck hold. They wore only what appeared to be baggy trousers, their sun-darkened torsos glistening with sweat.

Haha, Fyhnn thought to himself. *Those could have been skirts if they hadn't been tied off at the knees. Also...these sailors are most assuredly not women.*

"Come!" the woman called from a smaller open hatch.

It felt like he was moving in a dream. How strange to be aboard one of these ships. How strange that he was following this woman into its depths. The dark, oily sails and soaring gulls above disappeared from view as he descended the steep steps of the companionway.

Before his eyes could adjust to the darkness inside, he felt a hand on his shoulder and then stars exploded in front of his eyes as something hit him solidly on the head.

He had vague recollections of being dragged down steps, his body bumping roughly against the wood. Being unceremoniously dumped onto a pile of scratchy, musty cloth and where the slosh-slap sound of waves against wood jarred against his reeling senses.

When he came to his senses, the first thing he had tried to do was reach for magic. Though his small tear-shaped focus was still dangling from its fine silver chain around his wrist, he couldn't manage to pull together any magic at all. Rattled, he tried again. Nothing happened. Maybe the old words? Fyhnn searched his memory and dredged up the arcane words he had been taught as a child to learn his first spells. But the words fell flat as he spoke them.

Panic rose up like ice cold hands pressing into his very being. He'd never been without magic for a day in his life. It was the most treasured thing he had ever had. And he couldn't touch it.

Oh, Great Star, no. Please, Lord, help me!

But the Great Lord did not respond to his desperate prayers.

He had strained endlessly to pull himself loose from the biting shackles and chains that were fixed to the rusted ring of iron bolted to the stained wooden floor. Time and time again his head had banged on the low ceiling. He couldn't even sit upright. Like they had stored him on a shelf.

After that had followed a series of days trying to communicate with the man who came down once a day to feed him. The man didn't respond to anything Fyhnn said or cried or screamed. All he ever did was to bring a heel of stale bread and a small cup of water and to take the small bucket Fyhnn had been provided with to relieve himself in. Though, how they thought he was going to use it with any success in such cramped conditions was beyond him.

Eventually, he just watched and listened. What else could he do?

Though it was fairly dark where he sat, his eyes grew accustomed to the gloom. He was chained to a deep shelf on one side of the bilge hold. Though he could see the foamy bilge water sloshing below him, his chains didn't allow him enough leeway to get closer than the edge of his shelf. Towards the bow on the same shelf, there were wooden crates blocking his view further forward. On the opposite shelf, there were bolts of fabric towards the bow and smaller crates closer to the stern.

Over the heavy creaking of the ship and the constant slapping and rushing of the waves, he could hear muffled voices beyond the hold. Sometimes there would be shouting. When it got darker, he sometimes heard singing. He'd heard a low rumbling once or twice. Something he was fairly sure did not come from the ship or its crew.

The worst was the smell. Not the choking, sour rot smell of the bilge water. Not the sickly sweet stench of his own faeces smeared on the bucket and the surface below him. Not the overwhelming brine and pitch smell that permeated everything. It was the tantalising smell of food that seeped through to him. Soups of onions, potatoes and dried meat. Stews that smelled hearty and comforting. But none of it ever made it down to him. All he had were smells that made his stomach rumble and burn with hunger. Even his muscles seemed to burn with hunger. All he ever got were oily biscuits that barely smelt of anything besides fish oil.

One fateful day when he woke, he was shuffling around on his cramped shelf, trying to relieve himself in his bucket when he found the rusty ring significantly loosened. Whether by his own efforts or the help of some unknown ally, he had no idea. It took him all of ten minutes to wrench it all the way loose. He scampered from hiding place to hiding place until he surprised a deckhand by bursting up from out of the companionway and shoving the young man over. From there, it was a matter of a quick dash to the port-side gangway and over the rail to freedom.

Or back on the deck...as it turned out.

Surfacing from his reverie, Fyhnn saw the fight between the captain and the woman in red die down. He watched the captain turn imperiously on his heel and stomp off to disappear down the companionway.

The burly man holding him down gave his shoulder a shake. He looked up and followed the sailor's gaze to the woman. She was staring out across the waters, her hand resting at the base of her throat. That was when he noticed her hand. Its skin looked strange, like the wax built up on the side of a candle tinted with something green.

She turned around, starting to speak...but, as her eyes settled on Fyhnn, the words caught in her throat. Her gaze flicked to that of the sailor holding him and back.

The sailor grunted a short question and she nodded. Fyhnn was suddenly jerked to his feet and shoved unceremoniously towards the companionway.

Oh no! No. No. No. They were going to take him back down there! His stomach turned uncomfortably. He turned around, pitching forward to fight off the burly sailor, but he ended up getting shoved so hard that he smacked down hard onto his already-bruised knees. Another shove and he toppled sideways onto his forearms.

"No!" he heard the woman cry.

Looking up over his shoulder, the woman was holding on to the sailor's arm, pulling him back. He wasn't sure who was more surprised, him or the sailor.

She rushed around the sailor and knelt by Fyhnn's side. Her damaged hand rested on his shoulder for a moment and then she hooked her other arm around him to help him up.

"Come," she encouraged him.

He was too dumbfounded to resist.

* * *

She had led him to a small cabin furnished with naught but a narrow bed with a small chest by its side. Inside, it smelt of the flowers and spices from the markets at Kishnee.

Once she had managed to insistently coax him in, she had a small tub of hot water brought in and she gave him a clean rag and some harsh-smelling soap to clean up with...that and the unexpected luxury of privacy.

As the door closed, Fyhnn started inspecting the small room. There was no cupboard or closet and only the one door leading out. The round porthole window was smaller than his head, so, no way he could climb out there. Other than that, he could think of no means of escape that didn't involve magic. *Damned collar!*

He quietly slid open the door to peer into the narrow hallway outside. To both sides of the door stood a muscled sailor with a curved sword resting between his feet.

"Oh...uh...sorry to bother you," Fyhnn said. Not that they would understand that anyway. Not unless they had learned Ghennai all of a sudden.

He ducked back into the room, shutting the door quickly.

He looked at the tub, at the door and at the porthole. Well, then. Barring an attempt to break through one of the interior walls to an adjacent room, he was very effectively imprisoned in this little room. He looked down at his emaciated frame. A month of near starvation had reduced him from his already lean frame to barely skin and bones. Breaking through a wall indeed. He almost laughed.

* * *

It took him a good while to wash away the grime, the filth and the general stench he had built up during his month of confined captivity. When he was done, he wasn't sure the last bit of washing could have done much good. The water in the tub was so dirty, even a handful was too murky to see through. But he felt better.

Looking around for the dismal pile of clothes he had shucked before his bath, he found a large, mostly clean yellow shirt and a pair of the billowy pants the ship's crew favoured by the door. He had it on before he started thinking about whether it had actually been intended for him. Did that even matter, though?

The door opened just as he was about to put his ear to it.

The woman in red was holding out a copper plate of fresh fruit and cheese, presumably from the Kishnee markets.

"Food?" she said in the Beyonder trade language, offering the plate to him.

Well, there goes the next escape, he thought as his belly rumbled loudly. It took all his effort not to simply bury his face in the food but to take the plate from her instead. It really ended up being a wild grab.

The food was gone all too soon and, now, his thirst announced itself with a sour burn in his throat.

"Water?" he asked, looking up at her from the floor.

She was still standing in the doorway, her expression sad.

"No water?"

She shook her head as if to clear it and she blinked. From the hallway, she produced a bucket and a wooden cup.

That was more water than he had had in a week.

She took a step closer and crouched down.

The urge to get away from her almost overwhelmed him. It was the same reaction he would have had if a sword was being swung at him. It made no sense. Why was she suddenly trying to be nice to him? Was this some kind of ploy? To what gain?

Strands of her dark brown hair fell across her face. Her scarred hand was dipping the cup into the bucket. From where he sat, he could see no weapons on her. Then again, in the ample folds of that dress, she could be hiding half a laboratory.

A droplet of water splashed on the floor as she brought up the cup. He had never before really considered water as something that had a smell but, the surprisingly earthy aroma of the cup she offered him was so inviting, he found himself leaning closer. It reminded him of mountain streams. She raised it to her lips and took a sip, then she held it out to Fyhnn. He couldn't remember taking it but he shivered with pleasure as its contents slid down his throat.

* * *

With half the bucket gone, Fyhnn sat back against the small built-in bed.

The woman was looking at him intently. "Name?"

He looked at her and felt a burst of laughter bubbling up. "Name?" He chuckled darkly and then shook his head.

She inched forward and leaned a little closer. Her eyebrows were drawn up in what he assumed was intended as concern. She reached out gingerly and touched a finger to his arm. "Name?"

He felt a small twist of bitterness rise up from deep within. He jerked his arm away. "Slave. No name."

She rocked back. Was that shame he saw in her eyes? She looked down at the floor, her whole hand cradling the scarred one to her chest.

They sat in silence for a good few minutes.

After watching her for what seemed like ten minutes, Fyhnn felt his resolve waiver. At first he hadn't been certain but, there, he saw it. Her shoulders were shaking. Was she crying? He couldn't quite reconcile this version of her with the ruthless siren who had deliberately lured him from the docks to be taken captive and left to lie in his own excrement.

If she had been forced to do it, then why was he now ensconced in a cabin above the hold? Even with magic, it would have been hard for her to defend both of them against the whole crew of this ship. So, that meant that she was acting of her own volition. The captain wasn't about to barge in and take him below again. If that had been the plan, the crew would have done so the moment they had him back after his dip.

That left him with the rather perplexing problem of where that left him. Was he still a prisoner? It wasn't exactly like he could swim to shore. But they hadn't suddenly changed bearing either, so, they were still headed to wherever they had planned to go. Were they just going to leave him somewhere?

The more he thought about it all, the more questions he had. And the more questions he had, the more worried he felt. Time to stop thinking.

He reached out and touched her shoulder. She all but jerked back, her eyes wild as she looked up at him. Her eyes darted to his hand, to his face, around the room. He'd seen animals react like this when they were hurt. Right. Time to back off.

He held up open palms and moved back a little.

Her eyes widened a little and she actually started reaching out herself but let her hand drop. Suddenly, she looked tired, no longer upset, no longer afraid. Just tired, with shadows forming under her eyes.

He waited to see if she'd leave but she remained seated.

"Fyhnn," he said finally.

"Feen?"

He winced a little. "No. Fyhnn."

"No feen?"

"No. No feen," he confirmed. "Fyhnn."

She tested out his name a few more times, finally settling on a version with a short "ee" sound.

"Name?" he asked her.

"Phirae."

Chapter 2

"You can sleep on the bed." Phirae gestured to the narrow cot. "I'll sleep on the floor."

Fyhnn blinked. Did he understand her correctly? This was where *she* slept? He had imagined that she would have rich fabrics draped over her bed and a heap of luggage...maybe a few servants...

"It-" Fyhnn grasped for words. "...um... It yours?"

"What? The bed?"

He didn't know the word for cabin. He tried indicating the shape of the room.

"The cabin?" she asked.

He nodded.

"Well, yes. What did you expect?"

Fyhnn stared at her for a moment. "Money..." He tried gesturing "more" with his hands.

* * *

Over the next few days, Fyhnn spent his time following Phirae around. Of course, he kept looking for chances to make his escape but they were accompanied by two guards wherever they went. Well, that and the fact that he couldn't see land in any direction. There weren't even seagulls in the air.

She took him to the deck to absorb a bit of sun and feel the spray of the sea. They even helped out on deck once or twice.

The captain appeared now and then, casting disapproving glances at Phirae...sometimes sad glances. If Fyhnn had spoken more of the language, he would have tried to find out why.

He did slowly pick up more words. He actually managed to string together a few awkward sentences after the first week of his new "freedom".

* * *

"Where going?" he asked one evening as they were eating a meal of dried meat, hard biscuits and, what he presumed had to be, the last vegetables the captain had acquired in Kishnee.

As she often did, Phirae looked away, a look of sadness passing over her features. "Tajhnatai." After a pause, she added: "I live there."

"Why I going?"

She shifted uncomfortably. "I-" She cleared her throat. "To see a man."

"Why me?"

Her hand rose to the band of silver around her throat. "Magic."

"Magic?"

Her fingers wove a simple combination of motions and a small light appeared above her hand. "This is magic."

He had to stop himself from rolling his eyes at her. "Know word: magic." He gestured to himself. "Me magic. See man? Why?"

She looked lost for a moment and then nodded understanding. "You're a magician. That's why I must bring you."

His eyes narrowed. "You magician too. Why me?"

Phirae looked away. "It's complicated."

Fyhnn's skin tightened with a creeping sensation. He touched the collar around his neck. "You have collar. I have collar."

She didn't look up.

He tapped the one around his neck. "Stops magic." He reached out to her, stopping short of actually touching her collar. She still flinched. "You make magic light. So...what do?"

Her shoulders sagged even more. "It-" She shuddered. "It's a tracking device..."

"Find you?"

"Yes."

"Then what?"

She flinched again.

He moved a little closer and very lightly touched Phirae's shoulder. This time, she didn't pull away. More gently, he said: "Then what?"

"Cross will claim what I owe him."

"Cross?"

When she looked up, there were wet streaks over her cheeks. "My apprentice's father."

Fyhnn sat silently for a few moments. The tone of her voice had spoken volumes. "Blood debt," he said quietly.

She nodded.

He reached out and took her scarred hand. He studied the shiny, green skin. It was worst around her fingers and then licked up her arm in a spiral. "Apprentice dead. Yes?"

Phirae snatched back her hand. The look on her face bordered between bitterness and grief. "I tried to stop him. But the magic turned on us. And, because he cast the spell, it hit him first."

Fyhnn felt a pang of understanding and a little confusion. Though, it took many years to learn how to control spells once they were cast, the master could simply dissolve the magic into the air. Most humans did not live long enough to learn the basic skill of fine control. As an Alvari, he had had time. "How old?"

"He was twelve."

"Cross want life for life. Yes?"

Phirae nodded.

"He kill you?"

She looked up and seemed to consider Fyhnn for a moment. "It's not quite that simple. Do you know the concept of retromancy?"

Fyhnn blinked a few times and tilted his head a little.

"Bringing a departed soul back in a new body."

The words were like some dead thing slithering over his heart. It took him a moment to realise he had physically stumbled back from her in an attempt to put distance between him and the mere thought of what she was talking about. The Great Ones would strike down any that would tamper with the natural cycle of life and death. Not to mention the fact that the "new body" would still have the original soul in it at the time.

"Fyhnn? What's wrong?"

He couldn't get the words over his lips. How could she so blithely talk about it?

He flinched when she reached a hand out to him. She pulled it back hesitantly. He saw her studying him, considering his reaction.

"I see," she said quietly. "It's against your laws, isn't it?"

"Very bad thing. Never do. Never."

"Never is a long time, Fyhnn."

Fyhnn couldn't believe it. He'd just started feeling like he could maybe open up towards Phirae. And now this? He turned away, looking out the small porthole.

"Fyhnn." Her hand touched his back.

He shuddered.

"Fyhnn, I owe Cross a life. It is the law of my people. His son was an adept. That means I owe him the life of an adept."

"My life?"

She was silent for a moment and he felt her hand go slack and slip off his back. "I- I don't want to die."

He turned to face her. "Think I do?"

Though her head hung low, he could see her cheeks burning red.

"What if you no pay?"

"The collar will shut me down when my time runs out."

"Shut down?"

"I won't be able to move or cast spells or talk. It will basically allow me to eat, drink and breathe."

Fyhnn considered that a moment. "Why not use it..." He gestured to himself. "...me?"

"I didn't think of it. Wouldn't have been able to afford it anyway."

"Take it off?"

"I can't." She touched the silver band with her hand. "Not without it killing myself."

"How?"

"If you try to remove it, whether by force or by magic, it pushes spikes into your neck until you stop."

"Oh." He coughed delicately and pulled his head to the side to show the scabs on his neck. "My collar too. See."

She flushed again. "I'm sorry."

"How get off?"

"Without dying?"

He nodded.

"The person who put it on you must deactivate it."

A weight settled on his chest. She would have taken his off if she had been planning on it. That could only mean that she still planned to deliver him to Cross.

"How long before shut down?" he asked, his voice low.

"Two weeks."

* * *

Phirae looked miserable. She mostly sat on her little bed and stared out the porthole. She hadn't sent Fyhnn back down to the hold. He still slept on the narrow bed at night. Maybe it was petty of him but sleeping on the bed was the one thing that proved that Phirae didn't control him.

She didn't exactly make it easy for him to hate her, though. She had arranged for a change of clothes for him and she still stood up for him against the captain's continued disapproval of their new arrangement.

But, lately, she had stopped speaking to Fyhnn. The silence was eating at them both.

* * *

After three days of this, Fyhnn couldn't help but reach out to her. She was sitting by the porthole again, staring out. Her face was gaunt and her copper skin looked yellow.

"Phirae, talk with me?"

Her gaze weaved slowly to where he stood only a few feet away.

"You not say much lately," he said softly.

"Nothing I can say will make it better." Her voice was raspy, like she was really tired or maybe like she had cried recently.

"You try take off collar?"

"Why bother. I know what will happen."

"It work?"

She blinked slowly. "Sure it does. Look." She flinched in anticipation as she pulled the collar a bit to the side to show him the spikes starting to push out. Fine points of silver formed on the inside of the band and started pushing against the unmarred skin of her neck. A faint flash of blue danced between the little points and then flickered out in a pale green puff.

"My collar make blue?" He winced as the spikes bit into his neck. He hadn't even pulled it away all that far.

Phirae narrowed her eyes and shook her head a little. "What?"

"Blue light."

"Oh, you mean the wings. No, yours doesn't have a timer."

Fyhnn shook his head. He had seen the small blue wings that had been appearing on her collar, but that's not what he had meant. "No, spikes make-"

They both looked up as the door opened. The captain leaned in. "We're a week away from Jaht-Ni. I just did a few calculations based on last night's star positions."

"Thank you, Captain," Phirae responded.

The turbaned head nodded and disappeared again.

"Jaht-Ni is four days away from Tajhnatai," Phirae told Fyhnn when the captain was gone.

"Four days..." The air just above Fyhnn's arms felt charged with energy. Four days from Jaht-Ni until he might die. Four days from Jaht-Ni until he knew for certain what his life was worth. He had four days and a week to convince Phirae that there had to be a way around it all. A week and four days.

* * *

Fyhnn's skill with the Beyonders' trading language had improved quite a bit. He spoke mostly to Phirae but, he also picked up a bit of swearing and crude references from the sailors. The latter responding with raucous laughter when he tried out the words they happily taught him.

And the more he learned of the language, the more he ferreted out information from Phirae.

"So, how does a collar work exactly?"

"Well, it's of Yithnisian make. We actually just import them from there. All I really know is that you put it on your subject and set the magical signature. That seals the collar and also ensures that only you can take it off again."

Fyhnn waited.

She looked at him.

"Sooo, how do you take it off?"

"Oh." She hesitated a second. "To take it off, you just run the same signature over it again and it unclasps. It's really simple."

"And the mechanism that prevents you from removing it?"

"Well, that's really just a magical sensor that is set to detect when the inside of the collar moves away from the subject's skin."

"So, the sensor wouldn't trigger if you simply moved it around on the skin."

"Well, Fyhnn, the shape of the collar doesn't exactly allow for moving around all that much."

"Good point." He thought about it. "Is there a way to simulate the signature of the person who set it?"

Phirae sighed. "No. There have been many attempts to do that, but I have never heard of a successful attempt."

"What happens if you insert something flat between the collar and your skin. Wouldn't that confuse the collar's magic?"

"Have you tried that?"

"Well, no."

"Don't."

"But-"

"No."

Fyhnn considered Phirae for a moment. Obviously, he wasn't going to get further on that line of thought. "So, does the collar have a range? I mean, can you travel outside its area of effect?"

"The area of effect is centred on the subject. There is no way for the subject to move out of its range."

"What exactly happens when it shuts you down? I mean, you already told me that you wouldn't be able to do magic but you would be able to eat? Would you be able to move around?"

Phirae's copper skin went a little yellow. "As far as I understand it, it puts your mind into a semi-sleep state. Your body responds with instinctive actions to stimuli such as food or water. But you have no further conscious ability."

Fyhnn shuddered at the thought that the Beyonders had actually developed magic that would do such a thing. It really couldn't have much purpose beyond what had been done to Phirae. Immobilise a person so another can locate or maybe transport the subject without resistance. "Okay. So, simply avoiding Cross forever leaves you physically alive, but..." He shuddered again.

She looked at him. "You don't 'avoid' Cross."

"Huh?"

"He's not the kind of man that you can simply avoid."

"What, so, he's a bit more insistent?"

Phirae laughed darkly. "That's putting it lightly."

That brought Fyhnn up short. He hadn't considered Cross further than the basic blood debt. "How did you end up apprenticing his son if he's such a frightful sort?"

"You don't say no to Cross. He's..." Phirae paused, motioning forward with her hand. "Connected."

"Politically?"

"Among other things." The tone of Phirae's voice was not encouraging.

Fyhnn dropped the subject.

* * *

The squealing crash of splintering wood made Fyhnn jerk awake. He was on his feet before he had time to process exactly what the situation was. Voices were shouting and the ship was pitching to and fro. Was it a storm? Were they under attack?

"Phirae? Phirae, are you all right?"

He reached for her where she slept on the floor but his hands found only her empty blankets on the floor. Without any light, he couldn't see a thing. Was she out on deck or something?

Fyhnn stumbled out of the dark room, into the narrow corridor. He pitched unsteadily as he clambered up the steep companionway. What was going on?

"Bosun, get down below!" the first mate was bellowing as Fyhnn emerged onto the starlit deck. "Take those two with you! We need to stop that leak!"

"Aye, aye!" the bosun's voice cried from somewhere behind Fyhnn.

"You three by the foremast, get an oar or something and push us off that Pash-forsaken reef! And someone..." Fyhnn saw the first mate scanning the deck, his eyes finally settling on Fyhnn. "Fyhnn, go wake the captain!"

"Have you seen Phirae anywhere?"

"Fyhnn. The captain. Now!"

* * *

It took the rest of the night to stop the leak well enough for an emergency trip back to Jaht-Ni. They had passed Jaht-Ni just the day before.

By first light, Fyhnn knew that Phirae was nowhere on board. No one had seen her. He'd personally searched above deck and below, all the way to where the reeking and, now rather alarmingly voluminous, bilge water sloshed.

Fyhnn approached the captain as the sun cleared the horizon. "Captain."

"What?" the captain snapped, turning around.

Fyhnn rocked back on his feet at the hot glare. He cleared his throat. "Captain, I can't find Phirae. I've searched the entire ship."

The captain's brows drew together and he gave his head a tight little shake as if to clear his vision. "What do you mean you can't find Phirae?"

"She's not aboard the ship, sir. I think she went overboard. We need to look for her."

The captain spat out a series of curses. He looked out to sea and then back at his ship. "Damn that sorcelling bitch! Of all the rotten times to-"

"Captain, we need to find her."

The captain turned back abruptly, his broad frame casting a long shadow across Fyhnn. His face was pulled into a grimace of disgust. "No, little Yrthullian sorcerer. We *need* to get this ship fixed. That damned woman is probably at the bottom of the Saltwater about now. No point in looking for the dead."

Fyhnn's stomach turned uncomfortably. "But, Captain-"

"But nothing, Fyhnn. She's dead!" The captain turned away. "Make yourself handy or get down below!"

* * *

It took a day and night of sailing before the dusty red of Jaht-Ni appeared from out of the haze.

The captain had not spoken to Fyhnn, besides yelling orders, since the previous sunrise. So, when the captain put a hand on his shoulder that afternoon, he took a fright before he realised the man was looking at him with sympathy.

"Well, Fyhnn," the captains weather-roughened voice said. "Nothing against you personally but, without Phirae to pay for your passage, I don't really have any reason to keep you on board."

Fyhnn stared at the broad-shouldered man.

"We're approaching Jaht-Ni. It's a port city. You should be able to find work on one of the trading galleys if you want to head back to your homelands. By Pash, you can offer your services as an interpreter. I never heard a man from Yrthull speak the Trading Tongue so well. You could do well."

"But, sir... without Phirae-"

"She's lost, lad. There's no good in looking for the dead. 'Less you are one of them death magic sorts, eh?"

"But, Captain-" Fyhnn started objecting again.

"You'd better go pack your things."

"I don't have things."

"Good point." The captain bit off a laugh. "We'll be landing with the evening tide. See that you're topside when we dock."

Fyhnn just stood there. It felt like it was all happening to someone else. Like the captain's words were just flowing over and around him.

The copper-skinned man regarded him for a moment longer and then headed off to the forecastle.

All around him, the sailors were unfurling sails and tying off ropes on wooden pegs. They were shouting to each other and some were talking excitedly.

Eventually, his feet found their way back to the cabin he and Phirae had shared. It felt even more bare without her there. He felt more alone. But where else could he go?

He slowly sank to the floor where he had often sat talking to Phirae. The floor boards even felt harder now.

He had no idea how long he sat there, just staring around the cabin. Eventually, his eyes settled on the small wooden trunk Phirae had always kept by the foot of her pallet. It was kept shut by a simple but sturdy clasp. He hesitated for a moment but then realised that she wouldn't have a use for it anymore.

Chapter 3

That afternoon, Fyhnn was standing on the deck as the ship slowly floated right up to the pier. He had put the contents of Phirae's trunk into a piece of linen he had liberated from her sleeping pallet and it now hung over his shoulder.

"Good, I thought you'd take nothing," he heard the captain's voice just behind him.

"I left you half of what was in the chest on the bed."

"I saw, Fyhnn." The captain laughed quietly. "Half, you say."

"I have no idea what it's worth."

"I can tell."

"Thank you, Captain." Fyhnn said after a pause.

"For what, boy?"

"I'm not sure."

"Pash guide your steps."

Fyhnn nodded. "And may the Star shine on you."

* * *

The stink of the port was strong. Pitch, excrement and sour-sweet rot. If Fyhnn hadn't been so glad to see solid earth again, he would have swum out to sea to get away from the stench.

The moment the gangplank was in place, Fyhnn rushed across. The feeling of steady footing was divine even though his gait still rolled with the motion of the waves.

Jaht-Ni didn't feel anything like Kishnee. Besides the fact that all the people wore strange clothes and had weirdly pale copper skins, there was this smell in the air. Fyhnn couldn't quite put his finger on it but it made him uneasy.

His skin was sticky with grimy dust after only a few minutes off the ship. The way some of the strangers stared at him as he walked by made him walk faster. Maybe it was because they looked burly. Maybe it was because he was very aware of the collar around his neck. Maybe the memory of the last time he was on a dock was still very clear in his mind.

"That one's skin looks like the slaves they've been bringing in from that place, you know?" said a deep voice somewhere to Fyhnn's right.

"That place? What, that...um...what do they call it again? Eethu or something?" Fyhnn heard the reply.

It took all of Fyhnn's concentration not to turn around and look at them. He sincerely hoped they were talking about someone else. Either way, it would be better if they didn't know he understood them.

"Oh yeah! Eerthall. They've been going for good prices lately. Think we should nab him?"

"Might not be a bad plan. He's collared, though. Could bring down the price."

Oh, Great Star, they *were* talking about him.

The buildings to his left mostly shared walls. He'd seen only one passage past them, and that had been a few minutes back. Water sloshed against the docks and piers to his right.

Just then, a wagon came from around a corner ahead of Fyhnn. *Thank you, Great Lord Brannidyan!* As the wagon drew near, Fyhnn quickly swung around it, blocking him from his would-be captors' sight.

* * *

Crouching in a quiet alleyway, Fyhnn panted as silently as he could manage. It had been touch and go for a few seconds back on the docks. The wagon had veered away and he caught the two men spotting him just as he ducked into the opening the wagon had come through.

From there, he had just run all the way until he reached a crowd of people. There, he had lost them and sneaked off to find a bit of privacy.

The lid of Phirae's small wooden chest creaked open. He stared at the contents. Four more collars like the one around his neck lay inside, each still open and ready. His skin crawled.

Under the collars was a piece of deep red cloth loosely draped over the bottom of the box. He reached out to feel its texture and heard the telltale clink of coins underneath. His heart lifted. He might be able to barter passage back home. Back to Bish-Ghen. Back to the Uni-

He touched the cold surface of the metal collar around his neck. Of what use was it to go home if he remained collared for the rest of his life? He felt a stirring in his chest. A burning. Anger. She couldn't be dead. She still had to free him. Even if...

A wave of disgust washed over him. Even if he had to find someone to bring her back from the other side. Bring her back from the dead.

He'd probably need more money.

* * *

The markets had been easy to find. If not by the smell he associated with a dock-side market, he found it by the familiar sound of vendors calling out to passersby.

Wares of all kinds were displayed on tables and flatbed wagons. He couldn't put a name to half of it but that it was all for sale was quite clear.

He finally found a small table in the shade of a building that displayed what he had been looking for.

A tired-looking woman was standing behind it, staring passively at people passing by. The fabric of her clothes looked fairly rich, but worn. Deep blue and red velvet with an ochre shawl hanging from her elbows and an ochre and brown sash artfully tied around her waist with its frayed tassels arching up to the knot on her hip.

Fyhnn stepped up to her little table and put down his makeshift pack by his feet. The telltale shapes of the collars were easy to find. He drew out one.

"I was wondering if you could tell me where I can sell these."

The woman's darkly-outlined eyes widened, she reached out and then retracted her hand just before touching the collar. "How many do you have?"

Ah, good, Fyhnn thought. "Just one for now."

"But you'll get more soon?"

He almost laughed at her eagerness but he schooled his features carefully. "Possibly."

"What is its function?"

"It cuts the subject off from accessing magical abilities."

She hesitated. "It's a very specialised item. Very few have a use for a collar like this."

"But they pay a lot to get them." It was a gamble but he was going to try anyway.

The woman's face fell.

"Maybe you should direct me to someone who would 'have a use for a collar like this'."

She glanced at a spot behind him and then focused on him again.

176

"You're not from around here, it would take a while to find them."

He smiled benignly. "Oh, I have time." He started turning around.

"Wait! I'll give you three hundred Brado for that collar...and another two hundred for every other you can find."

He slowly turned back. By the desperation in her voice, he was fairly certain that she was offering him more than she would have earlier. Not that he really had any idea how much a Brado was worth. Hundreds sounded good, though. "Three hundred for the first and two hundred and fifty for every other. That's my final offer."

She nodded eagerly. "Deal."

* * *

On an impulse, Fyhnn decided to head in the direction that the trader woman had glanced when he had sold her the collars. The market area opened up into a large square packed with people. On a platform to the east side, a tall man in loose blue and red attire was exchanging money and papers with a man standing below. Behind him, two burly men wearing only loose pants and curly-toed shoes were restraining a young man chained to a ring affixed to the stage. Once the two men at the edge of the stage were done with their business, the young man's chains were unlocked from the ring and he was lowered to the square.

Fyhnn felt strangely violated. He'd never seen slavery in action before. Well, besides his time in the bilge hold. But he wasn't sure that that had really amounted to being a slave.

He was about to get as far away from the slave market as possible when the flash of red on the raised platform caught his eye. The next slave was being dragged onto the platform. The slave was struggling wildly against the two big handlers. It took almost three minutes for them to hold the slave down to fix the chains to the ring. In the struggles the slave's clothes had torn revealing green skin.

He hadn't been aware that he had been moving closer, not until he started pushing against the massing buyers to move forward. He suddenly broke through the throng and stood nearly close enough to the stage to touch it. Above him, Phirae was still doing her best to break loose. Another silver collar had been added to her neck. No wonder she hadn't used her magic, it was probably the same kind of collar Fyhnn had on.

The auctioneer turned to the crowd. "Bids are now open for this Aucrin spellweaver. She is of childbearing age; appears to be in good health; has been collared once before, though we were unable to establish the function of the collar; and speaks at least three languages. Can we start the bid on two-hundred Brado?"

The bidding began in earnest, Phirae's price climbing another two hundred Brado within the space of three heartbeats.

Fyhnn shoved his hand in the air as the bid passed six hundred. "Eight hundred Brado!"

Phirae's gaze snapped to him. Her eyes went wide and she went still.

There was a moment of stunned silence. The auctioneer gave him a scrutinising look and asked, "You good for that money?"

"Aye." Fyhnn patted the red cloth he had tied around the coins so they clacked together.

"Eight hundred Brado from the dark gentleman in the front. Can I have eight hundred and fifty?"

"Nine hundred!" Fyhnn called out with what he hoped sounded like bored confidence before anyone had the chance to respond.

"Nine hundred Brado from the dark gentleman. Anyone going to top that? Nine hundred going once, twice...Sold!"

Phirae let out a cry that was something between a whimper and a yell. Tears were streaming down her face.

The auctioneer kneeled at the edge of the platform and exchanged papers and money with Fyhnn. He carefully counted the full nine hundred Brado and then handed it to a servant who came to his side.

"What about the collar?" Fyhnn demanded.

"If you want that removed, go to the auxiliary's booth behind the platform. Just show her your papers."

The two handlers unlocked Phirae's chains and lowered her to the square. She fell into Fyhnn's arms, crying uncontrollably. He put an arm under her shoulders and led her away from the press of bodies and around the platform.

The skin of her wrists were bruised darkly and he could see that the cuffs were biting painfully into her. "Phirae?"

"Oh, Fyhnn! Fyhnn, how? Oh, merciful Mishni, I can't believe it. Thank you! Thank you! Thank you!"

"Come, we must get these things off you."

* * *

The booth was a tent just big enough to hold a desk and a few chairs. Inside sat an elderly woman with her grey hair pulled back into a tight bun. Her hunched shoulders pushed against the back of her chair as she shoved a piece of paper away from her. She only looked up at Fyhnn when he stopped right at the edge of her table.

He held out the papers the auctioneer had given him. "I would like to have her collar and chains removed, please."

The woman laughed. "I don't think you'd like that, son. We put those on the slaves for a reason."

Fyhnn cleared his throat. "Take them off."

She dragged the papers closer and got up with dramatic effort from behind the desk. "One magic restrainer," she read from the paper. She glanced up at Phirae's neck and clucked. "And an unknown restrainer. I'll do the collar last." She pointed at a spot in front of her and pulled a low stool from underneath her desk. Her hands started fiddling with a ring of keys that hung on her left hip.

Phirae glanced at Fyhnn and hesitantly made her way to the spot in front of the stool, the chains between her legs restricting her to a rattling shuffle. Her cheeks were still wet with tears.

As the shackles fell to the dusty floor with a dull clack, Fyhnn could almost feel Phirae's relief. A tremor ran through her body and she hugged her arms to her chest.

"Right," the old woman mumbled and clambered onto the stool.

Phirae shuddered as the old woman started fiddling in her neck. There was a soft crackling noise and Phirae's eyes went very wide.

"Oh, damn it!" The old woman muttered, and Phirae dropped limply to the ground.

* * *

"What's wrong?" Fyhnn demanded crouching down by Phirae's motionless form on the ground.

"This wasn't the one I meant to take off," the old lady said to herself holding Cross's collar. "How'd that happen?"

Fyhnn's heart lurched. "Phirae?" He touched her shoulder. "Phirae?" She wasn't moving at all. He couldn't even see whether she was breathing.

"Must have been defective. I hardly touched it." The old woman was now crouching next to him. "No help for it now. I'll need that magic restrainer back as well."

"What do you mean 'No help for it now'?" Fyhnn almost screamed. "You killed her!"

"Listen, young man," she said tiredly, "these things happen. I can refund half the money you paid for her. But that's that."

He stared at her in disbelief. How could she be so blasé about it?

She reached down to take off the magic restrainer. As it clicked open, she jerked back as if it had stung her. "Athus almighty!"

Phirae's chest arched sharply up and a moan pushed through her lips.

179

"Phirae? Phirae!" Fyhnn gathered her up. "The Great Lord be praised!"

Phirae coughed weakly. She pushed weakly against his chest. "What the-" She blinked and looked up at Fyhnn. "Where am I?"

"Did it hurt you?" was all he could think to say.

"Hurt?" Her scarred hand reached up to her neck and touched the open skin. Her eyes went wide and she put her other hand to her neck as well. "I don't feel anything... Is it off?"

Fyhnn didn't know whether to laugh or start crying.

"Fyhnn? I can't feel the collar. What happened? Where did it go?" She paused a moment. "Why aren't I dead?"

Fyhnn looked at the stunned auxiliary. She was sitting flat on her backside, looking pale and a little unsteady.

"What happened?" he demanded.

"I- I don't know. I was taking off the restrainer when that one-" She pointed to the Cross's collar which was now lying on the ground. "-stung me and some sort of smoke started coming out of it."

Phirae ran her hands over the skin of her neck a few times before she let them fell to her lap. "It's really off."

The three of them looked at each other.

After a while, the auxiliary asked, "Is this a problem?"

* * *

"We have to get away," Phirae said quietly once they were a few paces away.

Fyhnn looked at her. She stood stooped under his arm, her face was a palish yellow and her eyes were haunted. "What do you think we're doing now? Come, you really need to eat something."

She stopped, pulling him back as he took the next step towards the inn. "You don't understand. Cross is coming."

Fyhnn took her hands, pulling gently. "I'm sure there's time to eat."

"You don't know him." She pulled her hands back. A shiver shook her frame.

He looked at her. "What do you propose we do? Run for the hills? Ship out with the next tide?"

She looked over her shoulder and then down the road they were following. "I- I don't really know. My deadline is in a day or two...I think."

Fyhnn sighed. "Well, that gives us plenty time. Come, let's get some food."

She stopped resisting and allowed him to lead her to a nearby inn.

Once they were seated, Phirae reached over to Fyhnn's neck.

He started pulling back. "What are you doing?"

"I'm taking off your collar."

He sat completely still as she reached for it again. There was a soft click and then Phirae sat back with the open collar in her hands. Fyhnn's heart lurched as his senses reported the availability of magic for the first time in two months. He drew a shaky breath as the magic crawled up his arms.

Phirae looked him in the eyes and took his hands. "You gave me my life back. I will never be able to thank you enough."

Fyhnn stared at her mutely. Not too long ago, this would have been the moment that he hightailed it as far away from this woman as a he could. But he couldn't leave her now. He had the damndest urge to protect her at all costs.

"Where can we go that will be safe from Cross?" His voice sounded strangely triumphant to his own ears.

"What do you mean 'we'? You can go home now," Phirae said.

"Naw." Fyhnn shook his head and pulled his mouth high in an expression of refusal. "We've come too far to do something that mundane now."

* * *

The dock was slowly moving away as they stood by the rail of the passenger ship. Phirae had decided on a destination that would be a good point to start from and this was the only ship headed that way.

The moon was near full and cast a silvery light across the otherwise dark deck of the ship. Only a few hands were on deck, most being occupied with stowing away cargo and luggage.

A quiet calm was settling over him. They had made it.

Phirae, however, stood with her hands grasping the rail tightly. She'd been this tense ever since they had left the inn.

He was about to say something to put her at ease when a deep baritone voice laughed behind them. "Ah, so, you are running away, little Phirae."

Phirae spun around before Fyhnn had a chance to react.

"No blood payment, I see," the voice continued.

Fyhnn turned to see a big man wearing a rich red and gold waistcoat, a billowy cream shirt and loose brown pants with a subtle golden pattern. Dark, shoulder-length hair framed his broad face and obscured his eyes with shadow.

Four other men flanked him, their hands on glimmering weapons at their sides.

He felt a quiver in his stomach. A glance at Phirae confirmed it. The whites of her eyes were exposed and she was pressed tightly against the rail. A faint blue aura surrounded her. Some sort of spell, Fyhnn realised with a sinking feeling. This could only be Cross.

Cross looked from Phirae to Fyhnn and back. He huffed. "Oh, so you have even found someone to help you...well, well, well."

Phirae made a struggling noise and Fyhnn saw that she was trying to move. He looked around trying to think of something when his eyes settled on Phirae's green hand. Apprentices...spell control. He had it!

The small, hard shape of his magical focus slammed into his hand as he swung it forward. He gathered just enough magic to activate the effect and dissolved the spell on Phirae into the air just like a master would have done with an inexperienced apprentice's runaway spell.

Cross staggered back, his eyes widening. "What-"

Phirae sprang to action, weaving a spell of her own. She weaved her arms around her in a swooshing push and released the gathered power to fly towards Cross and his men.

Cross's eyes bulged and, with a magic-distorted wobble, he and his men flew across the waters back onto the wharf.

Phirae stumbled a bit and sat down unceremoniously. Her eyes were wide and her chest was heaving. "What just happened?"

"I was going to ask you," Fyhnn said. "I've never seen magic used like that before."

Phirae blinked. "I just meant to sweep them off the deck. I don't have the power to send them that far."

Fyhnn looked at her and then at the distant heap of bodies on the wharf. "You mean, you just cast that spell without factoring in the magic in the air?"

She shook her head. "I don't know what you mean. What magic in the air?"

Fyhnn laughed. "That's how I got rid of that spell that held you. I dispersed it into the air. It's a simple spell we use during training."

"In the air," Phirae said weakly.

"You must have sent your spell through the cloud and it was amplified."

"Amplified," she repeated dumbly after him.

Fyhnn looked back at the distant wharf that was steadily disappearing into the darkness. He could no longer see Cross and his brutes on the pier. "You don't suppose we scared them off for good, do you?"

Phirae laughed, then she shook her head. "Sadly, no. If anything, we've made Cross more determined."

"Damn," Fyhnn said.

Draca

♦ Andrea Vermaak ♦

He slowly opened his eyes. They had been shut for what many men would deem a lifetime. He breathed in deeply, allowing the cold, damp air to fill his lungs. It felt like the first gasp after being submerged in deep water for too long. It burned his throat more than the fire that lay dormant within it. A new scent hung on the air; it blended with the old familiar musty smell of saltwater and rotting kelp.

But it was not the scent that had stirred him from his long, deep slumber filled with dreams that now seemed like terrific memories of another lifetime; a dreamless, sleepless, restless life that tormented his mind while his body lay motionless, untouched between the stone pillars in his golden lair. No, something else had woken him. He then realised he was not alone.

His eyes adjusted to a new light; a tiny flame which shone in the corner of the enormous chamber. He heard metal slide against rusted metal, echoing faintly off the walls in the expanse of darkness, as if under water.

He took another deep breath and flexed the long-dormant muscles in his scaly neck and back. They ached with a lazy stiffness. The intruder stopped in his tracks. The unkempt man slowly turned to peer wide-eyed and foolishly brave into the dark, fiery face of the hoard-keeper. The man was perhaps a royal warrior once by the sight of the worn crest embroided on his woollen sea-green tunic. His body was sturdy and muscular, his jaw set and his eyes steady.

The dragon, as large as an old oak tree, was stunned at the sight of the intruder. He could not remember ever seeing such a creature in his lifetime, though he had met men many times before in centuries long gone. He held his breath for a moment, wondering what to do next.

Draca looked the man over and tensed at the sight of gold in the man's hand. He raised himself higher, gathering his strength. Draca saw fear in the man's eyes for the first time. The man dropped his torch and the precious jewelled cup he had so carefully nurtured in his rough hands and ran, faster than he had ever run, into the darkness of a tunnel.

Draca mustered all the decades of unused power which had gathered within him and released an almighty roar filled with flame and ash that entombed the entire space, and chased away the decades of pale darkness.

When his breath could pour out no more fury, the dimmed darkness wrapped itself around him once more like a thick ashen blanket. He could almost smell the offender's fear still lingering in the air.

His eyes, well adjusted to the eternal gold-lit night of his lair, eagerly searched the floor for his cup; his large reptile-like head swayed from side to side. His search grew more frantic as he realised that, like the thief, there was no evidence of his cup's existence, as if he had only dreamt of them being there. There were no cindered clothes, nor drops of melted gold upon the floor; no gemstones that glowed with heat in their bellies. The cunning fool had somehow escaped Draca's flame and fury with the cursed cup in hand.

How dare anyone enter my lair. How dare anyone look upon my hoard. How dare anyone look upon me without any fear, Draca thought with bitterness. *Do you even know what you have done?*

The gravity of the situation suddenly weighed on him. Before, he had only searched for his cup as a natural reaction. Now, with the realisation of what it meant for the cup to be gone, the more Draca scoured the chamber and found no cup there, the more the anxiety mounted in him like magma in a volcano about to erupt with all the anger of the earth. His whole lizard-like body shook uncontrollably.

I will find you, fool, and I will make you taste the curse that lies upon my cup!

He stretched his wings. They filled the expanse of his lair; leathery, old, but strong. Wings that had flown over rough, icy seas and lands; wastelands of tundra that creatures like the thief would consider hell. Wings that had felt the sharp piercing of arrows, which had torn in great storms long forgotten but remained unyielding to utter defeat.

He would seek out the thief, scour the lands for eternity if he must, to claim back his precious cup. He refused to be doomed. His search would become his new obsession, but no greater an obsession than that of protecting the rest of his hoard.

The heathen hoard of gold and meticulously cut gems, of battle-worn armour and rusted weapons was everything to him. Skilfully crafted by the hands of giants, a golden standard, the greatest of hand-wrought wonders, hung high over the hoard, casting an eerie light over carefully gilded vessels and plates, and beautifully wrought arm-rings which once brought great honour to many loyal warriors. These possessions consumed his every waking thought and had become his source of life.

Hundreds of years before, a wise king had hidden the ancient relics in this cave beside the Nordic sea to give them honour for their duties in blood-soaked wars. Many had died trying to plunder it.

Draca, naturally drawn to such hoards, sought shelter on a miserably cold and stormy night, when Thor had decided to wield his hammer and teach his people his law once more. The fire-breather could not overcome the temptation of such a rare find. He simply had to possess it. It soon became his curse. If he did not protect his hoard, every piece of it, he would surely die.

How then could he leave it now in search of the thief? His unguarded hoard would be a temptation to anyone who heard rumours of it, which were bound to spread far and wide like wild fire caused by a sudden lightning bolt of truth. Men would seek it day and night, unresting until they found his lair.

Draca folded his black, leathery wings back, and paced up and down his lair. He shook his head from side to side and lifted his eyes to the myriad stalactites that reached down like fingers from the ceiling. The thought of such dishonourable creatures raiding his lair would torture his mind while he was gone. It would cloud his thoughts, shroud his focus of reclaiming his cup and destroying the man who dared to even look upon it.

He stopped pacing, and sat down on his gold-covered floor and looked around. He had gold enough but the desire to find his cup would burn him if he stayed. It would brand his mind with as much pain and anguish as the thought of his unprotected lair, should he choose to leave.

He violently shook the thoughts from his mind with a shake of his head. All Draca could do was roar so that the walls and roof of his lair shook with his frustration. He stopped when pieces of mouldy rock fell around him.

"Why did I have to stumble upon you, you cursed gold?" Draca fumed at his hoard, which only answered with flickers of soft light.

He was suddenly overcome with exhaustion. He decided to sleep. Sleep would ease his pain. Perhaps his dreams would bring him clarity.

* * *

Wiglaf, son of Weohstan, the noble shield warrior, hid in the shadows of a small crevice in the cliff's face. He trembled as he waited as silently as he could for the dragon to emerge from its lair. He dared not sleep. He refused to be found.

He had abandoned his boat for the swiftness of his feet and had scrambled up the cliff face in a fit of fright. His fair hair lay flat and wet against his scalp. He rubbed his muscular arms and legs that tensed in the cold as he pulled himself up above the jagged rocks and rising sea below.

The dragon had taken him by surprise. He had expected to find an empty, cold cave. He reprimanded himself for being so foolish: *You should know better than to enter old caves without caution. Next time you will be better prepared to face anything and not run away like coward. You are not a coward.*

He waited for many uncertain hours, but the dragon did not emerge. He knew from legends that dragons preferred the shadow of the night. If the dragon had not emerged by dawn, it should be safe enough for him to leave and escape the dragon's wrath.

Wiglaf waited, but there was no sign of Draca.

I wonder why he has not come looking for me? Surely he has noticed that his cup is missing?

When the sun finally began to stretch its long fingers over the horizon, the young warrior, who had so gravely wronged the Bear

King of the Wederas, cautiously escaped his hiding place. He would travel south, from whence he came, and take refuge with kin in the villages until he reached the king's hall. There, he would present his prize, which he hid beneath his tunic, and ask the king's forgiveness.

* * *

Draca did not bargain on his dreams haunting him. They tossed and turned his mind into waking. He sat up and hung his head, forlorn, wishing he had never woken; that the thief had never disturbed him. Perhaps if he had not known that his cup was missing, it would not have worried him, he thought.

The sun had made its way across the sky and the dragon's mind remained clenched in anguish. He admonished himself for his procrastination; for remaining undecided. Between waking indecision and troubled sleep lies a destructive spirit determined to torture and destroy you. Draca fought this inner angst with all the strength that remained within his ancient being but failed. He collapsed to the ground, closed his eyes and tried to think of nothing.

Either way, he would succumb to the temptation of the hoard. If it meant that he would leave the majority of it behind in search of one piece to complete it, to save him from inevitable destruction, then so be it.

No one, until now, had disturbed him for three hundred years. He had only known the quiet seas and surrounding forest to feed his needs when he awoke for brief periods between years of dreaming that now blurred with his reality.

If he left, he would travel more swiftly, despite his age, than any creature on land and sea, including the thief. If rumour would indeed spread like wild fire, then his would be the fire to spread it.

Age, wisdom and strength would carry him in search of his golden cup. He would bring it back, secure in the knowledge of his life, and he would sleep away the memory of these events, as he had done so many times before. His hoard would be complete and safe under his protective wings and fire once more.

Draca opened his eyes. He knew what he had to do. His attention drew back to the thief. He wondered once more where the thief had gone; how he had escaped his flames. He could not have gone too far, though the past hours of torn horror had felt like days to the fire-breather. He imagined that the thief must be miles away by now.

Draca cast his wet, shining eyes upon the floor where the thief once stood. Draca could still see the man's face in his mind's eye; how the thief's defiance had melted into wide-eyed terror; and how his whole body had trembled.

A few wet foot prints, and disturbed gold and jewels gave evidence of the thief's trail. Draca scrutinised the place. It would seem that the man had fallen to the ground, cowering beneath a rusted shield to escape the dragon's fiery breath.

He's quick, thought Draca.

He followed the trail, sniffing the ground as he went. The thief had crawled away before lifting himself to his feet and sprinting towards the entrance of the lair.

As Draca followed the trail, he could feel the air grow colder. He cowered back, not for comfort's sake but out of fear. He could not remember the last time he had been outside his lair and did not know what awaited him. He looked back over his broad shoulders. His hoard and his haven tugged at his mind, willing him to stay. Yet, he knew he could not. More determined than ever, he took one step at a time towards the mouth of his lair until the icy winter air bit into his face and wings and flesh.

Shallow waves lapped large, jagged boulders which lay scattered across the cave mouth's watery path. Slimy green and brown kelp lay draped and dying like knotted locks of coarse hair over the boulders. If Draca had not been preoccupied with finding his cup, he would have found the night clear and still. He could almost hear his own heart beating.

Draca's eyes were drawn towards a small boat. Rope tied to a jagged outcrop of rock allowed the boat to rock gently, steadily in place upon the low tide. Draca took a step back. Curious, he slowly made his way towards the boat and, once near, peered warily inside. He found nothing but a pair of crudely carved wooden oars. He sniffed the boat. He lifted the oars carefully one-by-one with his teeth and tossed them into the water. When he found that neither his cup nor the thief were inside the boat, he shook his head and roared. With one angry breath, the wet boat glowed, then, grew in flames. The thief would not escape by water tonight.

Draca looked up at the stars as if to find the answers to his questions among them. All he found were what seemed like a million gems strewn across the dark sky. He turned to face the cliff, his eyes darting back-and-forth in search of his golden cup. The thief surely could not have gone too far; the cliff was steep and treacherous. His eyes, though old, were still keen enough to catch a glimpse of gold if it were there, despite the dark night.

When he was sure he had scoured the cliff up-and-down and back-and-forth as many times as his sanity would allow, and found nothing, Draca spread his wings to their full, terrifying expanse.

Determined, every muscle in his legs tensed in preparation. Like a tightly wound spring, Draca lifted off the ground. Pent up energy and fury surged through his veins, casting him into the night sky. His enormous shadow darkened the already blackened cliff face as he flew up and over in search of the thief and his cup.

He hovered above the cliff's edge for a moment, tensing his muscles, torn once again between leaving and staying. *You have made the decision to leave. It is the only choice you have. It is the right decision*, Draca tried to convince himself. *The creature is too afraid to return now. If he returns with others, you will be back by that time. Now, go.*

He took a deep breath and scanned the horizon. No, no one would disturb his hoard again tonight. He tried with all his might to ignore the sinking feeling in his belly and set off south, along the rugged shoreline. It was too cold further north for any creature to reside there of their own will, and Draca knew it. With every beat of his wings, the sinking feeling grew stronger, as if there were rocks in his stomach. He frowned and shook his head to be rid of his worries, and pushed on.

I've made my decision and it is a good one. This really is the only way.

He would begin with the lands he had known well before his long slumber and fly beyond them if he must. The idea of what he might find almost excited him; that he would discover newly carved scenes and unknown edges of wilderness, but he quickly reined in his thoughts and focused on his cup. He knew that he would fly further than he had flown in decades.

The thought of it in the thief's hand brought tears to his eyes.

He shook his head but he could not be rid of them. The more he saw the thief's face in his mind's eye, the more his vision blurred as he began to weep. He dropped in the air and bumped into a headland's face before he raised himself up in the air to lower himself gently onto the headland. He was not physically injured but he wept out of pity and shame.

Suddenly angered, Draca raised his head and roared at the sky.

"Don't worry, I'm on my way," he growled at the night.

With more determination than ever, he lifted himself from the ground and flew faster than ever along the coast, his eyes forever watchful. He flew over frozen hills and streams that had once flowed into the sea, and over white-frosted trees and mountains. It felt good to stretch his wings again and feel the sea air beneath them, lifting him higher and pushing him onwards. It had been a long time since Draca felt so in control.

Yet, every hour he did not find his precious cup, did not rescue it from the thief, Draca cast his mind back to his hoard. He wondered if it was safe from the prying eyes and longing fingers of the other thieves who would hear of it. He wondered if it was worth risking his hoard's safety without his protection for a mere cup. Yet, the thought of the consequences should he not find his beloved cup encouraged him to find it and take his revenge. He shook his head each time, trying not to imagine what would happen to him if he could not recover his cup, and pushed onwards.

* * *

The morning sun had just begun to rise when Wiglaf was prepared to be on his way. He could smell the wisps of smoke that curled into the crisp morning air. He could hear the distant clang of metal on metal as people prepared food and steaming water for their baths. All else was silent. It was as if the robins had warned the deer and the foxes to hide from a great silhouette in the night sky. He knew he could not stay but he was wary.

A villager's wife, who had prepared food for him, greeted Wiglaf on his way out. "Good journey to you, sir. It's a good thing my husband found you on his way home last night. You would've frozen to death out there and none of us would've known about that cave. Once you've presented the cup to the king, let him know that, if he needs a bigger raiding party, we're happy to help him."

"Thank you, I will. Thank you also for your hospitality."

Just then, Draca, who had approached the sleeping village and listened carefully for signs of the thief, rose from the trees. He roared so deeply and so loudly that the village was suddenly hushed. Wiglaf caught his breath and stared at the dragon. The woman beside him fell backwards into her home.

Seconds later, Wiglaf heard blades being unsheathed and doors fly open as men and shieldmaidens ran out to face the beast. Wiglaf gave the situation no second thought. He unsheathed his borrowed blade, raised his borrowed shield and joined the army of villagers. They gathered on the edge of the village to face their enemy.

A huge man raised his voice to the sky. "We thought you might come," he said. "But you will not defeat us!"

The people shouted their war cries into the air, raising their blades into the sky. The morning sun made their blades glow red like embers in a hearth. Although he only had a short, single-edged blade to defend him, Wiglaf felt invincible.

"Return my cup and I will not destroy you," snarled Draca, insulted.

"Never!" Wiglaf stepped out from the crowd. He saw rage swell in Draca's chest but did not allow his courage to fail him.

"What did you say?" raged Draca.

"I, Wiglaf, son of Weohstan and defender of the Bear King, said, 'never'." Wiglaf raised the cup to taunt the dragon. "This cup and all the rest of the hoard belong to our forefathers and it is our king's right to have it."

"It is mine!" roared Draca, entirely enraged. Mercilessly, he poured out his flames upon the nearest structure.

Mothers and children gave great cries and ran to hide among the trees, weeping silently into their winter-numbed hands. Armed men and women charged at Draca, shouting their war cries, but Wiglaf stood firm, his eyes fixed on the dragon, whose gaze would not leave him.

Draca darted towards him. Wiglaf ducked away from Draca's talons, raising his wooden shield above him. Suddenly, his shield was ablaze. He threw the shield aside and raised his dagger, arrogantly, staring into Draca's face; both were as defiant as the other.

Other men tried to distract the dragon, swinging their blades in the hope of piercing or slicing the beast's flesh but anyone who dared to venture too close met their unjust, fiery ends.

Wiglaf, more determined to defeat his enemy than ever, did not succumb to fear. He swung his blade with all his strength and will-power to protect the cup, once again hidden beneath his tunic. He hoped that its presentation to the king would bring him forgiveness and the comfort of the mead hall once more. He knew, however, that his fate was neither to die nor to defeat Draca that morning, much to his dismay. Neither flame nor blade would claim victory that day.

Wiglaf waited until Draca's eyes were elsewhere, the beast's talons warding off several men who rushed him at once. He ran as quickly and as silently as he could in the direction from which the dragon had come. He did not dare to stop or even look back but kept on running.

Soon, Wiglaf heard the distraught cries of the villagers as Draca set every remaining thatch roof alight in his search for Wiglaf. But Wiglaf did not stop. He refused to be defeated.

* * *

When Wiglaf did not emerge from the flames, Draca grew panicked. His breath became shallow and his heart raced faster than it had before.

"My cup," he said, almost timidly, "Where is my cup?"

The remaining pieces of his heart broke and he roared in such anguish that the still-standing walls of the burning houses shook with his fury and collapsed in flames and ash.

He did not hear the broken victory cries of the people as he flew away, shaking his head and weeping at his failure and loss. He would seek out and search every village, every home, every hall, to find his stolen cup, even if it took him a lifetime. He would leave no land unscorched by his scorn for Wiglaf.

Frustrated, Draca did not know where to turn next. He flew in a daze high above the tree tops, staring blankly into the distance, a great pit in his stomach. He sought the dark shelter beneath the forest trees a few miles south of the village. He felt cheated. He did not know, did not understand what he had done to deserve being disturbed. He had kept to himself, had not harmed any creature bar those he had hunted to sustain him.

He broke through the dense canopy of trees and came to rest on the dry ground beneath them. Draca did not know where to start looking again for the man that had caused him such grievous harm. He wondered how Wiglaf had come to find his lair, why he had ventured to enter a dark, unknown cave. Perhaps he did not value his life. Perhaps he had no riches of his own to watch over, to protect. Draca almost took pity on Wiglaf, but checked himself, reminding himself of his stolen cup.

He is a fool and a coward.

He was exhausted in every sense. He curled up beneath the trees and closed his eyes. He longed for the comfort, the familiarity of his cold, golden lair. He would just rest a while and then perhaps fly back to check that all was still untouched. If he could not control where his cup was, he could at least maintain power over the rest of his hoard.

His body tensed. No, he would begin his search anew in the morning. He hoped that sleep would bring him some clarity in the new day; that he would be focused and filled with new energy and motivation to continue his quest.

Silence surrounded him, silence so deafening that his thoughts began to shout at him, urging him to wake, to rise and seek his cup. His mind would not quieten, would not leave him be. His thoughts tore at each other, fighting each other and urging him to take action.

You're wasting time. Wiglaf got away again. Go. Look for him. What are you waiting for? Go now. Go.

Draca shook his head and roared. The voices in his head hushed. He hung his head, exhausted, though he knew that his thoughts would continue to haunt him if he did not obey them. He reluctantly got to his feet, his legs still stiff and unsteady after many dormant years. He lifted himself above the trees. The sun was just past its midpoint in the sky.

He glided over the tall forest trees, silently, swiftly as a cloud in a strong breeze. Nothing stirred beneath or above him. No birds could be seen among the trees. No deer, no fox nor rabbit stirred in the undergrowth. All had fled or were in hiding. He looked east towards the sea. The water was still, almost frozen.

After a while, Draca's muscles tensed. He shut his eyes tightly against the pain and started to veer to his left, dropping rapidly from the sky. He caught himself up again just before he hit the canopy of the forest along the coast.

He decided to settle beside a large boulder on a headland. It reminded him of his lair beside the sea. Its face was cold and wet against his back. It brought him a bit of comfort and he slid more easily into sleep. He slept fitfully, dreaming of Wiglaf and his cup.

His dreams began to piece together; a kind of path was forged in his mind. He saw the warm glow of a fire in the belly of a tall structure made of wood. It was at once like those he had seen in the village, yet not. It was grander, larger and finer; lavishly embellished with gold and gems. He had envisioned the hall full of men and women, including Wiglaf, all sitting, singing and eating together, while he looked on from the frozen world outside.

When the sun had, as many times before, mysteriously moved over the western horizon, Draca awoke. At first, he was confused, almost panicked. He soon enough realised that the nightmare of the past night and day were indeed no dream at all. He remembered too clearly Wiglaf standing in his lair, the golden cup in his hand.

He stood and flexed his legs, his wings. He shook the sleep from his body and his mind. He felt better, more focused, more determined, yet he could not help but wonder if his hoard had been found. *There is nothing you can do now. You have already come this far.*

He knew what he had to do and he would not be distracted again by his torn thoughts. His path was clear; a single pathway towards the recovery of his stolen cup. He would not go back to his lair until his quest was complete and he would not delay it any further.

He followed the line of trees along the coast until he reached a stream where the fresh water fell frozen from a height into the sea. He flew low along the jagged coastline where nature was still left untouched, raw to the elements. The silence of the dark hour filled his mind with thoughts of scouring the face of the earth forever, never finding his lost cup. He found it difficult to make peace with his loss and feared his impending doom should he not be able to recover the cup. He could not, he would not, rest until he found it. He would hunt down Wiglaf and destroy him in search of his precious cup. He lifted his head, certain of his victory.

He began to relax. His still stiff muscles began to ease as the monotony of gliding and soaring with the currents of the wind and the ocean let Draca's thoughts begin to slip into an abyss of silent memories. It was a long time since he had felt so free. It was as if he was seeing the world as a rippled reflection of what he once knew but had somehow forgotten.

He forgot for a moment about his quest, about Wiglaf and about his cup. He glided along the border of land and sea, and felt at peace. His soul felt renewed like a sleepy flower emerging from the thawing springtime earth. He spread his wings further out and rose from the ashes of his cursed hoard.

He did not know what lay before him but, in that brief moment of absolute abandon, he did not care. He searched deep within and remembered this feeling of undetermined, unlimited freedom and sudden joy from a time before he had discovered the cave. It was a time when the world was still being carved from solid, sheer rocks and ice; a time when he still fed on the tender roots of the earth.

It was a world in which anything was possible, when everything was fresh and new, and waiting to be explored and discovered; when new ideas beckoned curious minds.

He felt deeply nostalgic to the point of weeping, but reined in his emotions and wondered how much he had missed, how much he had overlooked, how much had changed. History is a never-ending chain of existence, thought and action that evolves and adapts, yet remains unchanging at its core. Draca took comfort in this but longed for days that would never be again.

Then, his bright world shattered like the waves that crashed on the rocks beneath him. His thoughts were drawn back to the present, to his lair and his hoard. *How much more would I miss if I do not find my cup, recover it and protect it from tempted hands and eyes?*

He gathered his strength and flew faster than ever, ignoring the pain of his tensing muscles, having felt alive in his remembrance and wishing to remain so. He focused all his renewed energy into seeking the hall he had seen in his restless dreams.

I will find you and destroy you. Every one of you. No one will ever enter my lair again, as long as I am alive.

* * *

Sooner than he had hoped, than he had imagined, Draca saw a grand sight; the vision from his dreams. Great raiders and warriors resided here on the edge of the sea. The Bear King was the most fearless of all warriors. He often led his men and shieldmaidens into irrefutable victories. They were seasoned fighters, ready for anything that faced them.

Draca slowed his course, uncertain, almost afraid of what he may face. He had not thought about what he would do when he had discovered the hall.

He flew between trees and came to an enormous boulder whose face had been carved for centuries by wind and salt and rain. He hid behind it, peering around it and over it to scout his surroundings. It would be an hour before Draca was brave enough to creep any closer.

As he watched under the dark sky, he saw a warm glow from within. Embers glowed in the hearth and tiny flecks of sparks grew into flames which licked the frozen air into submission. The golden eaves of the Bear King's hall sparkled in the fire light. All within ate and drank and sang within its warm glow.

They told embellished stories of a winged beast they had never seen before; a beast who had much wealth in its possession, a beast which breathed fire, a beast with breath more venomous than one-thousand snake bites. They sang songs of its defeat which was yet to come. Elders imparted their wisdom to the younger warriors, advising them on how to defend themselves against such a beast, although they had never encountered any themselves.

Draca watched, curious at such a wondrous sight, yet deeply offended by their arrogance and their ignorance. He snorted in disgust. *How dare they claim to know me better than I know myself.*

Suddenly, a giant, bear-like man dressed in wolves' skins, stood and placed his hand on a young man's shoulder. The Bear King raised his cup; Draca's cup. The hall fell silent as the giant man praised Wiglaf for his courage, and spoke inspiration and courage into his people's hearts. The men and their wives and children cheered, and the king lifted the cup to his lips and drank deeply.

Draca took a deep breath to steady his thoughts and shook his head violently.

How dare anyone taint such a precious object, he thought. *How dare anyone drink from this cup, albeit unknowingly.*

Draca was enraged. He unwittingly, uncontrollably, engulfed the nearest tree in flames and heat and light.

* * *

The sudden light of trees ablaze left Wiglaf and his companions silently stunned.

"It's the beast. He has found us," said Wiglaf as he rose to his feet, wide-eyed yet ready for battle.

The king's warriors sprang quickly to their feet, grabbing their blades and wooden shields that they knew would not protect them against the fire-breather. They had anticipated his arrival. Iron would fight fire tonight.

Wiglaf stepped outside, alongside his master and king. A dozen other warriors joined them, shields and blades ready. The beast roared and spewed his flame upon the hall. Women and children poured out every window and door to escape the blaze. They ran as fast as they could for the shelter of their surrounding homes. They would watch from afar.

Wiglaf frowned as he watched the beast turn his attention to the hall. The dragon appeared to be searching for his cup, as he frantically peered in at every window. Suddenly, the thatched roof collapsed, sending sparks and ash and smoke in every direction. Wiglaf covered his face.

"We must attack now," Wiglaf heard the king say.

Wiglaf followed the Bear King, who ran with his sword raised to pierce the beast's hind leg. Wiglaf tried to steady his legs as the king raised his bloodied sword and shouted at the dragon, "Fight, you coward!"

But Draca seemed to ignore the king and turned away to carry on his search. Wiglaf watched helplessly as Draca broke through a window, shattering the timber. Splinters flew in every direction, engulfed by the flames. The beast did not seem to feel the heat of the fire that surrounded him. Wiglaf ran forward as Draca reached out for his cup, lifted it gently and cradled it in his claw.

Suddenly, as if it could hold no more heat within it, the cup melted.

"No. No! It cannot be! No!" the dragon panicked. "No, it cannot end like this!"

"Beast, it is over." Wiglaf's voice was firm and steady, ready for battle. He would not run this time.

Draca roared in anguish and burst out of the hall. Wiglaf and his companions cried angrily into the dark sky. They cried "coward" and "beast" as Draca flew away, melted gold in hand.

* * *

Draca's strength faltered several times as he flew, heart aching, to his lair, weeping for his fruitless venture; for leaving his hoard for nothing but sorrow and pain.

His lair, filled with warrior's battle-beaten boards and blades, with crested helmets and battered byrnies, and elegantly engraved hilts and encrusted quillion, was his haven. No one could touch him there. Here, he and his hoard had been safe for centuries. One invader, one lamentable occasion, did not mean that more centuries would not pass unscathed by the mischief of men.

When he reached his lair, he tried to convince himself to sleep. He was exhausted. Yet his thoughts would not leave him alone. Though overtly deceived by the security of his lair and his war skills, inwardly he could not shake the sight of the men's fierce blades, and of their greedy hands and minds.

He wept too, between rage and silence, for the loss of his cup. He threw the now solid lump of gold angrily to the ground. He was angry with himself for not leaving it be. He was regretful of leaving his lair. He had destroyed the land in flame for nothing. He vowed never to let anyone near his lair again, for as long as he lived, albeit for not long now, for surely he was doomed now that his cup was lost for good.

Draca, once again, slept fitfully, wrestling with his thoughts. He dreamt of men raiding his lair, tearing into his hoard and drinking it in with their arms. Eventually, the agony of sleep became too much for him to bear. The fear of his hoard being taken away was too crippling. He stepped outside and looked up at the stars.

Somehow, their light comforted him but he was too wise to remain unwary of any potential danger that could linger in the darkness.

Still restless, he flew to the top of the headland. The sky's belly rumbled in the distance. Something was not as it should be. Draca became even more anxious, worried. He wished he knew why he felt so distressed. His cup was lost but his hoard was safe.

I don't need to worry any more. I'm strong and I'm skilled in the crafts of war.

He stood, looking out to sea; waiting, watching, listening. The winds had changed. They brought him news of flashing light, white blades against the dark sea; of shouts and cries of coming terror. They whispered a name he had not yet heard until now. It was not a name he had heard in his ancient tongue, yet somehow familiar, almost decipherable if the winds would not whisper.

Fear beat inside his chest like a war drum. *It must be the Bear King that comes in lust of my hoard. He surely seeks my life too. I will die defending you, my precious hoard. Not all will be lost in vain.*

He foresaw death and darkness, the end of his kind, and wept.

When he looked up, he saw, as if in a dream, a serpent-like creature rising out of the dark water, its silhouette sharply defined against the sky. Two dozen legs protruded from its belly, stroking the water simultaneously to push its body forward.

The serpent, with its crest-like head, turned toward the shore. Draca, having never seen the like of such a creature, stretched out his enormous wings and took flight. The winds beneath him whispered a warning. Yet fire would fight water tonight.

Draca flew toward his new foe, curious but cautious. He heard the anxious cries of many voices.

What beast do you steer, Bear King? What is this creature of the night that makes such a tumult?

Suddenly, what seemed to be giant barbed splinters flew toward him. He stopped in fright, though none seemed to scathe him. The serpent roared again with the cries of many men and Draca set the beast's crest ablaze. Fire conquered water.

Like tiny threatened spiders who take harbour on their mother's back, determined men and women leapt from the burning serpent into the shallow tides. Their muscular limbs beat back the waves as they waded towards the rocky shore. Among them were Wiglaf and the Bear King. They bravely fought the cold waves, conquering them to carry them to the foot of Draca's lair. Not once did either man take their eyes off Draca.

The biting winds fought against Draca's wings, pushing him toward his lair, his hoard. They whispered more loudly than ever the name of his new fiend.

More and more clearly could Draca see his death in the men's eyes. More and more clearly could he see his hoard fading, dwindling and scattering like dry sea sand on a breeze.

Panicked, Draca darted swiftly into his lair, faster than Thor's hammer's sparks that now lit up the distant sky. With blades held high, the king and his men followed Draca into the gaping jaws of his dark lair, fearless and willing to face the dragon's wrath. Man would fight beast tonight.

Draca knew that they were determined to slay him, their enemy, and claim every last item of his hoard as their own. Their desire to destroy him and possess his gold burned no less in them than his own desire to preserve his life and protect his hoard.

Draca stopped to lie low in the shadows, not far inside his lair. The angry clamber of men approached quickly but sounded no more to him than an army of rabid mice, running to attack his ankles with steely teeth. Still, he feared them but not for his own sake. He feared them for the sake of his hoard. One precious cup was already one too many pieces lost.

At the mere thought of Wiglaf, all the hurt and anger inside him welled up and he poured his fiery revenge out on the approaching men. They lifted their shields but soon had to throw them aside. Yet they advanced. These were no ordinary men. They were men who had seen battles so cruel that their stories and songs hardly seemed true.

When greed and revenge ran through their veins, nothing could stop them from inflicting pain of any kind. Though few weapons could harm Draca, he feared that his mind would completely unravel.

Soon, my curse will be theirs. They too will surely come face-to-face with equally greedy men and, suffering, meet their ends.

Draca watched the Bear King turn to salute his loyal warriors and friends. Draca strained to hear what the king said to the warriors but, somehow, he knew that the end was close for both of them.

Draca's fear intensified. His breath quickened. The fire in his throat seemed to burn a hole in his heart. He found it unfair to have to face such undeserving creatures in battle. Unlike the king, Draca saw his dreadful fate and the fate of his hoard.

Suddenly roaring and rushing, the king and Wiglaf turned and ran; their angry iron blades held before them in pursuit of flesh. Draca instinctively retaliated with flame. The sky split open with spiny splinters of bright light. Earth and sea roared. They swung their blades against the terror of flame.

Eager to seek revenge for such an insult, the king lifted his sword, an ancient, trusted heirloom that had survived many great battles. He indicated for Wiglaf to wait while he advanced on the cowering fire-breather, the protector of the earth's hoard.

The king stopped and waited. Draca, curious by the silence, cautiously stepped forward to investigate. Draca tempted fate and met it. Man would conquer beast that night.

The king, at the sight of the dragon, lifted his hand to plunge the metal into the beast's flesh. Draca roared in anguish and shame, humiliated by his naïvety. The king withdrew his ancestral weapon; the edges now less sharp, the blade now weakened, against the dragon's bones.

Angered now by the bite of the blade, Draca rained war-fire, bright battle-flames, over the king. Beast would conquer man that night.

Draca saw Wiglaf hurry through smoke and ash to his king's side to suffer the heat-blows with him. Enraged by the beast's impertinence toward his king, Wiglaf seized his yellow linden wood shield. With his other hand, he withdrew his ancient, legendary sword. It was a noble weapon that Draca found unfit for a cowardly heart such as Wiglaf's.

Draca, insulted by the sight of Wiglaf, hissed a warning. Neither Wiglaf nor the king flailed in fear but stood firm for their people. Draca began to fear their insolent nature.

Such men should flee at the sight of me. Why do they not fear me? Why do I fear them? If my hoard is to remain mine, I will need to fight despite my fears.

Panicked, Draca rushed forward to attack once more, flooding his enemies with gleaming waves of flame. As Draca lunged forward, Wiglaf tossed his burnt shield aside. It splintered beneath the licking flames. He courageously advanced though unprotected.

Draca, confused by the strength and resistance of the men, slunk back into the darkness of his lair, cowering against cold, wet rock.

No, I'm not afraid of pain or death. I fear for my hoard alone. I do not fear these men.

There was nowhere else to go but deeper into his lair where his hoard lay. He would not risk it. He would stand firm, so that neither warrior could even glimpse it.

The Bear King kept in step with Wiglaf. Closer and closer they came. Neither, like Draca, feared pain nor death. They would die killing the beast.

Draca roared in anguish at their continued advance. He spat at them in hatred. He would see them gone from his cave. The king, filled with renewed strength, ran at the cornered dragon. Draca felt the sting of the blade as the king drove it with mighty force into his head below his jaw. The ancient weapon shattered. The blade had seen too many battles, dealt too much violence at the hand of its wielder.

In utter animosity, Draca rushed at the king. He clamped his sharp, jagged jaw down on the king's arm. At his king's need, Wiglaf did not heed Draca's head. Courage came as naturally to him now as breathing. Though his hand was wounded with screaming burns, he struck Draca's belly. He drove the blade into his soft, vulnerable flesh. Draca roared in distress, in agony. He loosened his grip around the king and he tried to burn his injurer with his flames, but his lungs had weakened with the blow of the blade.

The king, wounded but always ready for battle, withdrew his battle-axe from his belt. His lesions had already begun to swell and blister. Draca's teeth had dealt the king deadly poison that now ran through his veins. It would be the Bear King's final battle.

To Wiglaf beside him, he would grant new leadership. The hoard would be left untouched in the lair for his fame. No man would dishonour the hoard unless he wished to be cursed. It would comfort Draca in his death to know this.

The king lunged forward for the final time. Draca stood firm, bold, though he knew no fire would come. He hung his head in sorrow.

I did my best to protect you but now I must face the fate of your curse.

Draca heard the king cry war and terror as he tore through Draca's belly.

With this final blow, Draca's heart broke. His enormous being collapsed. He lay still, eyes closed, breathing shallowly. He found himself among red rivers and flames. This was no longer his cursed paradise, though he was anxious not to leave. He still clung desperately to his world, to the thought of his precious hoard.

I don't want to leave you. No man must touch you.

Yet, for a moment, before he breathed his last, he felt the golden warmth of freedom, that had left him so long ago, return. Less and less did he care for his hoard or his lair. He was no longer anxious about kings and thieves. His curse had been lifted. He felt unburdened, as if he had worn a heavy cloak of thick darkness for three hundred years.

He heard the triumphant cries of men, as if from another world. They did not yet understand the nature of his hoard.

Draca opened his eyes slowly to nod a final, respectful farewell to his lonely, shining world. He had a new understanding that no man could ever take from him.

He closed his eyes and slept forever in his freedom.

Guardian Angel

♦ Richard T Wheeler ♦

Edge stared at the patterns that the flaking paint made on the ceiling, his scabbarded katana clutched to his chest. The bedside alarm buzzed for a brief moment before he gently turned it off. He slipped the earpiece of a comms unit into his ear before rolling upright. It was quiet in the house. He stared straight ahead for a moment, barely breathing. From the nightstand, he gathered the leather sword belt and strapped it to his waist. The wireless unit for the comms went into its pocket on the belt. He ran his fingers over the polished leather of the sword's scabbard and closed his eyes. His hands started shaking, his breath coming quicker. He squeezed his eyes shut and put his face in his hands, the tremor of his shoulders his only movement. Finally, he exhaled through his fingers, his breathing returning to normal. Only then did he rise.

Softly, stalking on the balls of his feet, he moved to the entrance of the basement of the house. Careful to avoid any noise, he opened the well-oiled hinges of the house's indoor storm shelter. Again, he listened for a sound. It was still quiet. He breathed out. There were no stairs leading up to the storm doors, so, he simply dropped down onto the carpeted concrete floor below.

With an exhalation of relief, he noted the only figure standing in the messy but fully furnished basement; a rail-thin woman. She stood in the farthest corner of the room, staring blankly at the wall. Her dark hair was flecked with grey and tangled; her only clothing, a satin gown, torn and dipping at her back. Edge walked up to her cautiously but she did not respond to him. Her fingers were bloodied and clutched to her emaciated chest. He briefly inspected her, noting the injured hands, and he adjusted the remains of the gown for modesty. The wall that she was staring at was scratched and stained with blood. He went to the nearest counter and collected some medical supplies stashed there.

He started with her hands, disinfecting and cleaning them; she did not flinch. Then he went to her hair, carefully brushing out all the knots. He washed her with a sponge, moving her – one limb at a time – to make sure he did a thorough job. He dressed her in yet another satin nightgown, collected from a chest of drawers containing several more in sealed packages, and discarded the torn one into a bin. Then he heated up a frozen packet of broth, from the little freezer, in the microwave to feed her. She mechanically swallowed whatever he put in her mouth and he was careful to monitor that she did not choke on any of it. He readjusted the furniture and cleaned whatever he had dirtied.

Edge glanced at her one more time and drew his sword. He cut the wire that held a knotted rope that led to the double doors. He ascended easily. At the top, he pulled the rope back up and fastened it again with some more wire, the same way it was before. He closed the storm doors.

In the basement, the woman glanced over her shoulder, then resumed staring at the wall.

He walked quickly to his dojo, rolling the knots of tension out of his shoulders as he entered. He stood in the middle of the octagonal room and studied how each wall was covered with every conceivable weapon, both modern and ancient. Decades old Kalashnikovs were side by side with centuries old broadswords and punch daggers. The floor was marked with concentric circles, starting with a red circle in the centre. With his eyes closed, Edge breathed out and drew his sword. He went through his *Taisu* and *Suburi* without opening his eyes. His movements were unrushed and precise. By the time a thin sheen of sweat covered his broad shoulders, he sheathed his sword and left the room.

Following a shower, his sword belt never out of reach, and after replacing the receiver in his ear, he headed to the kitchen. He heated up a pre-packaged meal for himself and ate in silence, allowing the air to cool his muscles. He cleaned up and strapped his knee heavily with supplies from the kitchen cabinet, covering the bandage with a light brace. He dressed in a loose, light pair of black combat pants and a black vest. Then he strapped the sword belt back into place and finished off his outfit with heavy boots.

The comms crackled in his ear. A pleasant-sounding, governess-like female voice spoke:

"Obsidian Edge, please comply."

"Obsidian Edge, ready for orders," he said.

"Good to hear, dear. Listen, things have been heating up in your area. How're you feeling?"

He silently awaited instructions, irritation flashing across his features. He headed back to the dojo.

"Central requests that you focus your patrols in UDZs near you," the comms officer continued.

He grimaced. "Understood. Angels in my vicinity?" He strapped on a thigh holster and two armpit holsters. He selected two semi-automatic pistols for the armpits and a third, heavier .45 pistol with a built-in scope for the thigh holster. The holster's straps had space for ammunition clips, and he filled each possible one.

"Emerald Scythe to your east, about five hundred metres; Garnet Shield to your north, one kilometre. Vermillion Sabre is to your west, but not yet in position. Two squads of contractors on standby."

"Aftershocks?"

"There were four minor tremors overnight. No blooms though. We're expecting trouble. That's why we're dropping that many resources in your area."

Edge nodded to himself, and clipped an additional ammo belt around his chest.

"Listen, Edge, there is something you should know."

He waited.

"Sapphire went home last night."

He stared straight ahead.

"If you need someone to talk to…"

Edge checked the straps of his sword belt, and the guns thoroughly and roughly. On his way out, he selected a scoped SR-25 rifle off the gun rack. "Obsidian Edge, moving out."

Edge slipped on his jacket off the back of a chair. It was deep red with a crest design on the back. A golden shield with white wings spread emblazoned with the motto "*Libertatem ex Alis Angeli.*" On the front pocket was a smaller design, a golden shield with a black, curved blade embroidered onto it. He slipped the strap of the SR-25 over his shoulder and left the house.

As he had expected, there were not many neighbours to greet as he walked. Most of the houses were empty anyway, their black windows yawning mournfully into the early morning light. Edge kept an eye out but more out of habit than any real reason. It was only when he reached the first market complex that he spotted the first person. It was a skinny guy, who ducked out of sight as soon as he was spotted.

Edge walked into the shopping complex; a restored pre-war centre, which meant it lacked the crescent shape that most modern buildings had. He checked the perimeter fences, and their gates and parking lots, and then headed into the interior buildings. The main thoroughfares had all the regulatory signs: "Don't run," "West is Best," "Thank God for Angels," all in good repair and with the required illuminated arrows pointing out the emergency exits to use. None of the signs were vandalised.

People gave him a wide berth, even if it meant treading on others' feet. They began whispering amongst themselves. "It's an Angel!"

"Come, hurry, we're leaving," another whispered. They always whispered.

Edge looked straight ahead, not making eye contact with anyone. Most passed him hurriedly, eager to get away. Edge felt like a wolf walking amongst sheep. He saw a mother trying to drag a little boy away from an ice-cream parlour. They looked like the sort that would not be able to afford such a luxury. The mother's eyes widened in horror when she saw Edge approach.

"Come away, we can't afford that," the mother said, trying to pull the small child away.

"But I want to try it!"

The boy seemed like the type not to be easily dissuaded. Edge allowed a brief twitch of a smile to touch his features. He fished out his wallet and thumbed through the numerous coupons there until he found one for luxuries. The mother was young, but tired, and the boy strong. Edge handed the coupon to the purveyor, and pointed to the kid. He nodded and gave a lop-sided grin, his brow knotted in puzzlement. The boy's smile filled Edge's vision. He curled the edges of his lips a little upwards.

"Come on!" the mother said through clenched teeth, "We can't afford this!"

Edge saw tears in her eyes. His attempt at a smile died. Wailing at the outrage, the child was dragged away by his mother. The purveyor gestured to Edge with the empty ice-cream cup, but he waved the offer away. The purveyor returned the coupon.

"You hungry?"

Edge glanced over his shoulder at the speaker. It was a large man, tall with broad shoulders and a slight stoop. He was wearing a chef's shirt and apron. Edge shook his head.

"A drink perhaps? Free of charge," the man asked.

"It'll cost you business," Edge said.

"Don't care. I hate how they treat you."

Edge looked at the man a little closer. The man's eyes were dark, sunken and defiant. Edge nodded. The ghost of a smile danced across the man's features, making him appear for an instant a little younger.

"Don't put stock in superstitions," he said. "They say that Events happen where Angels are."

"You don't believe that." Edge still had not broken eye contact with the man. To his credit, the man was only sweating a little.

"No, sir."

"Good."

"By the way, the name's…"

Edge put up his hand, closed his eyes and gently shook his head.

The chef apologised. "I, anything I can get you, you can rely on me. I run west."

Edge rewarded him a curled-lip smile. The chef led Edge to his restaurant.

"By the way," the chef asked. "What does 'Alis' mean?"

Edge looked at him impassively but didn't interrupt.

"I get '*Angeli*', that's 'Angels', obviously, and '*Libertatem*' means 'liberty' or 'freedom' right?"

"Wings," Edge stated simply.

"Liberty wings angels? '*Ex*', probably is some sort of connective word?"

Edge nodded.

"Freedom from wings angels? On?"

"Freedom on the wings of angels."

The chef was silent as he digested the phrase. "That's beautiful. I've always wondered. Folks aren't too keen to talk about it, understandably. Should have guessed by the wings on the back of your jacket."

Edge was seated at a nice table that overlooked the main piazza that formed the centre of the complex. He reversed the chair and sat down. He could feel the stares on the back of his neck.

"Yeah, this man is an Angel," the chef stated in a loud voice. "Yeah, he is in my restaurant. You want to leave, pay up and go. Go and be ashamed. If it wasn't for him, then..." he choked on his words. "Then many more of us would be damned lost. Many more. You want to run east, be my guest!"

Edge bore their stares. A few even got up and went, leaving coupons in their wake. The chef offered him coffee, which Edge accepted. It was the least he could do. Out of habit, Edge scanned his surroundings. The area around the restaurant was busy; maybe thirteen people remained. A dozen more wandered around the few shops that were still open. He could hear more close by but was not able to estimate a head count conclusively.

The comms earpiece crackled to life. A smooth male voice drawled. Edge recognised the voice of Vermillion Sabre. He pictured a lanky, dark haired man in his mid-thirties; a long scar across his left eye only added to his roguish good looks.

"Ah, Sabre in position, sorry for the wait. Was a little busy." He gave a contented sigh. "But I'm here now."

"Too busy for your duty? What an ass-hat," a woman's – no…a girl's voice retorted. Edge did not recognise her; must be Emerald Scythe.

The deep, rough voice of Garnet Shield cut in. "Duty? Really, you call all this standing around a duty? You're full of it, Scythe. Wait 'til it goes down; you're still a green-wing."

"Hey, keep it cool, you two. Relax," Sabre said. "Things all quiet, I hope?"

"Course it's quiet, you whoremonger," Scythe said. "You had comms in your ear the whole time, right? Right?"

"She got you to a T, Sabre; no chance with her," Garnet Shield said.

"Oh, ain't worried; the ones that protest the loudest are usually the loudest in bed."

Scythe shouted over the comms: "Shut up both of you! We have a living legend on our comms and you're embarrassing yourselves. And Garnet, baby? I've been in two Events; I'm no damn green-wing."

Sabre laughed. "Oh, Edge? I thought... Great to still have you. I mean that, I really do. I saw you on the comms and thought that... Sorry to hear about Sapphire. Heard you were tight. She rejected the hell out of me. Great gal."

The silence grew heavy. Edge broke it. "Thanks," he said.

Scythe spoke up, her voice subdued. "Edge, it's an honour being assigned to the same area as you. I've...heard a lot about you."

"They even give some info on you in the crash course now. You know that?" Sabre said.

"Of course he knows! There's an interview!"

"Ask him why it's so heavily edited and censored," Sabre laughed.

Edge turned down the volume of the receiver on his sword belt. The coffee arrived and he was intent to enjoy it, at least. He added sugar sparingly, tipping some onto his tongue to savour the sweetness.

One half-heard word made him turn up the volume of his comms again. "Garnet Shield, please state again," he said.

"I said, I got something. A tremor."

"Location?" all three asked simultaneously.

A siren wailed in the distance. Edge looked from patron to patron. They heard the siren as well. Each cycle of the siren was louder as a closer one added its wail to the toll. The ground under Edge's feet shook, rattling crockery, spilling the coffee still in his cup. A crack appeared in the wall near him. Edge silently counted under his breath. The tremor stopped.

Edge pressed the little red button on his receiver, activating the tracker. He whispered into the comms. "I'm on ground zero. UDZ designated SC 5-320."

The earth shook again, more violently this time, but for only a heartbeat. The shockwave tore at the structures, causing rends in the concrete. Loudspeakers creaked to life, repeating a pre-recorded message: "Head to the exits marked safe. Head to the west in an orderly fashion. May God be with you. Thank God for angels."

The comms operator spoke over the comms, her voice clipped and professional this time: "Acknowledged, Obsidian Edge, resources en-route. Outbreak logged, Urban Density Zone SC 5-320, at 10:43am. May God be with you, Angels."

Edge watched the disbelief dawn in the eyes of those around him in the restaurant. He breathed in deeply and said in a quiet voice: "*Libertatem ex Alis Angeli.*"

Scythe and Sabre echoed his words over the comms.

Garnet Shield swore. "On my way down to you, Edge, don't run east!"

"Me too, Edge! I'm on my way!" Scythe said.

"Stay where you are, Emerald Scythe!" Sabre said, "Stand-Op is that you're clean-up; any Edge misses will be up to you."

She swore. "I'm always on clean-up!"

"Position yourself directly east of Edge's beacon," Sabre said. "If memory serves, there is a crescent culvert there. You should be able to pick them off pretty easily as they run at you. God alone knows why they make it so easy for us."

"Confirmed," Edge said. "Should be three hundred metres from my beacon."

Edge saw people's eyes turn to him, their mouths opening in mute horror. He did not move a muscle. The last quake had torn open the concrete in the piazza and the hell-wind erupted from the cracks. It washed over him, smelling heavily of sulphur and brimstone. He fought to control his breathing; the wind stung his eyes. People around him were choking on the fumes, attempting to tug their useless portable gas masks over their faces. In between blinks, Edge watched the affliction bloom.

The first to turn was a woman and her two kids who happened to be closest to the main fissure. Her features contorted into a wide grimace and the howl erupted from her lungs; the two kids followed suit a split second later. Edge pushed back from the table, drawing the two lighter pistols from their holsters. His movement set the people of the restaurant off. They added their screams to the cacophony of sirens and the automated message, not to mention the inhuman howl. That sound carried clearly as the woman's incomprehensible shrieks were joined by others who were afflicted. The howl sounded almost like words shouted in a horrified mantra but mangled and garbled; the syllables wholly inhuman. The woman howled loud enough to do harm to her voice box; even the sides of her mouth tore from her screams.

He sighted for a brief moment down the barrels of the guns and squeezed the triggers. He was rewarded with a red flash that was the end of her torment. The explosive bullets made effortless work of her skull. He squeezed off two more shots, sending her children home to their mother.

More howlers arose, Edge started to have trouble tracking his targets. Instinct took over; he shot anything that looked like it wanted to move east. He steadily backtracked, discharging his weapons rhythmically. The afflicted charged past him, streaming towards the eastern opening of the centre. Edge cursed the fact that this place was not built into a crescent to corral them. He reloaded.

"Medium bloom," he said over the comms. "Thirty howlers, approx initial outbreak. Class 4."

"You call that medium?" Sabre said.

"Requesting contractors to reinforce east of my position."

"Loud and clear," the comms operator said.

"Edge! I've got your 9, I'm in position!" Scythe shouted.

"UDZ's 4-320 and 3-320 in first line with the bloom, approx population in one mile, one hundred and fifty-one," the comms officer rattled off.

"You'll be overrun, girl!" Garnet Shield shouted. "I'm circling around to reinforce."

"I got this!" she said.

"Survive this, girl, and I'll stop calling you green-wing."

Edge took another few shots; the afflicted steamed passed him, barrelling into him, biting and clawing at people trying to make it to the exits. He calculated roughly the amounts of people going down to the howlers compared to his remaining ammunition. He switched to the SR-25; the shots started coming more rapidly. One of the howlers was right on top of him as he pulled the trigger; the howler's blood sprayed over his face, into his eyes. He was wiping his face as something smashed into him.

"Stop talking down to me! I've been in two events!" Scythe was nearly in tears by the sound of her voice.

Garnet swore. "Two events? What class were they? Hmm?" Garnet was running, his voice slightly distorted.

"Class? Does it matter?"

"What class were they?"

Edge finally managed to get the blood out of his eyes when he heard a different howl nearby. One of the afflicted got onto a table and screamed a stream of incomprehensible gibberish. The tone was subtly different; this howl was not of horror but of rage – it was the chef. Edge reached for his rifle but the howler jumped off the table and threw a chair at him. Its impact knocked him away from the SR-25.

"One, okay! Is that what you want to hear?" Scythe said.

"Ohho, then you have no idea, no idea about-"

"Anom, berserker," Edge stated over the comms. The berserker shrieked at him, picking up another table to throw. Edge rolled out of the way.

"-that," Sabre said.

"Anomaly! That quickly?" Garnet Shield shouted. "Hang on, Edge. I'm five hundred metres away from your beacon!"

"Received, Obsidian Edge, Anomaly detected, berserker 10:44am," the comms officer said.

"Damn, that is quick! A first generation?" Sabre said.

Another table crashed into the space that Edge had just vacated. He leapt over the railing to the unstable ground of the piazza, then drew the heavy .45 from his thigh holster. The berserker seemed intent on tearing the place apart. He fired a warning shot into its arm to draw its attention away from the fleeing survivors. The berserker howled and charged at him, thrusting aside tables and chairs as he went.

"Obsidian Edge, I've got a VIP-" the comms officer started saying, but was interrupted by static and the rumbling sound of a microphone being manhandled.

"Don't kill it!" another voice shouted over the comms.

"What?" Sabre and Garnet Shield both retorted.

Edge pulled his headshot wide.

"That anomaly represents invaluable research data! We need to study it to learn from it."

The comms officer seemed to have regained control of her headset. "That's Doctor Ruben. He's a leading researcher on the affliction."

"Contact!" Scythe said. "First howlers in my sight." Edge could hear her shots ring out, her glee almost as loud as the Howlers. He wished that she would not leave her comms open.

The berserker charged at Edge, knocking him from his feet. Edge kicked the creature clear, and he rolled back onto his feet.

"I don't care who he is," Sabre said. "Berserkers are as bad as they come! We can't lose more angels to them!"

"Exactly why we must study it!" Doctor Ruben said. "I understand that you, Mister Edge, are a veteran."

"A freaking legend!" Scythe shouted in between shots.

"Quite. Can you, subdue the creature?" Doctor Ruben asked.

Edge picked up the heavy pistol and, just as he was about to take a shot, the berserker knocked into him again. The weapon clattered on the concrete floor. He looked at the afflicted, streaming away from him towards the east.

"How many limbs do you need on him, Doc?" he said.

"Oh no, just alive, if you please; as intact as possible."

Edge grimaced and drew his sword. "Make sure the contractors get here before it bleeds out."

The berserker charged. Edge closed his eyes and breathed out, letting the sword settle on his right side with the tip resting on the ground. At the last moment, Edge lightly stepped to the left and slashed upwards, the stroke cutting clean through the berserker's leg. It howled as it went down, seemingly oblivious to the wound. Edge spun on his heel and his down stroke took off the creature's reaching arm. The other leg took quite a few hacking slashes, as it was on the ground and not easily accessed. The last arm went in two more strokes. Edge grabbed the berserker by the collar of his shirt, trying to avoid the flailing stumps and the biting mouth, and dragged him into the kitchen of the nearby restaurant. He cauterised the stumps on the still-searing griddle.

There was a clatter as a pan fell from a washing tray nearby. Edge dropped the berserker and looked around. He silently moved around the rows of kitchen equipment, sword held low. He heard a muffled sound, like someone breathing roughly through their hands. He stalked closer.

Another clink of cutlery signified that he was close to his mark. He found her – a cook, or perhaps a dishwasher, was squeezed into the little space between the bottom two rungs of a storage shelf. She had her hands squeezed shut over her mouth. Her eyes desperately searched the area but she did not notice Edge. She tried to squeeze herself deeper into the shelf, some strong primal instinct forcing her to try to conceal herself. He crouched down at the opening – she had blood on her hands. Twitching suddenly, she flung crockery in his general direction, as if lashing out at unseen tormentors. She had to use her hands to manoeuvre and, when she did so, a low stream of incomprehensible growling escaped her lips, like a stray cat meeting another in its territory. Edge tried to stab her but the confines and the detritus made the attempt unwieldy. She thrust her way out, screeching and pulling things down behind her, tripping up his pursuit. He went down heavily.

"Anom, lurker," Edge said as soon as he could breathe again.

"Another? Second gen?" Sabre asked.

"Negative, probably first gen," Edge said. He heard shots fired nearby; a rapid rapport of gunfire – the type that contractors used.

"Received, Obsidian Edge…" the comms officer started.

"Anom!" Scythe screamed. "Leaper!"

"What the hell is going on?" Sabre shouted.

"Guys," Garnet Shield said. "Don't know if this thing was an anom but it blew up when I popped it."

"Sounds pretty anom to me," Sabre said.

"Received, Emerald Scythe…"

"Boom! Headshot!" Scythe shouted. "Don't worry about the leaper, anom down! He popped up like a duck in hunting season."

"For hell's sake, all of you!" Sabre shouted. "Clear comms! We need to report these anoms properly." There was a moment of silence, and Sabre took it to continue. "Ok, Edge? Is the berserker neutralised?"

"Yes," Edge said.

"Ok. That's great. Now, the lurker."

Edge picked his way through the carnage. "Unaccounted for. Heard contractor shots fired in the direction she ran."

"Central? Can we get confirms from the contractors?"

"I'm putting in a request now, Sabre dear, way ahead of you."

"Ok, and Scythe took out the leaper and Garnet has a new type to christen, Central?"

"Affirmative dear, there's no record of any one of them exploding on death as of yet. As custom, the angel who sent the anom home gets to name it. Garnet Shield?"

"Haven't thought of a name yet; will get a good one."

Edge saw movement out of the corner of his eye. He quickly made his way to a small pile of bodies that crowded the exit to the restaurant. As he got closer, he heard a muffled cry. He wiped his sword on a nearby body and, after inspecting the blade, sheathed it. He moved the bodies one at a time. The cries became more frantic. It sounded like a young boy or a girl. He moved another body and a girl struggled free of the press. Her features were obscured by gore and she clutched at her injured arm; she stumbled over a body and gasped for air. Tears made little furrows into the blood on her face. Edge walked over to her, hand on the hilt of his sword.

"Say your name," Edge said, his voice level.

The girl looked at him in mute incomprehension. Edge drew his blade half an inch. The shock of seeing the gleam of metal jolted her to semi-coherence.

"Tamaryn," she managed, her voice hoarse. "My name is Tamaryn."

Edge sheathed his sword with a click.

"Anom," Edge said into his comms.

"Another one!" Sabre swore, his voice getting strained. "What the hell is going on? Confirm type, Edge! What is it?"

He looked at the girl; she didn't seem older than thirteen. She was shaking, looking around at the carnage with wide terrified eyes. "Anomaly class confirmed: Angel."

Scythe hissed into the comms: "Don't do that! We're wetting ourselves out here!"

The comms officer cleared her throat: "Anom class lurker is still out there, Angels, stay frosty. I'll send an away team for the new angel. Edge dear? Can I ask you to take care of her until we can pick her up?"

Edge walked to the fridge and picked out a bottled drink. It took some time to find a glass that wasn't covered in blood and, after wiping his hand on a corpse, he poured the drink. He added a swirl of vodka to it.

"Tamaryn, drink this."

"I'm too young to drink that," she replied automatically.

"Least of your worries now, kid."

"You said you found a new angel, that true?"

He pressed the drink into her hands. "Yes."

She looked around. Edge hoped that she would not be able to discern any relatives or friends in the carnage.

"Drink up. It will help for the shock," he said.

She took a sip automatically and pulled a face. Edge led her deeper into the shopping centre, to a cleaner part where he had her sit down on a waiting bench. The flashing arrows pointing west bathed the area in a blue glow.

She took another sip. She did not look at him. "It's me, isn't it?"

Edge wanted to put his arms around the girl but hesitated. There were echoes of shots fired in the distance; the rat-tat-tat of the contractors' guns. "Yes," he replied.

A screech blared over the comms, signalling a new connection.

The comms officer stabilised the connection. "Comms merged, Angels. You're clear to speak, Captain."

"Roger that, Command, a bit of a mess you boys caused here. Sectors to the north of SC 5-320 getting a slew of new blooms."

"That's the lurker," Sabre said. "Captain, is it? Tell your men to stay cool. Lurkers move in random patterns; no way to predict where they'll go."

"We have the situation under control. You civilians can stand down."

"You've got no idea what you're dealing with…"

"Hah! Let them feel it on their hides," Garnet Shield said. He muttered something incomprehensible.

"Hey! Chill out!" Sabre said. "We're on the same side here! Captain, with all due respect…"

"With all due respect nothing, civilian, this is our fight now. You amateurs will soon be history anyway."

Sabre started saying something but held his tongue. Garnet chortled a rough laugh.

"Screw this," Scythe said. "Switching to local." Her comms clicked off.

Edge could hear helicopters overhead, in between the bleats of the alarms. Tamaryn nervously tried to clean her hands.

"Contact," Garnet Shield stated.

"Location?" the comms officer asked.

"Sector SC 5-319."

Edge stiffened. "Confirm location? 319?"

"Yep," Garnet confirmed.

"A new outbreak?" the comms officer asked.

Edge checked his remaining weaponry, mentally tracking where he dropped each one he didn't have on him.

"No, howlers don't get tired, remember? Could still be the lurker," Sabre said.

"It's heading north then, almost in a straight line," the comms officer said.

Garnet whistled through his teeth. "Contact again, Scythe's here. Way out of position but, damn, that girl can shoot."

"Scythe's with you?" the comms officer asked.

"That's what I said; she has a bike."

"Amateurs," the Captain said. "Our clean-up is in position to the east of ground zero, so, your ill-discipline will not cause many more unnecessary deaths."

Edge saw brown armoured men and women enter the complex. They were armed, ready for trouble. He got up and waved them over. The lead member of the away team unzipped the links of the bio-seal and took off her helmet. Her face was wrinkled and careworn; a wide smile etched itself onto her mouth but stopped short of her eyes. Edge nodded in the direction of Tamaryn and the away team got to work. He jogged to find his discarded weaponry. Members of the clean-up crew were already checking for survivors. Edge knew there would be none.

He searched the pockets of a man in motorcycle gear for the keys to his bike.

"Where the hell is the lurker?" Garnet breathed over the comms. "Edge? This is your valley here, isn't it? We could use your help here!"

"Got it," Edge said, looking for the corresponding bike. "I'm *en route*."

"Glad to hear it."

"You men stand down! We have the situation under control!" the Captain said, his voice unyielding.

"Switching to local," Edge said. He found the bike and sped off, heading north.

The comms receiver crackled as it switched channels. Edge could hear Scythe's heavy breathing; she had left the comms open again.

"Edge? Is that you?" she said.

"Yes."

"Listen, I think I know where it's heading. You better come north."

"I'm already on my way."

"Great, because there's like nothing here; this is the 'burbs – mostly depopulated. The only thing that's here is your safe house. I know, I know, I'm not supposed to know where you live. I've not been spying on you and all, it's just…"

Scythe fell silent. Edge opened the throttle of the bike, swerving in between the abandoned transport and cars.

"Edge?"

"I'm here," he said as he got a little clear of the jumble.

"Are you mad at me?"

"No, why would I be? I am almost there."

"That's good," she said.

Edge heard a shot go off over the comms.

"Contact," Scythe said.

"Where?" Edge felt his heart sink.

"Do you have anyone living with you? I think I just spotted the lurker."

"Where are you?" Edge said, emphasising every word.

"I'm going in; this is weird, even for a lurker! I've only read of them but, if I bag this, wow! I'd have two anom kills in a day! What do you think of that?"

"Do not go in, I repeat, do not!"

"I've got this, you just watch my back!"

Edge grimaced and spurred the bike forward. He spotted a howler as he entered his street but he ignored it. He slowed his bike down and coasted it into the driveway.

He looked up at his safe house, and checked his weapons.

Edge burst into the house through the already open window. He accelerated when he heard the rapport of handgun fire and the splintering of wood. Scythe's manic laughter rent his ears. With a growl, he drew his sword with his right hand and the heavy handgun with his left. He saw the double doors of the storm shelter had been torn open; Scythe was kneeling over the entrance with her rifle propped up for support. She was surprisingly small, the rifle seeming overly large in her hands; her dark hair, cropped close to her skull, gave her a pixie-ish look. Her red jacket was studded with little death's head badges. The sleeves were rolled up to her elbows. He levelled his gun at her.

"Stand up, no sudden moves," he said between clenched teeth.

Scythe glanced backwards. "Edge! I got it!" Then she jolted with surprise, her large brown eyes flashed. "Hey! Point that somewhere else!"

"Step away from the door."

"What? What's going on with you? This your place?"

His heart thudded in his ears; the tip of the gun shuddered as he tried to keep it on target. He heard movement from inside the shelter. He fired a warning shot into the ceiling right above Scythe's head.

Scythe flinched and swore, dropping her rifle. "What the hell is wrong with you? I got the lurker, ok? No need to hog my kills! It's dead! I thought you'd be proud of me!"

"Step away from the door; last call."

The sound of movement in the cellar grew frantic. A howl rose out of the hole. Scythe spun on her heel and drew one of her pistols. Edge pulled off another shot but it went wide because of her sudden change of direction. Scythe rolled, ducking behind the corner. She fired off a misdirected shot on instinct. Edge found cover in the door frame of the kitchen.

She swore. "What the hell, Edge! There's a howler in there, and you're shooting at me!"

Edge glanced at the storm shelter doors; he could hear the howler jumping in an attempt to reach the door. He changed position, moving to flank Scythe.

"Can we talk about this?" Scythe shouted. "What is that place, like a prison? A private lab?"

Edge moved without a sound, stalking around his furniture. He did not even dare to reload.

Scythe cursed. "Ok, I get it, you keep a howler as a pet. But why? That thing is dangerous! People'll die! Isn't that why we do what we do? To protect people?"

Edge glanced at the cellar door; he saw the howler's fingertips appear on the rim of the storm cellar but Scythe smashed the butt of her rifle into them, causing the creature to drop back down.

"Look, I'm not judging. That thing looks female, right? Is it a companionship thing? Talk to me, Edge!"

The howler attempted to gain purchase on the rim again. Scythe butted it down and kicked closed the shattered doors. With another curse, she stuck the barrel of her rifle into the looped door handles to bar the entrance and readied her sidearm.

"I don't want to kill you," she said. "We're on the same team! I just want to understand. Can you hear me?"

Her voice sounded strained with emotion; Edge still did not reply.

"I don't understand. You're a war hero! The last of Obsidian Company. They teach your tactics at the school; I learned all I know from you! I relocated here because…I know that you were an accountant or something when the first outbreaks hit. You fought from the beginning because your fiancé…" Scythe swore.

Edge leaned slowly around the corner; Scythe saw the movement and moved around the corner without hesitation.

She wore again. "Edge! That her in here? You kept her alive all this time?"

Edge leaned with his back against the wall, his eyes closing as tears filled his vision. His .45 clattered on the floor and he sunk down beside it. The knee-brace creaked as he went down.

Scythe risked a glance. She spotted the gun on the floor. Cautiously, she padded over, gun held in a low firing position. She rounded the corner on the balls of her feet. Edge sat on the floor with his back against the wall, his eyes squeezed shut. Tears freely ran down his face, his lips muttering something over and over. Scythe leaned closer to listen, lowering her gun slowly.

She strained to make out the words, then her eyes rounded in shock; she recognised it.

Edge was chanting: "*Libertatem ex Alis Angeli.*"

She did not have time to retreat. Like a rising tide, Edge moved.

"Edge, no!" she shouted.

In a shimmering arc, Edge's blade licked out. Scythe put up her hand in a feeble attempt at defence but it did not even slow the blade's trajectory. The blade whispered through her hand and across her throat.

She fell back, a look of silent shock across her features. Then, there was blood.

Edge cast the blade away from him and shut his eyes tightly. He heard Scythe thrash noisily for a moment longer, then there was silence.

"Why did you come here?" he said through clenched teeth. "Why did you have to come into my home? I warned you to stay away, I warned you."

The howler was rattling at the double doors. He scrambled over to the shelter, swallowing the bile in his throat. Edge attempted to shush her; the sound came out warped and mangled. "Please, love, be quiet, please, please, please. We have to be quiet; I need to move you before they find you. "

The windows rattled with the sound of a helicopter overhead. He shushed her again in between wracking sobs. The comms crackled to life again. Edge fought to compose himself. He ran to the kitchen to splash water on his face. He could taste blood.

"Edge, dear? Please comply?" the comms officer asked softly.

Edge struggled for a moment with the thought of destroying the comms unit in his ear. Instead, he breathed in deep and cleared his throat.

"I'm here," he said, surprised at how calm he sounded.

"That's cold," Sabre said.

"Edge dear, you're gonna have to trust us, ok?"

His heart thundered in his ears.

"Please, just come out quietly; there are contractors out front but, if you come quietly, they won't shoot." The comms officer's tone was level and steady, like someone talking down a bomb.

"Don't run," Garnet said. "We can help."

Edge looked at his reflection in the window; he was covered in blood, Scythe's blood. His legs wobbled under him and he caught himself on the rim of the basin.

"Her comms," he whispered.

"Was open the whole time, dear."

Edge walked to the front door in a daze. Through the window he could see vehicles driving up to join the ones already in place, the flashing green lights of the contractor's buggies and bikes joined by the blue of the militia police.

He took a few steps to remove himself from their line of sight and recovered his sword. The helicopter shuddered the foundations of the building again as it passed overhead. He headed to the back door, but the glint of the sun reflecting off a vehicle stopped his progress.

He heard the sound of glass shattering in another part of the house, most likely the living room, Edge thought. He gripped the blade tighter. He heard the heavy thuds of the breachers' boots stomping in his direction. Edge crouched low, struggling to blink the remnants of tears and blood out his eyes. The boots stomped nearer, right around the corner. Edge lunged, swinging the blade in an arc at whoever was around the corner. The impact rang loudly as the blade struck an immovable object; it shuddered through his arm and he barely managed to hold onto the blade.

He looked up, straight into the oncoming iron boss of a massive wooden round-shield, painted blood red. The shield impacted him, knocking him from his feet. The fall caused the blade to clatter across the floor. Edge's ears rang and his vision blurred. He struggled to get his breathing under control and to blink the tears out of his eyes.

His vision returned slowly. It revealed a mountain of a man, round-shield held loosely at his side. He was dressed in leather pants and a sleeveless cotton shirt covered by a red jacket matching Edge's own, only the sleeves were torn off. From a loop in his belt hung a single bladed bearded axe. His blonde hair was braided along the top of his head into a tail that hung over his shoulder, the sides of his head shaved close to the skin. He had clear blue eyes and a forked blonde beard. The mountain offered his free hand to Edge, blue geometric tattoos covered the arm.

"Garnet Shield," Edge managed to say.

"Good thing you're not yourself," Garnet Shield said. "The Edge I knew would never blindly bash into my shield."

Edge took the offered hand and was pulled upright without any effort.

Garnet glanced around and whistled through his teeth. He spotted the body of Emerald Scythe.

A crackle of a loudspeaker outside raked its nails across Edge's hearing: "Obsidian Edge, come out quietly, right now. There is no way out. Today, we close the Angels Project."

Edge looked at Garnet, searching his features. Garnet shrugged and walked over to Scythe.

"You here to take me in?" Edge asked.

Garnet kneeled by Scythe's body, and closed her eyes with a wipe of his broad hand. "Sleep now, little one," he said. "You fought like a Valkyrie and I'm sure that you died well. Odin waits for you in Valhalla."

Edge clenched his jaw and looked away.

Garnet stood up. "Clean kill. By the look of her, she does not believe she's dead." He wiped his hands on his trousers. "What you going to do?"

Edge felt the words catch in his throat. Garnet wandered over to the double doors of the storm shelter. Edge moved quickly but stopped as Garnet held out his hand. The howler in the shelter pressed quietly against the door.

"Anom?"Garnet asked.

Edge shook his head.

"Pity, Central loves live anoms." Garnet knelt by the shelter. "She's so quiet. Normally, Howlers scream their heads off."

Edge frowned and cleared his throat. "You think?"

Garnet shrugged. After a moment, he stood up and walked to the corpse of the lurker. It had a bullet wound in the centre of its forehead. He picked up Edge's sword and handed it to him. "What now?" he asked.

The comms in Edge's ear crackled to life. Sabre spoke. "Edge, come on out, just take it easy. The brave conquistadores are ready to charge in, both companies of them and they brought artillery. I'm out front."

"Time's up," Garnet said.

"Central sent an order for them to await instructions; the Captain would rather you resist. Your call."

"We're on our way, Edge dear, just don't get yourself into more trouble. Sabre, please stall the contractors from doing something rash. We're in the air."

"I'll come out," Edge said.

"Hold your positions!" Sabre shouted. "He's coming out!"

Edge walked out slowly, led by Garnet, shield aloft. The red shield blocked out the worst of the sights outside but Edge could see the little red dots of laser sights dancing over every uncovered part of him. The contractors had a rough perimeter around the property, simultaneously corralling him and keeping the curious at bay. The press had gathered and numerous onlookers had camera phones trained on the situation as well.

Sabre stood front and centre, facing away from the house,

weapons drawn. His sabre's gilded basket hilt glinted in the light and his unruly dark hair whipped about in the helicopter's wash. In his other hand was a stubby bullpup P90. He was wearing dark fatigues and an unzipped ammo jacket over his red jacket, and made it look like a fashion statement. A multitude of crucifixes of various designs and materials, ranging from simple wood to gold set with precious gems, dangled from around his neck; they glittered like the sun reflecting off the ocean. He turned his face toward Edge; the angry line of the scar writhed as Sabre treated him to a grin.

The Captain motioned his men forward. Several heavily armed contractors in their black bio-suit armour rushed onto the property; the suits' hard carbon fibre finish gleamed in the sunlight.

"Here they come," Garnet stated as he lifted the axe from its loop.

"Stop right there!" Sabre shouted. His voice clear and bright, like the sun, reflected from his sword. He levelled the P90 at the oncoming men. To Edge's surprise, the men hesitated.

"Take him now!" the Captain shouted over the loudspeaker.

"First man to move dies!" Sabre retorted.

The men hesitated.

"What's the meaning of this? That man is a criminal!" the Captain shouted.

"Not your jurisdiction, my lovely Captain. Your contract says nothing about this. I'd know. Sit tight, everyone; Central is on their way here to handle this."

"He's an accomplice; kill him if you have to!" The Captain's voice was getting high pitched.

"What, in front of all these good people?" Sabre motioned to the gathering crowd and to the media. "We are protectors of the people, their guardian angels made immune to the affliction by the Will of God. Do you want a riot?"

The contractors looked around uncertainly but there were many lowered weapons. The crowd started to sound unruly.

"Look at you," the Captain said. "You look ridiculous! Amateurs, the lot of you! Don't you see that you are a joke? Command lets you dance in front of the cameras so that people don't panic. God made you immune? Bull! You are all murderers and freaks! I know that you've got something to do with the outbreaks! We all do!"

Sabre's grin widened. An angry murmur spread through the crowd. "Now, that was the wrong thing to say." He muttered just loud enough for Edge to hear.

The Captain continued obliviously: "And you with the shield, do you think you're a Viking warrior? Give me a break! The criminal is the most sensibly dressed of the lot of you! But look, he still uses a sword. Amateurs!"

"Keep this up and we'll see where God's mercy falls, you idiot," Sabre said.

"You're all history! You just don't know it yet! You bastards will no longer have the licence to murder indiscriminately! What?" The Captain listened to something a subordinate was saying while motioning to a radio. He took it and stepped away.

"What's his beef?" Garnet asked.

"Well, our lovely military man has an onion to peel with the Angels Project."

"That much I got."

"He wants to shut us down, probably because he lost someone to a bloom, or an angel."

"Who hasn't?"

Sabre shook his head.

The comms officer whispered. "Sabre dear? I reckon you have control of the situation down there, right?"

"Well, control's a bit of a stretch at this point, Central," Sabre said.

"This could turn really ugly, dear; try to get that Captain to can it. Command is talking him down; just hang in there. There's a big can of worms brewing."

"Like the threat of cancelling the Angels program? Yeah, we know about that."

The comms officer sighed. "We've been fighting on two fronts here but this could be the nail in our coffin."

Edge swallowed. "I'll give myself up."

Sabre gave Edge a hard look. "Not sure that'll help," Sabre spat on the ground. "Not now, at any rate. Stand your ground, we'll get you out, for good or ill. If they charge, we'll fight."

Edge glared black, then dipped his head. "No point you sacrificing yourself. You know what I did?"

Sabre snorted. "Doesn't change anything."

"Why are you helping me?" Edge clenched his fists.

"I'm not helping you. I'm helping me. I'm helping the program. There's a special place in hell for people who hurt women, and without all this..." Sabre gestured at the assembled people, "... I'd have your head. But the program does a lot of good. We're in this together, until Central figures out the blooms."

Edge nodded. Sabre breathed out and rolled the tension out of his right shoulder.

"Is it true though," Sabre asked, "that you kept a howler alive in your basement?"

Edge hesitated for a moment, then turned his head away from them, towards the door.

"I'll take that as a yes. Who is she? Can't be a random girl. You're not the type."

Edge shook his head.

"Family then? It usually is."

Edge looked up in surprise.

"Yep, so family then. If I'd hazard a guess, I'd go for daughter."

Edge held Sabre's gaze for a moment, then looked away shaking his head.

"A lover?"

Edge paused for a moment; he remembered a smiling young woman, her eyes sparkling at the joke she made at his expense, about how serious he was about making the little numbers appear in neat little rows. He tried to swallow the pain away.

"You think I'm mad," he said finally.

Sabre smirked. "In case you haven't noticed, Edge, we're all a few apples short of a fruit basket. You'd have to be, to do our job. It's a mission from God. But...there's a reason that almost all of us clock out to go home sooner or later. Garnet, here, is a prime example. Do you think his whole Viking vibe is an accident?" Sabre shrugged. "Maybe he's descended from Vikings, maybe he was born right here in the 'burbs, I don't care, I see something of myself in him, the mask that he wears to do what we do."

Edge looked up at the bulk that was Garnet Shield. He saw the blue eyes stare back at him but, for the first time, he also saw the brittleness of the man's gaze, the haunted expression and, with the axe in hand, the mad willingness to dive into battle, secretly hoping that this one would be the last.

Sabre smiled at the big man. "I heard what you said for the girl; I'm sure she's waiting for you in Odin's halls."

Garnet nodded and fixed his gaze on the contractors.

Sabre continued, glancing at Edge. "Now we know what your big secret was. You've lasted a long time, Edge; it's fitting that it was love that brought you this far. That's why God favoured you."

Edge looked back at the front door again.

"Edge, I know what you're thinking," Sabre said, "but it cannot go any further. She's gone, man. She's gone. We're not, we can make a difference but only if we're all in. If the Captain wins, what will they do with us? Let her go, sit tight."

"Sabre dear? Can I speak to you on a private channel?" the comms officer asked.

"Why bother? He has to know. He's got to know that she's gone! He deals with howlers on a daily basis and, if there was any chance of bringing them back-"

"It's not as simple as that," the comms officer said.

Sabre narrowed his eyes, the grip on his sword tightening. "What's that?"

"I said the situation is not that simple."

"What are you hiding from us?" Sabre licked his lips. The comms remained silent for a moment longer before Sabre spat onto the pavement.

"Just a moment," the comms officer said. "I'm getting Doctor Ruben on the line."

"Don't bother, I get it." Sabre sheathed his blade.

Garnet Shield closed his eyes but his hands shook as if trying to fight off a fever. Edge turned his head back to the house; he could hear the rattling of the makeshift bar on the storm shelter. His mouth was dry and his breathing shallow. There was the blustering of a microphone being adjusted over the comms before, who could only be Doctor Ruben spoke. He seemed to be speaking to someone else at first. "What? Yes, yes, I'll tell them."

Sabre stared hard at the contractors, his expression hard.

"Can you hear me, Angels? Do you copy? Was that right?"

"Loud and clear," Edge said, his voice breaking at first but getting stronger. He stalked into the foyer to avoid the noise from outside.

"Edge, is it? Great work on the berserker; we have him safe and sound. You've contributed to humanity's victory in a great way."

"Is it true?"

"Yes! Wait, is what true?"

"That howlers can be rehabilitated?"

"What? Whatever gave you that idea, good man?"

"Can they? Answer me, Doc!"

"Theoretically, I suppose. No precedent, I'm afraid. But I have something more interesting here to consider…"

Edge stopped listening, his heart sank through the floor. He saw dimly that Garnet Shield, looking grim, and Sabre, his eyes hard, retreated into the house. Garnet hoisted him up bodily and dragged him back to the doors of the storm shelter. Sabre pressed his face close to Edge's and said something. Edge couldn't focus on the words, until Garnet Shield struck him across the face.

"Listen! No time to space out!" Sabre pointed at the door.

Doctor Ruben's voice scratched away in his ear but all he heard was the Captain barking orders to the men outside. "Right! These men are harbouring a howler! Do your duty! Open fire!"

There was a breathless moment, a hesitation. Edge could almost feel the contractors' reluctance. He used that moment to get behind cover. Then, a single burst of gunfire erupted.

The rapport of automatic gunfire shredded the air around them, followed by the tinkling of glass and the ricochet of bullets. Edge's reflexes jerked him behind cover, shielding his head with his arms. The firing petered out and then stopped as suddenly as it had started.

"Who said cease fire? Who said-?"

Then Edge heard it too; sirens – somewhere close by. Immediately, he looked at his watch. Another siren started up, this time much nearer. He looked up at Garnet and Sabre; they were both staring at their watches in disbelief, counting down the seconds.

"Central," Sabre said through gritted teeth. "We have tremors."

"Confirmed, Vermillion Sabre."

In the storm cellar, the Howler started keening. Edge counted down; a siren that sounded like it that was right by his head started up. Then there was a momentary silence. Edge could feel the tension of the people outside, already going into a mute panic.

"UDZ designated Sector SC 5-319, we're on ground zero," Edge said.

The earth shook one more time. The howler increased her keening. Edge could now clearly hear the shouting outside, adding to the cacophony of the quake. The howl nearby was joined by others outside and gunfire erupted once more.

"My God," Sabre muttered. *"Libertatem…"*

"Ex Alis Angeli," Garnet finished, his eyes glittered.

The tremor had stopped, but gunfire and stampeding feet rattled out erratically. Edge could the smell of the sulphur of the hell-wind.

"Edge! Can you fight? We need to contain this!"

"The armoury," Edge said, simply pointing out its direction.

Gunfire thudded and pinged into the house, much more erratic than the focussed fire from before. The front door thrust open as a contractor fell backwards into the house; another, screeching at the top of his lungs, scratched and clawed at the man's helmeted face, tearing away at the mask. The fallen man's back arched as the mask came away. Gunfire from outside ripped into both men, causing them to shudder and twitch with the impacts but they did not stop moving immediately.

"Listen!" Doctor Ruben shouted over the comms. "This just confirms what I've been saying! You have to protect the howler in Edge's basement!"

A fresh rapport of gunfire from outside tore into the wall above Edge's head.

"Are you mad?" Sabre shouted back, firing shots from his P90 in rapid succession, putting the two howlers near the front door out of their misery.

"Believe me! That lurker, as you call it, was heading straight there – no random, no nothing! We've got to know why, it's critical! There is something we can test; I have a theory!"

"Now, there's a bloom right here…" Garnet added.

"Yes! Can't you see? The howlers are trying to get to their kind! This has never been recorded before! It was just a hypothesis!"

A man in civilian clothing burst through the remains of the window. He was missing an arm but carried a contractor's M16 in the other. With a howl, he charged at them, swinging the gun like a club. Sabre pointed the P90 at it; squeezed the trigger. The gun clicked impotently.

"Damn!" he spat.

Garnet Shield stepped forward, shield and axe at the ready. "Anom, berserker," he grinned. The berserker smashed into the shield but Garnet bashed him back. The axe crashed down like Thor's wrath, striking home with shattering force.

"I wouldn't expect you to bring me another live one," Doctor Ruben said.

"Good," Sabre said, "Garnet just took its head off." He discarded his gun.

"Protect the howler; we're coming with some reinforcements for you, is that right?"

"Perfectly," the comms officer said.

More gunfire ripped into the house, and Sabre yelped in pain. He clutched at his thigh, the blood bubbling up through his fingers.

"Damn it, artery," he said.

Edge tore off his sword belt and looped it around Sabre's thigh.

"No use doing that here! We're in the line of fire!" Sabre said through gritted teeth.

"Storm shelter," Edge said.

"No good, we need guns, here they come." Garnet smashed into the howlers careening into the house from the front door and the ruined window. "You two go down! I'll get you covered and armed!" He kicked Edge's discarded gun at them.

Sabre grimaced at Garnet. "Don't be a hero," he said. "Get the guns and get into the shelter."

Garnet smiled, the afternoon light making his blonde braid and beard shimmer golden. "Don't know any other way," he said. "Odin waits for me."

Edge pulled the belt on Sabre's leg tight, scooped up the gun and handed it to Sabre. Then, he nodded at Garnet Shield. The big man grinned and stepped out into the open, shield up. Edge dragged Sabre behind Garnet's cover and tore open the storm shelter's doors. The howler tried to climb out but Edge dropped Sabre on top of her – both landed in a tangled heap. Garnet grunted as a bullet ripped through the shield and into his shoulder. Edge dropped down into the hole.

Sabre dragged himself and the violently struggling Howler to the back of the basement. "Your woman's feisty," he smirked through a pained wince.

Shots rang out upstairs; they heard Garnet's voice bellow out and then get cut short.

"Hah! That's one!" the Captain shouted over the loud speaker. "Sweep team six, cover the back entrance! Anyone still active? Damn, I'll deal with this myself!"

"Godspeed," Sabre said, pain splayed across his features. "Have a drink on us in the great hall."

Edge walked up to him, his expression neutral and drew his sword out of the scabbard in Sabre's hand. The first howler dropped through the hole. It was a civilian. Edge removed its head in a single movement.

"Last chance, Edge!" the Captain shouted. "Bring out the abomination and we'll leave you alive. She's a threat, you know that!"

Edge didn't reply. He cast a questioning glance at Sabre.

"Not backing out on you now, old war horse," Sabre said. "It's a beautiful thing, devotion like that."

"I promised I'd watch over her," Edge said.

"A guardian angel," Sabre laughed mirthlessly.

Guns sputtered outside. Two more howlers fell in. Edge spun around, sword levelled. A gunshot rang out next to Edge's ear, too loud to be real. The howler on the left's head opened like a popped water balloon. The other was dead when it hit the ground, its body riddled with bullet holes. Edge's ears rang with a high pitched whine; his eyes watered from the assault of the nearly physical sound. His head throbbed and he was sure his ears were bleeding. He looked around to Sabre, who clutched at the sides of his head, the .45 miraculously still in hand. He saw the howler stagger up – Sabre was not holding her down anymore. She was quite off-balance but intent on escape. He stumbled to intercept her, barely able to keep himself upright through the ringing in his ears.

She stopped, her eyes on him. She looked right at him. He looked into the black caverns of her eyes, searching for a flicker of recognition. She tilted her head to one side; her eyes were focused on a point somewhere behind him. Edge felt a chill run up his spine. He positioned himself between her and the exit and spread his arms. The howler moved to pass him but he wrapped his arms around her. Then, an icy stab of pain stabbed into his lower back, then another and another. He saw Sabre attempting to rise, wincing as he struggled to aim the handgun, shouting something through his pained expression. Edge's legs gave way, his arms still holding on to the howler. Her mouth was moving of its own accord; he could not make out any words. She did not hold him up and he slid to the floor, his body feeling distantly cold and weak. He let go of her. She took a step over him; he could not stop her.

Sabre raised the gun again, aiming with his eyes squeezed shut, his free hand clutching at the side of his head. Edge reached out to him, stretching towards the weapon. Sabre opened his eyes and lowered the weapon, surprise blooming on his features.

With an effort of will, Edge twisted around to look where Sabre was looking. He saw the howler crouched over the Captain's struggling form, straddling him, her hands wrapped tightly around his wrists. He still clutched a gun with both hands. With glacial grace, she dragged at the fabric of his sleeve, tearing it. She leaned over and bit him on the exposed hand. The Captain screamed. It was the first sound that Edge heard through the ringing in his ears. Then there was pain. He tried to move again but a shock through his chest jolted him to stillness.

Sabre hobbled over to him, one hand grasping the tourniquet belt tightly. When he started to kneel, Edge shook his head as vigorously as he could manage and motioned towards the struggling pair. Edge became aware of a low disquieting chant, punctuated by feeble moans from the Captain. Sabre picked up Edge's dropped sword. It was drenched in blood. Edge looked at the floor and saw a growing puddle of it. It was spreading around him. He closed his eyes for a moment and tried to breathe in a calming breath. But instead of air, all he got was pain from his chest.

The howler let go of the Captain, still chanting.

The comms crackled in Edge's ear. It was nearly at the edge of his hearing. He closed his eyes to try and blot out the pain, and to focus on the voice from the little device: "Is it speaking?" Doctor Ruben said. Edge was sure. "Get the receiver closer! Yes, yes, like that! What is it doing?"

"Uh, it's just standing there, saying the same thing over and over again." Sabre's voice sounded far away.

"Got it! We'll start right away!"

"What? Start with what?"

Edge heard the chant from the Howler in his earpiece.

"Mihh eam morf eeaawa eeaats. Mihh eam morf eeaawa eeaats."

He felt a weight fall on him; it knocked what little breath he had left in him out. He opened his eyes and saw her lying on top of him, her cheek right against his face. She looked at him, a flicker of emotion showed around the edges of her eyes. She was chanting something else now, her voice barely a whisper but it was the sweetest sound that Edge has ever heard.

"Eead tnod eeselp eeselp! Eead tnod eeselp eeselp! Oee eval eea!"

"That's great, Mister Edge, we're getting really great audio now! Almost got it!"

Sabre tried to move her off of him but she slipped out of his blood-slicked grasp with ease.

"She- She bit me!" the Captain said.

Sabre peered at him for a moment and then snorted. "Yeah, couldn't have happened to a better person. Central? Got another anom here, angel."

The Captain's eyes nearly popped out of his skull and he made a strangled sound. More figures entered the room; not the black-armoured contractors but the brown-armoured volunteers.

"Got it! Commencing playback!" Doctor Ruben said.

The voice over the comms sounded alien, the inflections at all the wrong places. But Edge recognised her voice.

"Staay awaay from him! Staay awaay from him!"

"Oh Edge," the comms officer said but not over the comms. He looked past the weight on him and saw a familiar gaunt older woman in the volunteer's gear kneeling nearby. Her helmet was in her hands.

Sabre bristled. "What the hell? How long?"

The comms officer placed her hand on Sabre's shoulder. "You have to understand-"

"Understand what?! That you've been lying to us? That you can *understand* howlers?"

"It was purely theoretical up to know," she said. "But Doctor Ruben was confident there was merit. Never expected this."

"And what, we've been…they're…oh, God." Sabre allowed his legs to fold under him, his eyes wide open as he tilted his head back. For a moment there was a wash of emotion in his eyes, then, after a blink, he stared blankly at the ceiling.

"This is it, Sabre dear," the comms officer said. "This is where we turn the tide-"

Edge opened his eyes, sound growing dim around him; it wasn't even cold anymore. The comms officer helped the howler off of him. She didn't resist.

"Playback on track two," Doctor Ruben said.

Edge could barely make sense of the voices, then, nothing. He smiled, and closed his eyes.

The alien feminine voice sounded again over the comms: "Please, please, don't die, please, please, don't die, I love you!"

ELMIEN GROVE

Elmien figured she has had enough crazy experiences in her life to fill several novels; so, she first started writing a blog where she spoke candidly about the highlights and the shadows she has faced prior to turning 30.

After turning 30, she got bored writing the truth and decided to start writing fiction instead, which brings us to the present.

Connect with Elmien Grove
Blogger: http://ellenell.blogspot.com/
Facebook https://www.facebook.com/elmiengroveauthor

RYHEN E KNIGHT

Ryhen was born in Pretoria, South Africa in 1976. He received his doctorate degree in engineering in 2003 and has been working in the field of engineering since 2003 to pay for his addictions: travelling and coffee.
An engineer by trade, a writer at heart, with a passion for history, dragons and Lego. Short stories are one of his preferred writing formats but he has dabbled in poetry and travel writing. The dream is to publish a series of fantasy novels from his cottage in Scotland. He and his wife have two young squires that resemble sons and they live happily ever after in Pretoria.

Connect with Ryhen E Knight:
Facebook: https://www.facebook.com/pages/Ryhen-E-Knight/806565216045505

H J KRUGER

Born in South Africa in 1981, H J grew up in a house filled with books. From an early age, his love for literature became apparent and soon he started to write his own stories. Architect by day, writer by night, he lives in Pretoria with his partner and a collection of cats. When he isn't writing, he likes to draw, travel and make movies. This is his first published short story.

Connect with H J Kruger:
Facebook: https://www.facebook.com/hjkrugerwriter
Goodreads:
https://www.goodreads.com/author/show/7272133.Hernes

Isibindi is a little Rhino who lives in Africa. But when poachers attack, Isibindi is forced to flee into suburbia and befriends a little boy named Nkosi. Together they embark on an adventure to get Isibindi to the Sanctuary over the mountain and ultimately to safety.

CALDON MULL

Caldon has had a long publishing career in technology and various game publications under different *nom de plumes*, and in his own name. He has travelled extensively throughout Africa and Central Asia, and has even worked in Antarctica. In this time, he has become a sous chef, a therapy counsellor, a technician and a consultant for business and military sectors. When he is not currently working in a Technology field, he is usually writing science fiction and fantasy, and looking to expand his genre work into new directions. He is an unrepentant petrolhead with a weakness for classic Italian cars.

Connect with Caldon Mull:
Goodreads: https://www.goodreads.com/caldon
Print paperbacks: www.createspace.com
Smashwords: www.smashwords.com/profile/view/Caldon

The Memoirs of a Faun
Quirky, odd, thought-provoking and off-beat. The book is about Dreams and dream-stuff and concerns Arteus the Faun, and introduces the characters. The author takes us through layers of symbol, in short sharp, scenes reminiscent of an actual Dream together the paranormal bounty hunters of the Numinous Constraint Agency.

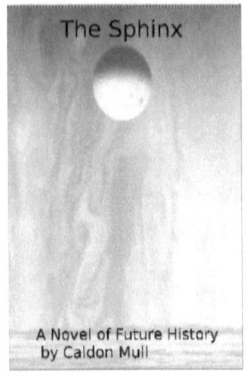

The Sphinx
The Sphinx is a fast-paced, brutal and disturbing read with as many moving moments as I have come to expect from this author, I couldn't stop thinking about it. Set in the Solar System in the Sixth Extinction, humanity struggles to overcome its base nature in order to survive.

The Estuary Tales
The world has ended, but still it carries on. The Estuary Tales takes you into a stark vision of the future as each of the next five centuries brings forth its own champions to steer humanity through the perils of the Sixth Extinction on Earth and beyond the planet.

NATALIE RIVENER

If Natalie had been born a few odd centuries earlier, she would have been burned as a witch. Her nonconformity has branded her as not-a-sheep and she loves exploring new things without caring too much about what others may think.

She currently spends most of her time running after her toddler and looking after her newborn but she's really a Jill of all trades…everything from sewing to pole dancing to painting to calligraphy to baking has taken up her time, but her favourite remains writing.

She lives with her husband, two children, cat and tarantula in a quiet part of Gauteng, South Africa.

The Mystic
In the magical realm of the fairies, EL Tianne, queen of the fairies, is watching the sand of a young adept's life running out. The young man is about to die in the storm of his own power tearing him apart. Only one can be sent to save him. Only one has the power to bring him back alive. But the Mystic is late. He might not make it in time.

Beyond
The Myrrh of Yrthull are dying but, if they can fill Birr Rhellor's prophecy, they will be freed of their doom. A small group of warriors now head out on this quest and ahead of them lies the fearsome Serpent Storm. Will they be able to cross this deadly barrier and return to fulfill they prophecy?

The Gravic Exacerbation

It is a day like any other when the ripples of two greater castings shake the grounds of the University of Yithnisia. No one pays it much heed...except for Corvic, arguably the most hated person at the University. It is now up to him to convince everyone of the mortal danger they have landed themselves in. But...will they listen?

ANDREA VERMAAK

Andrea had already published two poems by the end of high school, as well as teen-related articles in *Saltwater Girl*. She continued to write for *Saltwater Girl*, as well as for *Hip2B2* magazine while studying her BA (Journalism) Languages degree at the University of Pretoria. Andrea also wrote articles for the 'Buzz' section of *Perdeby*, the university's student newspaper. Andrea honed her creative writing skills as the Director of Creative Writing of The Inklings, the University of Pretoria's Literary Society, which she later chaired. She also completed a semester module in Creative Writing during her BA (Honours) English degree.

Andrea has since written many articles for several publications, but enjoys working as the editor of *Supernova, the mag for curious kids*, a general interest magazine published by BK Publishing. She has also edited self-published books and students' theses.

According to Andrea, her greatest accomplishment is completing a 50 000 word novel during the National Novel Writing Month

(NaNoWriMo) challenge.

Connect with Andrea Vermaak:
Facebook page: https://www.facebook.com/AndreaVermaakWriter
LinkedIn: http://www.linkedin.com/profile/view?id=47213899&tr
k=nav_responsive_tab_profile
Smashwords: https://www.smashwords.com/profile/view/AndreaV
83
Twitter: @AndreaVermaak
Wordpress: http://andreavermaak.worpress.com/

RICHARD T WHEELER

Richard T Wheeler is the co-author of the Sanguinem Emere series, the author of *A Girl Called Storm* in the STORM anthology and *Guardian Angel* in the Flight of the Phoenix anthology.

He is also the owner of, and lead-contributor and CEO of, DauntlessWriting.com, where he provides practical guides to the organisation, the craft and the marketing of professional entrepreneurial novel writing, using his own experiences as an indie authorpreneur with a day job as a basis. Unlike other guru's and professional writing teachers out there, his content focuses on a ground-up, step-by-step approach to firstly creating a saleable manuscript and then getting it into the hands of readers, and then turning them into a loyal, sustainable fan base in order to live the writer's life full-time.

Born in Pretoria, South Africa, Richard lives behind computer screens, working towards the perfect story. That is if, and when, he can pry himself away from the novels of Jim Butcher, Sergei Lukyanenko and Terry Pratchett.

When not reading and writing fiction or about fiction, Richard spends time at Sushi shops and in the gym where he plots away for the day when he could write that "Dear Boss" letter.

Richard holds a BA Degree in Language and Literature (with a specialisation in Creative Writing) from the University of South Africa and is currently pursuing further degrees.

Connect with Richard T Wheeler:

Amazon Page: http://www.amazon.com/Richard-T.-Wheeler/e/B008UM5WG2/
Facebook: https://www.facebook.com/richardtwheelerauthor
https://www.facebook.com/dauntlesswriting
https://www.facebook.com/SanguinemEmereBoughtInBlood
Goodreads: https://www.goodreads.com/RichardTWheeler
Twitter: @RichTWheeler
Smashwords: https://www.smashwords.com/profile/view/RichardTWheeler
Websites: RichardTWheeler.com
Dauntlesswriting.com
SanguinemEmere.com

A Girl Called Storm
What can change the nature of a man? In John's case, it was 90 seconds. His life before was not a savoury one, but now it contained a new force, a change agent, *A Girl Called Storm*.

Sanguinem Emere Book 1 – Nightfall on New Babylon
In a city built on sin, the Lords of Night move all the pieces.
New Babylon is a city of sin, build on lies told over generations. The inhabitants think they are the masters of their own destiny at the dawn of the Scientific Revolution, but as night falls on New Babylon, the true Lords of Night once again move their pieces across the playing field - Devika Templeton is a girl who has it all, including a nightly visitor; Roald Black has lost it all, but the truth is even more painful than the loss will ever be; Dalla Arnessen must rebuild her scuttled career, a tenuous feat in a city set against her; and Victoria Campbell has a secret that she must share with her rich suitor if she has any hope of escaping the streets.

Binding all four together with strings of obligation and pain is House D'Asur, the disgraced Lords of the Glass Manor, those who would be Lords of Night again.

Be the first to know when the authors of this anthology write more!

If you would like to receive news of further publications by Siygrah Books or any of the authors featured in *The Flight of the Phoenix*, please visit our Facebook page and leave a message.

www.facebook.com/siygrahbooks

We have a very strong no-spam policy, so, please rest assured that we will not abuse your contact details in any way.

From time to time, we will feature promo codes on our Facebook page that will give you discount on certain publications for a limited time. So, stop on by to make sure you don't miss out!

www.ingramcontent.com/pod-product-compliance
Lightning Source LLC
Chambersburg PA
CBHW020555180626
46810CB00007B/2513